ATHENA STUMBLES

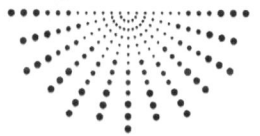

KIMBERLY A. SCOTT

Eyes That See Publishing

Athena Stumbles

Eyes That See Publishing
Newburyport, Massachusetts

ISBN 9780990741381

This is a work of fiction. Except as otherwise noted herein, names, characters and incidents are either a product of the author's imagination or are used fictitiously. Any resemblance to actual events or people, living or dead, is entirely coincidental.

Printed in USA

DEDICATION

For Jeanne DeFilippo Scott,
the epitome of a good mother.

CHAPTER 1

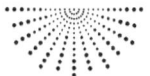

Spring 2006

I am no longer afraid of myself. I do not know when this happened, when I stopped feeling the tremors inside. The reflection that stares back from the mirror now does not blink and shrink away as it once did. Except in the late afternoon, when the dusky shadows shift and scurry, seeking a home for the evening. In this percolating murkiness, this gray gloom that reigns before the full darkness of evening extinguishes it, I can see the secret, hidden essence of me lurking in the unlit recesses of the room. And when I turn away from it, I feel its clammy fingers caressing my neck, inviting me back. There are days when I wish to let it take me.

Yet I cannot go, any more than I can erase the years from my face, infuse my heart once again with sweet anticipation for a life yet unlived, or press an ill-fated child back into my womb. Or, sadly, breathe the life back into a dead man.

"Earth calling, Nonny." The voice is high and slightly squeaky, and is housed in the skinny body of a nascent adolescent that I can see before turning around to face her.

Hands atop hips, blond hair high in a ponytail with wispy strands slipping in front of her face, she challenges me to step into this moment.

"I'm here, Amber," I whisper, though I intended to speak louder.

A quick shake of the ponytail. "Not all of you."

No. Not all of me. "Sorry. Just thinking. What do you need?"

"Grampa says he's making his tofu scramble for dinner, and I'm going to Emma's."

"Has she invited you?"

"Not yet," she shrugs, pointing a telephone at me. "I was just about to call her."

"You can't invite yourself to someone's house for dinner, Amber."

Amber taps in numbers on the phone's keypad as she speaks. "Normally, I would agree. But exceptions must be made in cases of extreme emergency."

"Tofu is not an emergency," I feel obliged to point out.

Amber's blue-green eyes widen in disbelief. "Remember what happened last time? You couldn't deal with that on your conscience again, Nonny."

My face breaks into an unanticipated smile at her playful impudence. She is more right than she knows. This conscience is filled to the brim, thank you. A granddaughter's tofu-induced illness could shatter the vessel. But still. "It's just not right…"

"I'll bring you a doggie bag."

Really? Do I succumb to bribery? "Call her," I sigh. *Was there ever any doubt?*

And so I live this existence, wallowing in this so-called domestic bliss nearly every living soul strives for, pressing down memories of turmoil and animosity and blinding righteousness, and I congratulate myself. For I no longer live with the fear. It is the peace I never believed I would know. Because the honest, bared-soul truth of it is, I never intended to murder Robert Dechesney.

"I thought you were switching to green tea," Charlie says as the deep black coffee sloshes into my favorite oversized mug with the Peruvian chinchilla on one side and a chip on the rim from Amber's first attempt at dishwashing when she was four.

I need a sip before I can answer, before my tongue and lips and brain can work in unison to form words he will understand. "I am. Tomorrow."

Charlie presses his lips together and eyes me with sympathy and poorly concealed amusement. "You're going to have to ease off gradually," he tells me in his smooth, purring voice. "You can't handle cold turkey."

"I can't handle quitting at all," I agree. "It's the only addiction I have left. Why can't you just leave me to it?"

"Antioxidants, blood pressure, insomnia, fibroids. Do you need more?"

"What I need," I raise my mug to him, "is this."

"You won't, once you wean yourself off it and start sleeping better." He kisses the tip of my nose, something he has been doing for so many years I no longer bother to wipe away the dampness left behind, and instead let it dry there, a little cool spot as it evaporates in the air.

The tiny wrinkles around Charlie's eyes when he smiles were not there 37 years ago, and the curly blond hair that was has now vanished from all but the sides of his head. But I find I like him better this way. Now, he looks more like the kind and gentle soul he has always been. The love I hoped I could believe in almost four decades ago is now plainly visible in every glance and gesture. Then, I hoped his love was true because it would afford me some measure of safety. Now that I have come to take the safety for granted, it is the love that I cherish.

"You going to be able to meet for lunch?" he asks, setting two plates of whole-wheat waffles with fresh blueberries on the dark, knotty pine table.

I pop a plump blueberry into my mouth, and then another, before answering. "I don't know, there's a chance I may have to run up to Chesterford. Can I call you around eleven?"

"Of course," he shrugs, and grins his toothy grin at me, the one that reveals the latent dimple lurking in his left cheek. Perhaps he thinks I do not see the doubt and disappointment in his eyes. Certainly he does not want me to see it. It is the reason for the grin.

"Delicious," I tell him truthfully, around a mouthful of waffles. "As usual."

"I know."

My turn to grin. "You do, do you?"

"Your oh-so-finicky granddaughter ate four of them. Although maybe she was just trying to make up for cutting out on my tofu last night. I should commend you, by the way,—and thank you— for not cutting out with her. I know it's not your favorite either."

"I would *never*," I say in my most indignant voice.

He raises his eyebrows at me. "You thought about it."

Busted! I wave my fork at him while finishing a swallow. "Pleading the fifth."

He nods, smiling, and I think I see the doubt in his eyes again. But I cannot be sure because of the grin.

Stenciled on the clouded glass door are the words, Food Recovery of Greater Springfield. Those of us who work here, with varying degrees of affection, refer to it as FROGS, although never to outsiders, lest it be inferred that it alludes to the foodstuffs we recover. It is my way to do good things, working here. My way of being a good person. A better person, anyway. The several tons of food thrown away each day by supermarkets, hotels, restaurants and convention centers of central Massachusetts are recovered, repackaged, and redistributed to hundreds of our neediest citizens in the city's shelters and soup kitchens. It is not how I imagined I would change the world when I was a young woman. I had much grander plans, much more revolutionary plans than this! It was at no small cost that I discovered I did not possess the heart of a revolutionary, and now I find myself content to save the world one hungry belly at a time. It is certainly safer for all concerned.

Inside, the big black bulk of Jarvis Chandler, all three hundred pounds of him, most of it in a bulging, pillowy belly, hovers over Lindsey McCullough's skinny blonde frame, seated at her desk. The program director of FROGS, Jarvis is a huge man in every way. His appetite, obviously. His presence in a room, his command of every micron of attention, is just as obvious. Much more covert, and often inaccessible, is his huge heart, his enormous capacity for kindness. But his kindnesses he bestows sparingly, as though they were only so many coins jangling in a pocket. When he decides to open the pocket, he reaches first for the big, shiny silver dollars, the acts of kindness that will change a life. When those are depleted, he generously sprinkles the good deeds that bring a smile or a small dose of hope, like scattering half-dollars and quarters into a crowd. But he saves not even one tarnished penny for Lindsey McCullough.

Lindsey, sugar-sweet and fizzy as soda pop, was raised rich and privileged and sheltered enough not to be accustomed to people treating her with the scorn and derision heaped upon her by Jarvis. And she is young and naïve enough not to understand why he would do so. She is, however, observant enough to notice that he does not treat everyone that way. And to her credit, she is tough enough, or perhaps foolish enough, not to give up and give in and go back to her cushy life in the suburbs.

Lindsey raises faded blue eyes at me as I enter the room, Jarvis' harsh voice berating her from above. Her eyes say "Help," or "Why me?" or maybe "Oh brother, the big lummox is at it again." Whatever they say, her mouth says nothing as she lets his words fall over her. I cannot help but have sympathy for her. It may well be, as Jarvis believes, that she works here helping the poor to assuage her guilt at being given so much. But I am not one to judge her, when I have my own dubious reasons for being here. What would Jarvis think of me if he knew the truth of me?

"Jarvis," I interrupt his mumbled tirade. "Good morning."

Jarvis lifts his heft up to its full, towering height and nods, his dark eyes softening as they shift from Lindsey to me. "Morning, Annie."

I walk past him and settle my old macramé purse among the stacks of file folders and photos of Charlie, Amber and Darlene strewn about my desk in a neat, organized clutter. "Am I going to Chesterford today?"

Jarvis' head shakes a no, the fat in his cheeks wobbling slightly. "I'm meeting with a possible new donor in North Stockton, so I'll do the drop-off in Chesterford."

"But—"

"I know," Jarvis holds his beefy palm up toward me, "I know you like to do the drive up there, for whatever reason, but I need you here today. We got a mostly new crew of volunteers handling the pickup from the Marriott, and it's all perishables, so it's gotta be packaged and distributed today, and somebody who knows what they're doing has to coordinate all that. And that's you."

I nod and dip my head so he cannot see my face. He does not know what he has caused me to miss today.

So I stay here in Springfield all day and supervise the little squad of earnest and bright-eyed volunteers as they do their good deed for the week, or maybe the month. Maybe the year. Lindsey is competent and helpful, and I think that maybe she can handle this alone someday soon, and I will not have to forgo another trip up to Chesterford, and to nearby Dunlee Mill, the place I really wish to go. I call Charlie at his photography studio as promised, to tell him I can grab a quick lunch with him, but he has had a job pop up suddenly, and cannot make it after all. So I nibble on a flax and soy nut energy bar, which tastes more like tacks and sawdust, but that is merely evidence that it is good for me, according to Charlie.

Early in the afternoon, as some of the volunteers are just heading out with four SUV-loads of repackaged food to take to the shelters, a pudgy young man with red high-top sneakers opens the front door. He allows himself to be jostled and bumped by the people with packages exiting the building, then stumbles his way in.

"Hi Sean," Lindsey greets him brightly.

"Hi," Sean mumbles. "I'm late."

Lindsey smiles at him. "Are you? It's okay. Whenever you come in, we're happy to have you."

"I'm sorry I'm late."

"Don't worry about it. What have you got today?"

"Liverwurst and pickles on rye," Sean says, holding out a brown paper bag. "It's my favorite. Sorry I'm late."

"Yumm," Lindsey flashes a quick grimace at me that Sean cannot see. "Sounds delicious. That's awfully generous of you to give up your favorite."

She has more patience with him than I can muster on busy days, this little boy in a man's body. This man with a child's hopeful heart who comes in every day at one-thirty to donate half the lunch his mother made for him that morning.

"There's hungry people need it more than me," Sean says, sliding chubby fingers through long brown bangs that flop in his face. "I got lots to eat. Give it to somebody needy."

"We will, Sean. Thank you."

"You're welcome. Give it to someone needy." He glances briefly at me, raises a hand in a tentative wave. "Hi, Mrs. Pulkowski."

And though I feel buried under the mountain of food still to be processed in the ever-shortening day, I stand and walk over to him. "Hello, Sean. Thank you for your donation. Your generosity is very much appreciated. You are helping many people in need."

Sean's face brightens and he smiles shyly. "Okay, well, have a nice day."

"You too, Sean," I say, throwing a smile toward Lindsey for reminding me why we are here. Sean is just as needy as any of the hungry, Jarvis likes to say, and in fact, says often. It's just a different thing he's in need of.

And this is what I focus on, as the day wanes into evening. The childlike smile on Sean's face. The many people in this city who will fall asleep tonight without the hunger that normally torments them. I try, and I fail, not to think about Chesterford and Dunlee Mill, and what my day would have been like had I gone there, where my secret heart lives. I try to press down that jittery, restless sensation of being trapped here in this spiritless city. I do not succeed in suppressing it, but I can live with it. I have grown accustomed to feeling trapped in the ordinariness of my every day.

I am careful not to congratulate myself as I leave the bank. The money I have withdrawn represents a substantial chunk of my paycheck, and I am happy about that, but I will not be proud. This money will go where it is needed greatly. It is meant to fill a void that is unfillable, to ease a burden with its callous practicality.

At the post office, I slip the cash into a plain envelope, affix the typed mailing label to its front and drop it into the Out-of-Town slot. *Go. Do what you can.* Charlie's business has been doing well and so I am able to send more each month. I am pleased to be able to be so generous. Devastated that I must. So there is no room for pride or congratulations. It is nothing, this token I send. Nothing in comparison to what I have taken.

I know before I reach the door of my house that something inside is different. A small, white Cape-style house with black shingles on its steeply sloping roof, the home I have shared with Charlie for most of the past 30 years looks like many others here in this part of Massachusetts. All that distinguishes it is the counterfeit wood-shingled wishing well in the front yard that looks quaint and charming but does not actually harbor a well or hole of any kind inside its pretty casing. All of this is very much in place, just as it was when I left this morning, and yet as I walk the few steps up the short front path, I know that something is not right inside. I would call it a disturbance in the force if it did not sound so much like those science fiction space movies Charlie likes so much.

I push the door open slowly and look for her. She is there, on the living room couch next to Amber. Her hair is a yellow found only in sugary soft drinks and cream-filled snack cakes, except for two inches at the very top of her head where the dark roots have begun to grow out. The skin of her face is pallid and blotchy, with puffy dark spots under her eyes. It is a face that surely must have seen five or six decades of harsh living, and yet I know with certainty that she was born just thirty-six years ago.

She turns as I close the door and drills heavy, black-rimmed eyes into me. "And there she is." A sneer crosses slowly over her face. "My mommy dearest."

"Darlene." It is all I can say at the moment.

"You remember me. That's very heartwarming, really."

I take a few heavy steps into the room and drop my purse onto a polished cherry sideboard. "How—?"

"How?" she mocks me, her short skirt riding up on her thighs as she crosses one stiletto-heeled foot over another. "How can I be here? Why am I not in jail? They had nothing to hold me on. But hey, thanks for bailing me out, by the way. Very decent of you. Earned yourself a mother-of-the-year award for that one. Put it with all your other ones."

This hits me harder than I would have liked to believe possible and I hide, as usual, behind the well-rehearsed mask that has become my face. "I thought that maybe a night or two in jail...would..."

"Would what? Be good for me? Smack some sense into me? Great strategy. And hey, you know what? It worked. I'm totally reformed. Clean as a whistle." Her eyes flash, her mouth torques into a twisted smile. "And I'm a virgin again too. Yup, jail time really works miracles."

I turn my eyes from Amber's face so that I do not have to see how it registers this remark by her mother. "Why are you here, Darlene?"

"To see my loving family, of course. Can't say I'm sensing too much love, though."

Charlie walks in from the kitchen carrying a steaming bowl of beans and rice, one of my favorites and the item on tonight's dinner menu, apparently.

"I take that back," Darlene says. "Charlie loves me. He took pity on my poor, starving self."

I see Charlie wince at the sound of his name. Up until Amber was born and Darlene had needed an accurate family medical history, she had called him Dad. It had caused him such pain to have to tell her he was not her biological father. But nothing like the pain she caused every time she called him Charlie.

Darlene takes the white porcelain bowl and scoops food into her mouth with a primal, urgent hunger. Who knows when was the last time she ate anything decent. Amber watches her mother devour the food in silence for a moment, then places a tentative hand on Darlene's leg. "I love you, Mom."

Another spoonful is shoveled into her mouth before Darlene seems to hear her daughter's words. Still gripping the spoon in one hand, she presses the other on top of Amber's. "You do, don't you honey? I know you do." She slips an arm around Amber's shoulders and turns to me. "My daughter loves me," she says, her eyes never straying from me, even as she gives Amber's shoulders an affectionate squeeze. "Maybe you should come live with me, Amber. Would you like that honey?"

She says this, I know, to anger me. Or to frighten me. She hits her mark on both counts.

Amber's face lights up with hope, but I can see that she is nervous, unsure. "Well, maybe," she hesitates, "you could come live here with us. If you want. Couldn't she, Nonny?"

"Why do you do this to her?" I hear in my voice a sharp hiss, like an enraged cobra.

"Huh," Darlene rolls her eyes upward and picks up her spoon again. "Your grandma doesn't like me very much, Amber. She doesn't want me here."

At this, Amber turns her open, trusting face toward me, hurt and suspicion darkening her big eyes. So here I am, caught between Darlene's manipulative sneer and Amber's innocent hope, accused by both. Darlene has trapped me here, as Jarvis trapped me in Springfield earlier today, but this chafes more because she has done so intentionally and with malice.

"Your mother," I say in as steady a voice as I can muster, "will be welcome to stay here when she is able to obey the rules of this household."

"Jesus fucking Christ," Darlene snaps, setting the now empty bowl on the table. "What am I? Five years old?"

"And that's just one of the many rules you are incapable of following," I say with forced calm, although I can feel the eruption coming. "No swearing. And your so-called adulthood has nothing to do with it. Your father and I would not let anyone live here—adult or child—who didn't abide by our rules and who treated us with such blatant disrespect—"

"Disrespect?" Her chin thrusts forward as it always did when her temper flared. Which it frequently did. "You have to earn respect, lady. You don't just automatically get it because you gave birth to me. You get treated the way you deserve." Her voice is low, condescending, as though she is teaching a slow-witted child, and this feeds the fury building inside me. "It all comes back," she continues, "all that shit you dished out over the years. So if you get treated with disrespect, then trust me, you've earned it. And you own it."

"No!" The rage in me has burst out and filled the room, and I know that I have lost again. Even as I know that I can not let her win, that I can not let Amber see me behave this way, I cannot stop myself. "You will *not* put it all on me. *You* made a mess of your life, not me. *You* poured your life down a hole, not me. So whatever misery you live in that makes you come here and torment us, that is all your own doing. And you," I lower my voice, "own that."

There is an awful quiet filling the room, and I will not look at Amber because I cannot bear to see the fear that I know is in her eyes. I know it is there because I have seen it before, every time Darlene comes into our lives and incites an agonizingly familiar emotional battle. This is not new to us, this black parody of familial affinity. We have lived it many times, and always I am resolved to remain detached, untouched by my daughter's vicious and unpredictable malevolence. And every time my resolve proves no match for the old fire of my previous self that burns like a tiny pilot light inside me.

Eventually, after her regular—and regularly rejected—request for money, Darlene leaves our home and it is quiet, peaceful again, although not happy as it normally is. She leaves behind a bleakness when she goes, a somberness that permeates every room, every sound and smell, and each one of us. I know that Amber is angry with me for what she perceives to be my inexplicable cruelty toward her mother, and this saddens me, and I wonder if Darlene will someday succeed in poisoning Amber against me permanently. And I feel a tiny pebble of guilt scratching at me because I wonder if maybe my daughter is just a little bit right. I wonder if maybe the mother I was is in some way responsible for the woman she has become.

Only Charlie seems able to put these incidents into a separate compartment. He is certainly quieter than normal this evening as he serves Amber and me the meal he has prepared. But I sense that that is in deference to our desultory moods. He asks Amber about school and soccer practice and tells us both about the photo shoot he did today of the two-year-old twins and their cocker spaniel. Not a one of them could sit still for more than twelve seconds, and never all three at the same time. And by the way, some of the guys were organizing a little fishing trip this Sunday, and did I mind if he went along? I would have to bring Amber to her play rehearsal and then I would be alone for much of the day.

He knows that I will say this is fine, and he knows I will mean it. I am not unhappy alone. He cannot know that I feel a lightness inside, the trapped feeling that has burdened me all day lifting off of me. He does not know how elated I am that he is going fishing and I will be alone.

CHAPTER 2

Catherine Whittendon was aching to get out of church. Every shuf-fling step forward in the line to shake Reverend Sanders' hand was an almost unbearable delay today. She could have gotten out of the line and foregone her weekly handshake and chat with the good reverend, as many of her fellow congregants did on a shockingly regular basis. But that would have been as unthinkable to her as not wearing her best shoes to church, or the gray tweed hat with the satin rose on the side. Some things simply were not done. Not by her, God knew.

Ahead of her in the sluggish, plodding line was Donna Pearson, blathering on and on to the reverend about her son in medical school. Twenty years younger than Catherine, that woman prattled on like an old biddy. And behind her was Enid Claybourne, doddering old empty-headed fool that she was. A full minute of vigorous handshaking with a silly grin on her face, another minute of *Praise-the-good-Lord-Almightying*, and then one more minute of silent handshaking. Same thing every week. The good Lord might want to consider instating some basic minimum standards. For the good of the flock.

Seven agonizing minutes later, Catherine approached Reverend

Sanders as June Wilkins pressed his hand and smiled at him. Catherine tapped a toe on the stone step impatiently. *Move it along, move it along.*

"Mrs. Whittendon," Reverend Sanders turned his wispy gray head toward Catherine and clasped her hand in both of his. "I'm always so glad to see you here. How are you meeting God's challenge?"

"Fine, Reverend, just fine," Catherine felt an honest warmth wash over her that slowed her down a bit. She truly did like this good and caring man. "But I am in a little bit of a hurry. I'm meeting my great-grandson for the first time today."

"Oh, congratulations! That's just wonderful," the reverend's face brightened, "and so comforting, isn't it? How God will bless us with a new life just when we need it most?"

Catherine nodded, and water filled her eyes involuntarily. "They named him Sam," she whispered.

The pastor smiled. "That's lovely. Your husband's spirit will live on in your great-grandson. I think that will be of great comfort for you."

Catherine's eyes glistened. "It is. It already is. Thank you, Reverend."

"May God go with you, Mrs. Whittendon. And enjoy your day!"

Snickerdoodles with chocolate chips. Vanessa's favorites. Catherine arranged the little cinnamon cookies on the white paper doily set on her good bone china plate from England. Her granddaughter would be happy to see her favorite cookies, but not surprised. In fact, she was probably expecting them.

All the way from San Diego, she was coming with Catherine's new great-grandson. And the husband too, of course. Jason with the weird last name. Luvius. What kind of name was Luvius? She never had figured that out, but it wasn't American, that's for sure.

She could ask, but then it would seem as though it mattered to her, which of course it didn't. But it definitely wasn't American. He seemed like a nice enough man anyway. And now he was the father of her only great-grandchild. So he would be welcomed like family.

She pushed open the back screen door with a perfectly positioned thrust of her hip and carried the plate of cookies and a large ceramic pitcher of iced tea out to the picnic table under the sprawling maple tree. She counted chairs. Colin and Cindy, her son and daughter-in-law, would be coming too, so there would be six of them altogether. But only five would need chairs.

"Hellooo," a singsongy female voice rang out from behind her and she turned to see Vanessa, beautiful as ever, striding across the yard, a small blue bundle in her arms. Strung out behind her, as though attached to Vanessa by a string, followed Colin, Cindy, and Jason with the weird last name.

Catherine felt the grin spread over her face and held her arms wide as they approached. "Hello!" she exclaimed, folding her arms around her granddaughter and squeezing gently. "How are you my dear? I've been so excited you were coming." She bestowed brief hellos and kisses on the rest of the adults, then turned quickly back to the little blue blanket in Vanessa's arms. She tugged carefully at its corners and peered into its folds.

Tiny, round and pink, with small blue eyes that blinked lazily up at her, the cherubic little face, new to the world and bursting with incipient potential, stirred a sensation inside Catherine she could not fathom. Something between joy and grief, wonder and loss, that she could neither make sense of nor contain, and it spilled out in a breathy wave of tears.

"Oh. Oh, just look at you," she whispered, clamping a hand over her mouth, awed by the miracle of this fresh new soul to love. "Oh, you're just..."

"Would you like to hold him?" Vanessa asked.

"Oh," she breathed, "yes! I would love to hold him."

Vanessa transferred the baby gently into her grandmother's

arms, then raked her fingers through her wavy brown hair. "He was just five months old yesterday."

"I know exactly how old he is," Catherine said, brushing her lips lightly across his soft pudgy cheeks. "The little angel. Little Sam."

Vanessa and the others watched silently for a few moments as Catherine nuzzled the baby, then Vanessa stepped toward the picnic table and dropped into a chair. "Oh. I need to sit down,"

Catherine looked up at her granddaughter and nodded. "You look tired, honey. You all right?"

"Oh, yeah. It's just those middle of the night feedings. They're a killer."

Catherine darted a glance at Jason. "I remember."

"Luckily, Jason's been just great," Vanessa said quickly. "He gets up as soon as Sam cries and brings him to me. If only he could lactate too." She laughed and reached out to Jason, who took hold of her hand.

Catherine sat down in the chair next to Vanessa. "They sure are hungry little things, aren't they? Your dad was up every two hours for what seemed like an entire year, although I'm sure it wasn't quite that long." She grinned up at her son and Colin smiled back.

"What can I say? You obviously were putting out a fine brew." Colin offered a chair to his wife, then sat himself. "Speaking of which, what have we got in here?" he said, peering into the pitcher.

"Iced tea. There's soda and beer in the fridge if you want."

Vanessa eyed the plate of cookies with raised eyebrows. "Snickerdoodles?" she asked Catherine.

"With chocolate chips," Catherine winked. "For the lactating mother."

As her family bustled and laughed around her, munching snickerdoodles and sipping iced tea or beer, Catherine watched contentedly from her chair. It was a good family she was left with here at the end of her life. There was her beautiful, vibrant granddaughter with the long, long hair and laughing eyes. Her son, hair graying now, was still a handsome man. And even better looking these past several months, it seemed, as he'd been beaming with pride about becoming a grandfather. And Cindy too, although she had whined once or twice about how being a grandmother made her feel old, was obviously overjoyed with little Sam. Even Jason with the foreign name seemed to be a good man. He made her Vanessa happy, and that would have been enough. But he was polite and considerate and actually nice to have around.

Catherine snuggled the tiny baby in her arms a little closer, breathed in his little baby smell. Her family had changed so dramatically over the years. There had been such terrible pain, such awful losses. But these people here, those who were left, and those who had joined, were her family now. And it was a good one.

I watch them from behind my tree. This giant old oak has become my tree over the years because I am the one who cowers behind it, hiding from those who must never see me, often hugging it in pain and longing, for want of a true, human hug. It shelters me from both sun and rain; it shields my face from those who must surely despise it, even though, or perhaps because, they once loved it. It allows me to see what I have lost, what I no longer can be a part of, and it unfailingly offers up its wide, rough shoulders for me to cry against, when the enormity of the hugs and kisses and joy and sorrow and love that I have missed out on overwhelms me. By all these measures, this is my tree. It certainly is no one else's.

For almost 30 years I have been coming here, forced to sneak in like an intruder to this place that once was my home. I park my car a quarter of a mile away and trek alone through the wooded bird sanctuary which had been my childhood playground, and which abuts this backyard so that I may watch this old woman with gray-white hair and stooped shoulders. My mother. She was younger than I am now the last time we were together. Her laugh has not changed in all these years; I can hear it clearly from behind my tree, and it makes me think of splashing in the pond and pancakes flipping through the air. But she is sadder now than when I was growing up. And even more so these last six months, since my father died. My smart, charming, and masterful-storytelling father, whose funeral I could not risk attending, not even secretly, not even in disguise. I stayed home from work that day and cried the entire time, not because he was gone, but because for the last 37 years of his life I was nothing more than an unwelcome ghost to him.

My mother is happier today than I have seen her in some time. She is profoundly moved, I can see, by this new baby. He is my great-nephew, and he will never know me, just as his mother, my niece, Vanessa, has never known me. Does she know that I ever existed? Have they told her even that?

And the handsome, salt-and-pepper haired man is Colin, my brother. I know him to be Colin because I have watched him grow and change all these years from behind my tree. But he is a stranger to me. My brother will always be Colley, the shaggy-haired fifteen-year-old he was when I last spoke with him. When he last knew me.

My brother has a very beautiful wife. Cindy is perhaps a little overly coifed and primped and made-up, although she seems to love my brother, and he most certainly loves her. I do not believe my mother was happy with Colley's selection of a wife originally. But over the years I have watched her slip an arm around Cindy's shoulders, walk with her, confide in her, laugh with her. I wonder now if she thinks of Cindy as her daughter. Just the thought of this causes a hurt so strong it sucks the breath out of me. I am fortunate, I realize, that I will never know the answer to this question. I do not feel fortunate, however. I feel alone.

CHAPTER 3

"Good morning, Mrs. Pulkowski."

"Hello, Chris," I say. Chris is the perky twenty-something with the lifeguard looks and the slightly excessive ebullience behind the front desk of the RealFitness gym where I miserably haul my reluctant self three times a week. Chris has been instructed, I believe, to greet all customers by name, and he does so, with a cheer and verve that is both admirable and cloying at 5:30 in the morning. I do not blame him, not really, for addressing me as Mrs. Pulkowski when he calls people twenty, even ten years younger by their first names. It does not bother me in the least. I would just like to know what the cutoff age is. Just curious.

"How's everything going today?" Chris says as I pass my membership card by the scanner.

"Once I get through this next hour and a half, everything will be just fine," I tell him and head for the locker room.

"Have a good workout," he calls after me. Was he not listening?

Out on the gym floor, an orderly row of silent televisions descend from the ceiling like flickering drill sergeants commanding a huge array of treadmills, cross-trainers, stair climbers, and stationary bicycles. Rows of human legs pedal and climb and run, all furiously going nowhere.

I stroll unenthusiastically among this stalled army, trying not to see myself in the giant mirrors that line all four walls of the colossal room. But there I am. I cannot help but see the middle-aged woman looking grumpily back at me. She is still slender at 56, and that renders a slight, contented satisfaction. But her hair is almost entirely gray and faint lines have begun to etch her face, as though chiseled by some divine, yet sadistic, artist.

I am troubled, still, about Darlene, and this makes me crankier than usual. In some way, my recent, secret visit to my mother and my first family deepens my agitation. I do not fault my mother for my failings; surely I am not to blame for Darlene's. Still, I have not been able to be the mother I would have wished, and I will never fully escape that guilt. Add it to the list.

My favorite cross-training machine with the perfect view of the political analysis channel is occupied by a young man in flowered shorts, flip flops and sunglasses. He is unaware, perhaps, that no beach exists for miles. I choose another machine nearby, but as I step onto it, a foul stench of sour human exertion engulfs me. The obscenely overweight man on the next apparatus drips sweat onto the display and pedals of his machine, and I feel swamped by his putrid mugginess. I will not last a minute here.

I settle, finally, onto a third choice and, as I am unable to see my political analysis program, I scrutinize the people on the gym floor. Regulars, most of them, that I have studied many times before. There is a well-muscled man in a loosely hanging muscle shirt and fuchsia Lycra shorts lifting free weights. Earphone cords dangle from his head and his body bops and sways between lifts. Across the floor, a young woman wearing not much more than a bikini and heavy makeup chats and giggles with a middle-aged man sporting a graying comb over. Her largely exposed cleavage is enormous; does she realize he is not looking at her face? I believe she does. Young women flip through beauty magazines or furtively catch their own shiny reflections in the mirrors while the elderly woman who wears the same black Bermuda shorts over cloudy beige panty hose every day shuffles about slowly, perpetually falling further and further behind.

Challenging though it often is, I regularly admonish myself not to judge myself superior, either to those gracelessly fighting time and aging, or the slim hard bodies crudely celebrating youth. Theirs are defects of vanity, insecurity, or hygiene. I could only wish for such trivial faults.

"Hey Grampa."

Charlie looked up from the newscast he was watching as Amber bounded into the room. "Hey pumpkin. Finish your homework?"

"Almost. I needed to take a break from staring at the periodic table or my head was going to, like, spin right off my body."

"You truly are the master of hyperbole," Charlie grinned as she plopped down on the tan and green striped couch and snuggled in close to him.

"Thank you. What's for dinner?"

"Broiled trout, freshly caught yesterday by the fisherman extraordinaire of the house," he tapped his chest proudly, "served over wilted red chard and arugula with whole wheat couscous."

"Okay. I can live with that." She propped her feet up on the dark wooden coffee table next to Charlie's and crossed them at the ankles exactly as his were crossed. "I could use a snack in the meantime."

"Soy nuts?" Charlie offered, reaching for a cellophane bag on the side table. "Honey roasted."

Amber raised her eyebrows at him. "Have you ever even, like, *tried* a potato chip?"

"Sure. When I was young and naïve and ignorant of the havoc it wreaked in my body. But I'm over that now. Lucky you can benefit from my wisdom and not make the same mistakes."

"Lucky me." She took a few nuts, gingerly placed one in her mouth and chewed without enthusiasm. "Lucky, lucky me."

Behind them, a key sounded in the front door lock and Charlie turned to watch Annie come in. As always, his heart thumped out a little extra beat of joy when he caught sight of her. For all of their entire life together, he has felt exactly the same little surge of excitement at seeing his wife, only slightly faded with time. "Hi, hon," he said casually, betraying none of the delight he felt inside.

"Hi Nonny," Amber called out without turning around.

"Hey," Annie said, walking over and collapsing on the couch next to Amber. "What a day. Can't tell you how happy I am to be home." She kissed Amber on the top of the head, then leaned over her to kiss Charlie on the mouth.

"That bad? Well, at least your timing is good," Charlie said with a grin. "You just missed your favorite president talking about his war."

Annie shuddered, releasing a breathy groan. "That would have sent me right over the edge."

"So let's hear it." Charlie offered sympathetically. "Unload on me. That's what I'm here for."

"Oh, you know, maybe later. Right now I just want to relax and unwind with—"

Her voice broke off as her eyes caught and focused on the television screen. Charlie turned toward it to see a black-and-white photograph of a young man, his hair and clothes obviously outdated. The photo disappeared and a female reporter appeared, speaking into a microphone.

"...were called to the hospital bed of a man dying of terminal pancreatic cancer. This man, Steven Roberts of Cambridge, told a fantastic story. He told police that his real name is Michael Strickland, and he was involved in a robbery and murder that took place thirty-seven years ago in New York City. In 1969, a group that called themselves Soldiers of Democracy attempted to rob the Federal One Bank in midtown Manhattan. Security guards foiled the attempt, and the group fled, although not before shooting one of the guards, who died the next day. Steven Roberts, or Michael Strickland, if his story is true, told police he drove the getaway car in the failed heist."

The reporter disappeared from the screen and was replaced by a uniformed police officer with an assortment of microphones fanned out before him. "It was really your typical deathbed confession," the policeman said. "The guy is dying, a week or so to live, they say, and he wants to get this off his chest. He's gonna die there in that hospital bed, so there's nothing we can really do, other than check out his story to see if it's true, and try to get him to help us find the others involved."

Just as quickly as he'd appeared, the police officer was gone again, and the reporter was back. "The identities of the others involved in the crime have been known for years. One of the group, James McDonough, was injured during the robbery and was captured, and had been incarcerated in maximum security Sing Sing Correctional Facility in Ossining, New York, until he died in a prison fight in 1987. McDonough cooperated with police at the time of his arrest in exchange for leniency in sentencing, and provided the names of his co-conspirators." A series of black and white photos appeared on the screen, all as outdated as the first had been. "They are," the reporter continued, "Michael Strickland, whose photo we just showed you, originally from Long Beach, California, Gordon Blackwell, of Green Meadow, New Jersey, Pamela Mercurio, of Dunlee Mill, Massachusetts, and Lucinda Whittendon, also from Dunlee Mill."

"Dunlee Mill?" Charlie said. "That's not far from here. Just up 91 a bit, isn't it?" He glanced at Annie, but she stared at the screen, lost in it. "Annie?"

She turned toward him and blinked. "What?"

"Isn't Dunlee Mill just up 91? Near where you have to drive for work every week?"

"Um. No," she said. "I mean, yeah. I guess so. I think I've seen a sign for it up there."

Charlie studied her face. "You all right? You seem...out of it."

"Yeah," she said quickly, her eyes flickering. "Yeah, I'm just—like I said, long day. I um, I'm going to go change and wash up for dinner."

Charlie squinted at her. "Yeah. Okay."

"It's trout again," Amber informed her.

"It's going to be trout all week, honey," Annie said, heading toward the bedroom she and Charlie shared.

Amber spun her face, a dramatic mask of panic, toward her grandfather. "Really?"

Charlie laughed silently a moment, enjoying yet another one of her over-the-top expressions. Destined to be an actor someday, that one. "No. I froze the rest of it or it would have started to spoil. Besides, we can't have you running off to Emma's house for dinner all week. Her family would have begged for mercy."

"I have other friends."

"I know. But the truth is, we'd miss you." Charlie kissed the top of her head, then got up and headed toward the kitchen to work on dinner.

He turned on the broiler and watched the flames spring to life, licking the roof of the oven. Something was up with Annie. He'd known that face, and loved that face, for almost 40 years, and the look on it just now was not one with which he was familiar. It was closed to him, keeping him out. They'd always been completely open and honest with each other. No secrets. No lies. But now, there was something she was keeping to herself. And that, as much as he tried to push it aside, that hurt him. He stirred the greens around in the big wok on the stove and watched the leaves sweat and wilt. Maybe she just didn't want to discuss whatever it was in front of Amber and would tell him later. That must be it. She would tell him later.

By some perverse kink in the cosmic laws of physics, I have managed to get myself out of that room. My heart, upon seeing that photograph of Michael, declared a work stoppage and refused to beat. My legs seemed to liquefy under me, and had I not already been sitting I am sure I would have fallen. And then Charlie would know for certain there was something truly wrong. Perhaps he knows anyway. He is so perceptive, and he watches me all the time and carefully. Surely he must know.

It has taken me by surprise, this moment. I have always known it might come; at times I expected it and was on guard. And yet now it has crept up on me with stealth and celerity. I have seen that picture of Michael before, of course. When it was first flashed on television sets around the country in the summer of 1969. I have not seen it since, and I believed his image had simply faded from my memory over time, like old upholstery in a sunny window. Yet when his face appeared on that screen just now, I felt his entire person was sitting before me. I could hear his voice, see his sideways smile and the loping, impatient gait of his walk. I was there myself, in 1969, completely.

I did not hear much of what the television reporter just said, so completely was my body fighting not to shut down entirely. Other than that Michael was dying, which immediately filled me with shock and disbelief because Michael is so young and healthy and vigorous. But of course, he is not anymore. He is middle-aged like me. I am glad they did not show a picture of the sick old man he is now. I prefer him to always exist in 1969.

I believe I could have recovered from this shock, and fooled Charlie into believing nothing was wrong beyond my tiring day at work, had it not been for that last set of photos. The very last one in particular. Seeing my own face peering out from the screen, my own young, innocent, untainted self, filled me with such a profound sorrow for the life I could have had and threw away, for the person I could have been. It is my high school portrait, and the enthusiasm and optimism, the pure *life* in me, radiates out from it like an ethereal halo. A person could believe a good and decent heart lives inside that smiling girl. Had a photograph been taken of me immediately after the robbery-turned-murder, would the loss of innocence and goodness be readily apparent? I do not know. I did not allow pictures to be taken of me for many years after that horrible day.

I could not bear to look at that photo on the TV screen, and yet I could not turn away from it. Hearing my name astonished me, alarmed me. I have not heard it spoken in all these years, and I no longer answer to it. I always liked my name, until it became synonymous in the country's mind for ruthless murderer. I was Lucinda Whittendon. I remember her, that passionate, idealistic young girl who was going to change the world for the better. I remember her and I miss her. But I am frightened of her, too. Because whatever my life could have been, that sweetly smiling face could destroy the life I have now. This life with Charlie and Amber, so wonderful in so many ways, except that I must constantly hide my true self from them. They do not truly know me, and I cannot allow them to discover the genuine me, for how could two such wonderful people love such a monster? Who could love the notorious Lucinda Whittendon?

So I congratulate my legs for getting me out of that room and into this one, despite a lack of any real solid bones or muscles or cartilage to rely on at the time. And I am grateful to my heart, which I know has now resumed beating because I can hear blood pounding ferociously in my ears. I am frozen here, afraid to go out there and let them get a good look at me, for surely they will be able to see right through to the depraved core I harbor inside. Yet I cannot hide in this room forever. I must go out there and be Annie, steady and even and boring, as I have been for more than three decades. I will have to tell Charlie something. I will tell him that I recognized someone from long ago. I think he will believe me. He will want to believe me. I can only hope they will not continue to show Lucinda's picture in the media. Certainly he will recognize me eventually. How much of Lucinda is still discernible in Annie?

CHAPTER 4

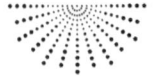

For once, I am not able to get out of the house fast enough for my morning run. Normally, I procrastinate. I sip my coffee, listlessly pull on clothes, linger over the newspaper. Then finally, when I am about to make myself late, I drag myself out the door, only slightly less miserably than on those days I go to the gym. But today I am eager to get outside where I do not have to pretend I am comfortable making normal eye contact with Charlie. Where he cannot peer into my face, and maybe right down into my truth.

Even the running itself feels good today. This straining of my legs, the wheezing of my lungs and pounding of my heart; this exertion seems to consume the anxiety that's taken hold of me since last night's newscast. The light breeze cools the sweat on my face and it is strangely familiar, and I immediately know why. I woke up in the middle of the night last night, suddenly and somewhat bewildered. The darkness was so complete that my eyes beheld the same nothingness whether they were closed or open. And then it came upon me, the realization that I could no longer visit my mother. I could no longer watch my life that could have been from behind my tree. This insight struck me abruptly, and I languished in it, this fresh new aloneness, until it filled me entirely.

I felt a coolness on my face and found that it was wet with tears, and I made myself stop because Charlie can always tell when I have been crying. And he can not know. I will not let him know any of this. If he ever does discover the truth, I will have lost him.

I told Charlie, because I knew he needed some explanation, and because I believe it is always preferable to have some tiny particle of truth within a lie, that I had briefly dated Gordon Blackwell while at a summer camp when I was a teenager. Charlie believes that I grew up in New York State, and so this story will not seem so farfetched to him. I hope.

I need Charlie to believe my lies, although a part of me aches to unburden my truth on him. It would be such an indulgence to swaddle myself in his wisdom and level-headed perspective and his precious kindness right now. That kindness would evaporate, however, if I were to confide in him, as would his love for me. And so, as I did 37 years ago, I endure this alone.

One misguided, poorly aimed, fateful squeeze of a trigger finger, one whizzing bullet that all of us wished could be put back in the barrel, mutated us from righteous crusaders into malevolent killers. It happened so quickly. The thunderous blasts of the gunshots stunned me. I did not know how many were fired, although the newspapers later said nine. One went into Jimmy's back, and one, the evil one, went into the neck of one of the security guards. I saw him fall, slowly, as though crumbling from the ankles upward.

Gordon was screaming for us to get out. To run. I stumbled after Gordon because we always did what Gordon told us to do. And because I was terrified of being left behind. Dumbly, I wondered why Jimmy did not get up off the floor and come with us.

As we approached the entrance, Gordon pulled off the bandana covering his face, and I did the same. Outside, Pam was waiting at her post by the door. "What happened?" she said, alarmed. "I heard shots."

"We gotta split," Gordon snapped, dragging her by the arm.

We jogged across 51st Street as nonchalantly as is possible when the gun in your hand is still hot, to the banged-up white Pontiac Star Chief where Michael waited behind the wheel. Gordon jumped in the front passenger seat. "Go!"

Michael craned his head to scrutinize Pam and me in the back seat. "Where's Jimmy?"

"He got hit," Gordon said. "Just go."

"What?" Michael spun around. "We can't just leave him!"

"Go goddammit!" Gordon roared. "I don't even know—he might be dead. We gotta split, Michael. Now."

Michael stared for a brief, awestruck second, then shunted the car into gear and eased it out into traffic. "What the hell happened?"

"Bad intel is what happened," Gordon muttered. "Take us to the other car. Fast as you can go."

"What the hell is that supposed to mean, bad intel?" I demanded, my fear turned to anger.

"It means you chicks don't know how to count, apparently." Gordon shot back. "You said there was only one guard."

"We scoped that place eleven times in the last three weeks. We never saw more than one guard. The second one must stay in the back or something until he's needed." I glanced at Pam and saw her face stricken with dismay and fear, tears brimming in her eyes. "No way," I shouted at Gordon, "can you blame this on us!"

"Is Jimmy really...?" Pam asked.

"I don't know. He got hit in the back and just went down on his face." I looked at her and I was crying. "I don't know." She stared back at me without sympathy.

I could see Michael's eyes framed in the rectangle of the rearview mirror and he was watching me. "Shit," he said quietly and looked away, back toward the road.

"Lucinda," Gordon turned and faced me. "Wipe your gun clean of fingerprints. We're going to leave them in this car."

I found myself surprised that I was still holding my revolver, and the sight of it, still clutched tightly in my hand, caused a searing pain through my palm. It smelled pungent, smoky, and in my ears echoed the fierce blast of a few moments ago.

"What? Why leave the guns?" Michael asked.

Gordon shot a look at me, then turned his attention to his gun, vigorously wiping at it with the hem of his shirt.

"Oh," Michael breathed. "Oh, no. Shit! The guns weren't supposed to be loaded. We agreed on that!" He looked to Gordon, who slid the gun from his shirt onto the floor. Michael's eyes appeared in the rearview mirror again, their fury trained on me, and I ducked my head like a coward. "Goddammit!" Michael shouted at the windshield. "What the hell did you think you were doing? You shoot someone?"

"Just drive the goddam car," Gordon ordered.

"Don't you tell me what to do!" Michael swatted at Gordon's head, smacking him hard in the temple.

Gordon grabbed Michael's arm. "Get off me!" The car swerved abruptly; a horn blared. "Shit Michael, drive the fucking car! You're going to attract attention!"

Michael turned his eyes back toward the road, both hands back on the steering wheel. "Goddam shithead screw-up."

Gordon pretended he did not hear this, and we rode in grim silence until we reached the second car, a new, bright blue Chevy Corvair, parked on 55th Street. Michael parked the Pontiac across the street, and we all disembarked, leaving nothing in the Star Chief but Gordon's and my literally-smoking guns.

As we drove up the West Side Highway in the Corvair, Gordon tapped his fingers against the window. "We're going to have to split up," he said, looking out through the glass. "Nobody go home, or to your parents' or friends' houses. Nowhere the police might look for you. Nowhere you would normally go." He ran a hand down his long black ponytail. "In fact, we should probably all get as far away from this city as possible."

There was silence in the car as Gordon's words echoed fiercely in my head. I could feel the fear welling up inside me and I looked at Michael, then Pam in desperation. Michael's eyes were focused on the road, and Pam refused to look at me at all. She spoke forward, over the seat, to Gordon. "They don't have any of our names," she said, her voice tiny. "And you and Lucinda had masks."

"They got Jimmy. And if he isn't…dead, well, he knows all our names."

"He won't talk," I said. I felt strongly that since we didn't save him, we should at least defend him.

"Maybe. Hope not. But we can't take that chance."

"So what's the plan then? When and where do we hook up again?"

Gordon turned sideways in his seat, looked at Pam and me, then at Michael. "Depends on Jimmy. If he talks, you can bet our pictures will be all over the TV and newspapers. If he keeps quiet, or if he's…if we haven't been identified, well, then we can meet up again in let's say, a month. Exactly. At Bethesda Fountain in Central Park. Five o'clock."

"Right," Michael snorted, and I knew that he had no intention of rejoining us.

Pam's dark eyes were big with fear. She, like me, had never before been alone. "Oh God."

"Let's just see, okay? Maybe nothing happens. Maybe nobody ever figures out it's us, and then we all make excuses about what we were doing for a month and everything goes back to normal. Just keep your eye on the news. And hope Jimmy is…quiet."

We said goodbye in Utica five hours later. I was crying again, and still. Still because we had lost Jimmy, one way or another, and because the sound of gunshots still rang in my ears and terrified me. I was crying again because I was nineteen years old and I had never been on my own, with no one to turn to. I was frightened of leaving everything I knew and being completely alone. Even though it was just for a month.

Pam and Michael snuggled together for a long time at the Utica bus station. They wanted to go away together, but Gordon was insistent that we all split up, at least for the first couple of weeks. I do not think he had a reason other than that he had already made and announced this decision, and he did not like to make a change to an already-issued command. But I could hear Michael and Pam making plans to meet somewhere in a few days. This made me feel even lonelier, and I turned away to cry by myself.

The next day our pictures were on every television and newspaper in the country, the security guard had died, and they were saying felony murder. Life imprisonment. Never-expiring statute of limitations. So I cut off my long blonde hair and dyed it black, and wore baseball caps much of the time so that I looked like a clean-cut young man, not one of the crazed, drugged-out counterculture hippies that had botched a robbery so badly they turned it into murder.

From a distance, I no longer looked like the girl in the photograph. Her face, however, was mine, and I could do little about that. I avoided, as much as possible, being anywhere in the vicinity of where that photograph was displayed, and I avoided eye contact with anyone, but watched everyone for excessive interest in me. I would not smile. Ever. The girl in the photograph was smiling and my face would look more like hers when it was smiling. This was not difficult to do; I did not ever feel happy. I felt terrified. I was afraid to go to sleep at night, for fear that someone might sneak up on me and catch me by surprise. I was afraid of the daylight in the morning that allowed people to see me. Over the years, as I first welcomed the uneventfulness, then became bored by it, then numbed by the tedium, the fear dissipated like early morning fog in the heat of the sun, and finally disappeared. Now it has returned.

In the dark, Charlie's hands expertly unrolled the film he had shot yesterday. Here in his darkroom he felt cut off, isolated from the rest of the world. Not in a bad way. It was comfortable and familiar here in his own private cocoon. Normally he was happy to be here.

Today, though, he was feeling shut out from not just the world in general, but from Annie's world in particular. This was not someplace he was used to being. Not at all someplace he enjoyed being.

She had been like this, closed to him, way back in the beginning, when they'd first met. But of course, that was because of what the poor thing had been through. And Charlie had been a stranger to her.

In so many ways, it seemed like a lifetime ago. It was the fall of 1969 in Chicago. She was sitting alone, on a bench in Grant Park, eating a muffin like a five-year-old would eat spinach. Her straight black hair was cut into a short little bob, which set her apart from so many others her age, females and males alike. Charlie raised his Nikon F Photomic to his eye and centered her face in the viewfinder. Her head inclined slightly, the curve of her jawline unfolding delicate and enticing against the shabby wooden bench on which she sat. His index finger pressed, again and again, snapping several pictures. The girl looked up, startled, at the clicking sounds. Her bright blue eyes were alert, with a fragile, naked melancholy. Looking at her, Charlie felt the sudden and urgent craving for a seat on the shabby wooden bench.

"Hey," he grinned nervously, walking toward her. "Sorry. I was just taking your picture. I guess I should have asked first."

She watched intently as he slid onto the bench, her arms wrapping themselves tightly around her slender body. Her eyes roamed over Charlie's blond curls, falling in ringlets past his shoulders, his tie-dye shirt and faded jeans with wide bell-bottoms. "Why?" she said finally, her voice low, suspicious.

"Why what?" Charlie smiled amiably, and the girl's eyes fell on the dimple in his left cheek. "Why take your picture?"

She nodded silently.

"It's for a class assignment. Intermediate Photography." He raised the camera to his face, focused, and shot two more frames quickly. "We're supposed to shoot images of beauty in the natural world." The shutter blinked one more time, then he lowered the camera and looked at her shyly. He pressed his lips together and raised his eyebrows, embarrassed now at his own words. "That was, um, the assignment."

The girl ducked her head down, as though inspecting the muffin in her hands. After an excruciatingly silent eternity, she glanced briefly up at him. "That's nice. Of you to say."

Charlie exhaled loudly, then smiled with surprise that he had been holding his breath. "Charlie," he said, extending his hand. "Charlie Pulkowski."

She looked at the hand, then up at the dimple, then at the clear blue eyes. "Ann," she said, and placed her hand gingerly in his.

"Ann," he repeated, grinning happily. "Groovy. And I wasn't just saying that. You really are…one of Mother Nature's finest works."

"Don't," she said, shaking her head. "I don't know how to talk to you when you say things like that."

"Okay. We don't want that. Do you live around here?"

She turned her head away, watched a pair of squirrels chase each other before turning back to him. "Tell me about you."

"Okay," he nodded. "I'm a senior at Northwestern. Majoring in fine arts. Photography. I grew up in Winchester, which is north of St. Louis. Two parents, one brother and a dog, those last two being indistinguishable from each other sometimes. I like to cook and play baseball, although I'm not very good at either. I'm against the war, of course, and adamantly in favor of Grace Slick." He leaned back and looked at Ann intently. "You look a little bit like her. Can you sing?"

"No." Her face twisted into an involuntary smirk, a half-smile, then quickly became serious again.

"Whoa," Charlie said. "Was that a smile?"

"No."

"You got something against smiling?"

She stared at him dolefully. "I need a job."

"What?"

"I need a job but I can't use my social security number or even my own name because…because I can't let anyone find me." She frowned an apology. "And I need you to destroy those pictures of me."

"Who," Charlie said slowly, "are you hiding from? The fuzz?"

"No," she blinked. "My...my family."

"You ran away?"

She nodded. "Had to."

"Hairy scene?"

Her eyes closed tightly for a moment, and when they opened they were damp and shining. Slowly, deliberately, she opened her mouth to speak, and the words stumbled out dry and raspy. "A nightmare."

She'd turned those sad turquoise eyes on him and he knew at that moment that he would help her. It was weeks before she'd trusted him enough to open up to him and let him in to the hell she had been living. Almost a month before she could bring herself to tell him about her abusive stepfather. About his visits to her bedroom in the dark, bleak hours of the night, visits that left her sore and sobbing alone into her pillow. About the alcoholic mother who wouldn't believe her daughter's words, who blamed her own child instead.

She'd slept in Charlie's bed, while he'd curl up in a pile of blankets in the corner of his tiny apartment. As beautiful as she was, and as much as he found himself captivated by her, she was just too fragile, too damaged for him to even contemplate approaching her in that way. Besides, she was still a child.

So he would keep her, he decided. He would keep her and care for her until she was whole again. He ventured off campus to the seedy apartment of an enterprising student with dubious undergraduate status who was known for trafficking in everything from illicit term papers to acid, and purchased her a fake ID with a false last name. He found her a job at an ice cream shop near campus. He listened when she wanted to talk, and talked when she could not put into words the terrible things she needed to say. And then, when she started to show and realized she was pregnant with the beastly man's baby, he held her while she cried.

Opening the door, Catherine was struck by the dazzling sheen of sun on the front walk, by the warmth of the morning air, and she breathed in deeply, inhaling the day's promise and vitality. The world was in full bloom this late spring, coming to life in bright colors and the soft, jazzy music of birds and breezes. Catherine stooped to pick up the daily *Boston Globe*, being careful not to spill her coffee, and brought both out to the picnic table.

It had been Sam's favorite place, this picnic table. Basking in the sun early in the day, it was an oasis of warmth in the cool morning gusts of spring and fall. In the afternoon and evening, shadows from the sprawling maple tree overhead spread across it and it became a breezy refuge from the summer swelter. *Just perfect*, Sam said just about every time he sat here, and Catherine looked across at his empty seat as though she'd just heard those words again.

Catherine sipped her coffee and unfolded the newspaper. Sam would be so proud of his namesake, baby Sam. Little Sam, who enabled the entire family, although they would never forget big Sam, to look forward rather than back. Her eyes drifted down the headlines of the front page as she put the coffee cup to her lips again. And almost gagged. There, at the bottom of the page, was her daughter's picture. Her long gone, often cursed, uneasily remembered, lost daughter. Lucinda. *Oh dear God.*

Catherine's hands shook the paper violently; the coffee spilled over its rim and she dropped both on the table. She hunched over the newspaper. The black-and-white photograph stared up at her, reproaching her. This beautiful, smiling, cheerful girl; so lovely, so perfect. The once-cherished high school photo lined up to the world like a mug shot. Catherine ran her fingers over the fuzzy picture. *Whatever became of you, my girl?*

She'd been lost so long ago. Physically taken away, yes, but also removed emotionally, morally. She was a killer, they said. A perverted monster that shot a bullet into a thirty-two-year-old man just doing his job. Leaving three young children fatherless. Leaving Sam and herself daughterless.

Nothing like when they'd lost Ray. Lucinda and Colin's older brother had been killed in the war, serving his country. There had been a body to bury and a proud military funeral, patriotic flags and men in uniform. It was tragic, but there was closure, and they could be proud of their son. Their daughter was different in every way.

Catherine allowed her shoulders to slump under the sheer weight, the relentless fatigue of disavowing the love in her heart for so many vacant, incomplete years. She let the tears come, rattling her body, drenching her face. She was despised, her girl, and with good reason. There was no good reason to love her. For years, Catherine had hoped that it had all been a mistake. That Lucinda would show up and prove to everyone they had been wrong. Mistaken identity. She'd been miles away at the time. If everyone had been wrong, and it had been a mistake, Lucinda could have— would have come forward and explained herself. But Catherine had waited, and the years had passed, and her daughter had not been heard from by anyone. So everyone was not wrong, and Lucinda was the terrible killer they all said she was, and there was not, in fact, any good reason to love her.

Much later, inside the house, Catherine dialed Colin at his office. "Is he in?" she said to his secretary. "It's his mother."

"One moment, Mrs. Whittendon."

Catherine listened to the dead, empty hiss for a long moment, then her son's detached voice broke through the void. "Hey Mom."

"Colin. Did you see the paper this morning?"

A pause. "Yeah."

Catherine waited for more, hesitated, then said, "They've got one of them. Do you think he knows where she is?"

The airy sound of a loud sigh shushed through the line. "I don't know, Mom. I don't know. But even if he does...I mean, do you still care after all this time?"

"No," she breathed. "Of course I don't."

"She's not Lucinda anymore. Not the way you remember her."

"No. I know she's not." Catherine looked down at her smiling daughter.

"She's gone, Mom. Even if they do find her, it's been thirty-seven years. I mean, after what she did then, who knows what kind of stuff she's been doing since?" Colin paused, listened to his mother's strained breathing. "It's better just to think of her as gone, Mom."

Catherine choked down a sob. "I always tell people that my daughter died when she was nineteen."

"Well," Colin's voice was serious, "that's the truth."

Jarvis has been toying with his newspaper all day, torturing me. The picture of me and the others, all in a row as they'd been on TV last night, is splayed out on the bottom of the front page. When he is not reading it, he leaves it on his desk, my face exposed to the world for all to see. I want so desperately to get up and flip the paper over so I do not have to see her staring at me. And surely, Jarvis and Lindsey and the others will look at her and see me. How could they not? But I have no excuse to touch his paper and I cannot risk bringing attention to it, so I force myself to sit here and pretend to be focused on my work. And so she continues to stare at us all.

I see Jarvis turn toward me, call my name. Did he just call me Lucinda?

"Annie!" Jarvis spreads his thick arms wide. "What is with you today?"

"Sorry. I don't know. I'm just distracted, I guess."

"Ya think? You're like a zombie today."

He looks hard at me, and I cannot help but look away. *Do not look so closely.*

He eases his huge bulk onto the edge of my desk. When he speaks, his voice is soft, kind. "Everything all right?"

I have to look at him now, and I do. I see Lindsey glance over quickly, then away. *Does she know?* "Just…some trouble at home," I lie. Or maybe it will be the truth.

Jarvis looks away, flustered. "Aw, jeez, I'm sorry. Jeez, I hope you work it out. You and Charlie are so perfect together. Or," he stops himself, switches gears, "is it Amber?"

"You know, Jarvis, I'd really rather not talk about it."

"Yeah, yeah, of course. I'm sorry. If there's anything I can do…"

"Thank you," I say, but am sure not to smile. Thirty-seven years later and I am back to not smiling so that I do not look too much like my high school photograph.

The fact that I am here, all these years later, and not in prison, is evidence that my disguise was effective. Now, the years have provided me with a different disguise. I am a gray-haired, middle-aged-almost-senior-citizen with wrinkles and a somber smile, and there are countless people who have always known me to be Annie Pulkowski and would not be easily convinced that I was someone else. Least of all Lucinda Whittendon, infamous murderer. Yet it is possible that someone may recognize me. Jarvis or Lindsey or a neighbor or Amber's teacher or the checkout girl at the supermarket or *anyone* could recognize me from the photograph. So I must watch them as I once did, with paranoia and fear clouding my vision. I must watch them all.

I stop for gas on the way home and the attendant is looking at me funny, I am sure of it. Just as everyone has been looking at me funny all day. The gas pump in his hand looks like a revolver, and I feel a stabbing pain shoot through the palm of my own hand. There is no gun in my hand, I know, but I look anyway.

"Have a good day, Ma'am," the attendant says, staring into my face.

Go away. "Thank you, you too," I say. Without a smile, of course.

I am so relieved to drive away from his prying eyes. He is watching my car as I pull away. My heart thumps heavily in my chest. Is he noting the license plate number?

Out here on the road, I feel better. More anonymous. My heart settles down a bit and my mind can venture out of its smothering cloak of paranoia. And though I don't want to, I think of Michael.

Michael is here in Massachusetts. Cambridge. Has he been here all this time? After fleeing New York all those years ago, and living for a while in the Midwest with Charlie, I felt drawn to come home. As close to home as possible. Close enough so that I could go visit home, watch it in secret. And it had not been difficult to convince Charlie to come here. For Michael, though, home was California. He had come about as far away from home as he could get. And yet, Cambridge was a natural place for a young, idealistic, so-far-left-leaning-bordering-on-revolutionary hippie fugitive to make a home in three decades ago.

Had I known he was here, just 100 miles away…what? What would I have done? I know he is here now, in Massachusetts General Hospital, and I will not go see him. Of course, partly that is because I know they will be watching his visitors and a trip to his room would end in a prison cell. Even if that were not the case, however, I would not go see him. I no longer know him. We are not those people we were back then, those revolutionaries. I am ashamed of those people; I do not want to see any of them again. I wish I did not have to torment my soul with the one who stares back from the mirror every day.

As I steer my little Toyota Prius up to my house, I notice something. A little blob on the lawn. Walking up closer, I see the blob is Amber, lying on her back, hands under her head, legs crossed at the ankles.

"Hey," I say.

"Hey, Nonny."

"Grampa kick you out of the house?"

She turns her eyebrows up at me. "You think I'd stand for that? I'm looking at shapes in the clouds," she says. "It's very relaxing. Very therapeutic. Stress-reducing."

"Is it?" I say. "I could use some of that."

"Well, pull up a patch of grass," Amber says, eager for me to join her.

I drop my bag and stretch out on the warm grass next to her. "What are you in need of therapeutic stress-reduction for these days?"

"Nonny, I'm an *adolescent*. In *middle school*. The social pressures alone are astronomical. How to reconcile the responsibility to be a good person and a good friend, build a college admission resume of extracurricular activities, yet still fit in and not be like, a dork. Not to mention the overwhelming need to know if Peter Quigley likes me or Janine Harris. Then there are the academic pressures. MCAS exams are next week, and the grade-point average must be maintained, preferably improved upon, for the aforementioned college resume. And through all of this, the hormones are simply *raging*, encumbering me with a precarious emotional instability." She turns her head toward me on her pillow of grass. "And I've got a zit coming out on the tip of my nose. Need more?"

"No," I laugh. I cannot help it. "I get the vividly-painted picture, thank you. But, nothing in particular, or extreme, though, that you need help on?"

"Just your typical teenage angst, Nonny. Just a stage, right?"

"So I hear. Too far back for me to remember myself." She does not mention, in her retinue of stress-inducers, that she is forced to live with her grandparents because her mother is an unstable and volatile drug addict.

"Ooh, see that one over there?" Amber points overhead to the sky. "A giant computer mouse chasing a little dragon. Or maybe it's just a lizard. See it?"

I look, but just see formless wispy blobs. Pretty, but no dragon, and definitely nothing high-tech. "Mmm," I mumble noncommittally.

"And over there," her extended finger shifts in the air, "see the lion with the hump on its back like a camel?" Her arm drops down to her chest and we are silent for a moment. "So what's stressing you out?"

"Oh," I say, sounding more startled than I would like. "It's nothing. Just work stuff."

She says nothing to this, just lets my lie hang there in the sky like the shape-shifting clouds above.

"Nothing to worry about," I say, simply because I cannot tolerate the silence any longer.

"Grampa's worried."

A loud thump in my chest as my heart stands still for a moment. "Is he?"

"Well, he didn't say so, but...you know. A pterodactyl!" Her arm shoots up once again, pointing at this new figure.

I want to ask her what Charlie said, exactly, but that will only lend credence to her—and therefore his—concerns. Or are they full-blown suspicions? Theories, maybe? In any case, this is not a subject I can safely continue discussing. I search the clouds, desperately, for some secret thing to emerge from its hiding place and reveal itself to me so that I can make a contribution to the menagerie in the sky. As a child, I saw endless objects and creatures up there, shifting constantly, in a languorous, theatrical dance. Now they will not show themselves to me.

"An ice cream cone, right over there," says Amber. "See it?"

I look. They are clouds. Nothing more. "You know," I tell her, "I think there must be a certain age over which you can no longer see shapes in the clouds. And I am most definitely over it."

"Really?" Amber turns toward me in surprise. "Not everyone. Grampa sees lots of shapes still. And he's older than you."

"He does?" This makes me sad for some reason I cannot name.

"Yeah, he sees all kinds of weird stuff. Moldy cheese and elephants on tripods...weird stuff like that."

"Oh," I say, hoisting myself back up to standing. "Well, speaking of your weird grandfather, I'm going to go in and see him. You staying out here for a while?"

"Yeah. Little while longer."

I pick up my bag from the lawn where I had dropped it and head toward the house, wondering what Charlie has that allows him to see magic like a child when I no longer can.

Inside, Charlie relaxes on his favorite overstuffed leather recliner. His feet lay on the extended footrest, elbows on the cushy armrests as he turns a page in the newspaper he holds. *The newspaper.*

He lifts his eyes over his black-rimmed reading glasses to look at me. "Hi hon," he smiles. "How's everything?"

"Hi," I breathe, force a smile. I cross the room and lean down to kiss him. "I'm good," I say as he plops a quick kiss on the tip of my nose. "How are you?"

"Fine. Just reading about your favorite president," he says with a grin, knowing my abject abhorrence for our current commander-in-chief. "Even die-hard Republicans in the Midwest are turning against him. Comparing Iraq to Vietnam."

Vietnam. Do all my terrible memories of that time show on my face? "It's about time," I say. "What took everyone so long?"

Charlie presses the footrest down and it folds into the chair with a smack. "I don't know." He flips to a different page and hands it to me, pointing. "And here. I was also reading about your buddy, there, Gordon Blackwell. I can't believe you dated him. How come you never mentioned it before? Back when we met?"

I was too busy telling you other stories. And I didn't know I needed this story yet. "I don't know. It was years before I met you, and we didn't go out very long. We were just kids. And I guess I was kind of embarrassed by it. I still am."

Charlie grins at me. "Hadn't yet developed your stellar taste in men."

I smile back at him before I remember my new no-smiling rule. Can I apply the rule to Charlie? Or Amber? They, who infuse the only authentic, ardently savored life into this shell of an existence I lead? No. Charlie and Amber, the two loves of my counterfeit life, must be exempt from the no-smiling rule, and as I realize this, I am relieved.

"You might get to see him again," Charlie is saying.

"What?"

"It says in the article that they have reason to believe this guy in the hospital might know something about some of the others."

They do? Panic surges through me again. "Why would he tell them anything? He's dying."

"That's exactly why, I guess. He obviously wants to cleanse his soul; he's already confessed. Why not help bring the others to justice if he can?"

Why not? If he can. Can he? I do not believe Michael knows where I am; I certainly do not know where he or any of the others have lived their lives. And I do not believe Michael would tell the police if he did know. But of course, I don't really know this present-day, fifty-seven-year-old Michael.

I summon up my best casual shrug and nonchalant voice for Charlie. "I guess." I reach what I hope to be a very dispassionate hand out for the newspaper he is holding. I look at it, up close for the first time all day. Five killer children. Gordon, who I had never really liked, was only intimidated by, and would never have dated. Jimmy, poor sweet kid who was never really comfortable with our steal-from-the-banks-give-to-the-poor schemes, but who was also intimidated by Gordon. Michael, charismatic and charming, and maybe the only one of us who was truly good-hearted. Pam, my best friend from high school, joining me in my save-the-world adventure. And me.

Above the five of us murderers is a picture of the man we killed. Robert Dechesney. *He is so young.* At the time he seemed like an old man, part of the Establishment, the enemy. But I see now that he is younger than Darlene. Younger, and working a real job and being a good parent. Until a bullet in the neck bled the young life right out of him.

Does this man not deserve justice? Do the reckless, self-righteous renegades who killed him deserve to be punished? Of course they do. I have known this for years. I think I knew it as I watched the poor man fall. But I was scared then. I was a coward and terrified of jail. Now, I believe I have the courage to face what time I have left in my life without freedom, but not the courage to face Charlie with the truth. Or Amber. And what about Amber? Her mother is a mother only biologically. What harm will it cause Amber to learn that her only other female role model is even worse than a pharmaceutical-sodden mess? A killer. A stealer of life. Me, whom she has always turned to for kisses on booboos and snuggles to ward off the monsters in her nightmares, and whom she still occasionally confides in once in a while. Where will the love and trust in her soul go if she ever learns the truth of me? I know only this. I will not be able to stand face to face and watch that trust turn into something ugly as she looks upon me. That is something for which I have not the flimsiest trace of courage.

CHAPTER 5

The last, watery gulp of gin was already gone from the glass, but Darlene tilted it up to her mouth and sucked at the ice cubes. Slowly, reluctantly, she set the glass down on the scarred wooden bar and stared mournfully into its emptiness. She reached out absently for the pack of cigarettes in front of her, tapped one out and fumbled with a green plastic lighter until the tiny orange glow flared in front of her, familiar and comforting. Inhaling deeply, the hot, acrid smoke filled her lungs.

Darlene shifted slightly on her barstool and lifted her head as she exhaled a crooked pillar of gray. The dim haze in the dreary bar was alive, swirling and dancing to the discordant music of drunken voices.

"Hey gorgeous."

Darlene lifted purple-shadowed eyelids at the voice. Three-day-old beard, blood-shot eyes, mean smile. "Fuck off."

"Kinda what I had in mind." A rough, sandpaper hand shot out and slid inside Darlene's v-neck shirt, bristling against her breasts.

"I said fuck off, asshole!" She twisted away, wrenched his hand out of her shirt and bit down hard on a callused fingertip.

"Ahh—shit!" he yelped, clutching his finger. "What the fuck you do that for?"

"What the fuck you cop a feel for?"

He glared at her with unconcealed disgust. "Fucking bitch," he spat, "Ain't worth it."

Darlene watched him walk away, fading into the turbid, melancholy gloom and then stop. He stood motionless for a moment, then turned and shuffled back to her. "Look. Baby. We started out bad."

"You started out bad."

He shrugged an acknowledgement. "Okay. I did. So let me start over. My name's Frank. What's yours?"

Darlene sucked deeply on her cigarette and turned to stare at her empty glass.

"Come on, honey," Frank persisted. "We could be good together. We both got something the other one needs."

"I need another drink." She glanced at him. "You gonna buy me a drink?"

"Sure. Sure, I'll buy you a drink if that's what you want. But I got something better."

She turned, curious, and didn't try to hide it.

"You like ice?" The question on his face morphed into a grin as he watched her process his words. "Oh, yeah. I could tell you were a crystal meth girl. I knew it."

Darlene examined Frank again, who actually possessed a nice, square jaw under the scruffy beard, and teeth that were all present and lined up relatively neatly. Not so bad. She offered a thin smile that gradually grew broader and more genuine.

"All right, then," Frank bobbed his grinning head. "Let's go. My car is just outside."

She nodded assent, slid off her barstool and tugged down the hem of her short skirt. "Okay."

Frank watched her adjust the little denim skirt, then put a hand on the small of her back and directed her toward the door. He glanced around the smoky bar, nodded to a dark corner on the other side of the room, and followed Darlene outside.

"Over here," he said, leading her toward a decrepit blue Dodge Stratus parked in the shadows at the edge of a mostly-empty lot. Frank grinned over the roof of the car as he fumbled with the keys in the lock of the driver's side door. He climbed in, leaned over the seats and unlocked the passenger door.

"So," Darlene said as she settled into the seat next to Frank, "I'm Darlene."

"Darlene. Yeah. Good." Frank turned the keys in the ignition and the car sputtered, then rumbled unwillingly into service.

"Where we going?" Darlene said. "Let's just do it here."

Behind them, the back doors of the Dodge creaked open loudly and two men fell onto the seats. "Yeah!" one of them whooped. "We got ourselves a party!"

Darlene spun around, startled. "Who the fuck are you?"

"They're just friends of mine," Frank said, grinning into the rearview mirror. "You'll like them. They're the ones with the ice."

I have tripped the burglar alarm and it is shrill, piercing, head-splittingly loud. Red lights flash in the darkness at me, warning me or berating me, I cannot tell. I cover my ears with my hands, but the trilling bores through my mere flesh and bone and finds its way into my head to torture me from the inside out. The red lights flicker, then fade, and are suddenly gone completely, and I find myself prone on my bed in the blackness, the telephone at my side braying obnoxiously.

The digital clock glows 3:22 in cool green, and I know before I pick up the phone that it is Darlene. Needing money or a ride or a sucker to post bail. My hand pauses over the receiver. I should not even answer it. I am tired of it all.

"Hello." My voice sounds sleepy and I am glad of that. Not that she has any qualms about disturbing my life.

"Mom." Her voice is thin, weepy. As I would expect when she is asking a favor at this hour.

"It's 3:22, Darlene. Whatever mess you've gotten into will have to wait until the sun comes up." This is my opening shot, and I know that she will eventually convince me to give her what she needs, but I must make her earn the favor. It is, as has been eloquently said, this dance we do.

"Mom, I need...will you come get me?"

This I can say no to. "I will not. It's the middle of the night, and I'm sleeping, like you should be. Call a taxi."

"I don't have any money, I had to beg just to use this phone." A muffled whimper comes through the line. "And I'm...hurt."

Hurt? I breathe in the suddenly heavy night air. Charlie stirs next to me; I feel his hand on my arm. "What, exactly, is hurt?"

"I'm...everything," Darlene sobs. "They beat me, and I...Mom, I really need you." The sound of sobbing stops abruptly, and the new silence is terrible to hear. "Please Mom. I need you."

She is waiting for me. Alone and huddled against the ripped green vinyl of a booth near the window, she waits. She watches me as I enter the all-night diner awash in harsh lights and the smell of old grease. I stand and look at her. She does not move. We are at a place, a time that neither of us chooses to be. She is mortified to tell me what has happened, and I am terrified to know.

When she stands and comes to me, I can see that she walks with difficulty. There is a dark purple bruise under one eye and her lower lip is swollen. I think the dark smear on her short denim skirt is blood.

She is watching me, and I can see something changing in her face, behind her eyes. It is fear becoming shame. No, not shame. Remorse. I do not know. Perhaps I am wrong altogether and am seeing only what I have been hoping to see all these years. Her shoulders shake and she hugs her arms around herself, seeking solace from her own battered body, weeping quietly as though not to disturb. I am not thinking when I wrap my arms around her, nor am I feeling. I am just doing. I hold her frail, trembling body and let her cry against me, just as I did when she was six and had gashed her knee on her bicycle. This embrace feels utterly the same to me. And although I do not know what has happened, I find myself crying along with her.

It is morning, just a few hours after I brought Darlene home, but it is light out now and so feels completely unconnected to the eerie drive home from the diner. Except that Darlene is now sleeping on my couch. She would not let me take her to a hospital. She would heal on her own she said, and she couldn't face them poking and prodding her for hours. She wanted to sleep, somewhere comfortable and safe. She wanted to go *home*. I knew she did not mean her dingy, roach-infested apartment in Springfield.

I will skip my workout this morning. The early morning rescue of my bleeding, traumatized daughter has sapped my energy and my resolve. Charlie has compassionately allowed me as much coffee as I can siphon down, even making it and serving it to me himself. She would not tell me what happened to her, and for once, I believe she truly is trying to save me some pain.

She is going sober. That is the one thing she will tell me. No more drinking, no more drugs. It is true she has said this before. It does not matter if I believe her, I have come to learn, only that she believes herself. So far, she evidently has not.

In another hour, Jarvis will be at FROGS and I will call him and tell him that there is a family emergency and I will not be in today. I do not know if Darlene will want me to be here when she wakes up, but I want to hear her repeat her vow of sobriety in the light of day. I think it is important for her to say it, and to hear it herself, when there are no shadows in which to hide. So I sit down with my third cup of coffee in the overstuffed recliner that is Charlie's favorite, and I wait.

CHAPTER 6

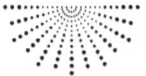

A battered red Ford pickup truck rolled into the rest area off the Massachusetts Turnpike in the town of Lee. Its sides and undercarriage were spattered with old mud from the South Dakota fields where it had spent its entire eighteen-year existence until this trip. Stopping abreast of the line of gas pumps, the driver side door opened and a stocky woman with tight blue jeans, work boots, and gray-flecked hair emerged. She reached her arms up high and stretched, the past sixteen-hundred miles weighing heavily in her cramped back. She smiled though. Massachusetts at last.

She paid cash for a full tank of gas, then headed into the combination fast food and convenience store for a giant cookie and a package of vanilla snack cakes for the rest of her trip, which she estimated to be another couple of hours, then headed for the McDonald's counter.

"Can I help you, Ma'am?" The boy behind the counter was several sizes too scrawny for his white uniform, and his childlike face was dotted with red, pimply splotches.

"Uh, yeah. Let me have a super-size fries and a chocolate shake." She dug a hand into the pocket of her tight jeans with difficulty. "Make that two fries." Same pathetic story since she was a kid. Always ate too much when she was nervous.

"For here or to go?"

The woman pursed her lips as she considered this question. It would be nice to stay and take a break from driving. But who knew how much time she had? "To go," she said finally. "I'm in a rush."

The baby-faced boy passed her a white paper bag overflowing with fries and a large paper cup. She tucked a straw into the plastic cover on the cup and took a deep pull as she turned to leave.

"Have a nice day," the boy called after her.

"Mmmm." Shuffling forward, her head down, she sucked hard on the straw, feeling the icy chill slide down her throat, through her chest and into her belly. Delicious. She headed toward the exit, slurping the frozen shake as she walked. Almost at the door, she lifted her head just as two people were entering from the parking lot. A jolt of electricity sizzled in her chest. The bag of fries slipped from her grasp and fell to the floor as she gaped at the huge black man and the thin, gray-haired white woman. As the woman turned and locked eyes with her, she shivered from a coldness that had nothing to do with her chocolate shake.

Jarvis insisted this morning that I make the trip out to the western part of the state with him today, and now we are in the blue FROGS van traveling eastward on the Mass. Pike back toward Springfield. Like everything else about Jarvis, his foot is heavy, and so we are speeding along significantly faster than the official 65 mile-per-hour limit.

I could not very well protest making this trip after he was so understanding about my need for two days off last week to be with Darlene. My daughter had been quiet, subservient and agreeable when she woke just before noon that day. That is to say, nothing like her normal self. She ate whatever Charlie prepared for her and answered every question we asked her that did not pertain to the previous evening's events. She even thanked me for coming to get her.

And she willingly reiterated her determination to stay away from the drugs and alcohol. I am not so naïve as to say outright that she is a changed person. I can be forgiven, perhaps, for hoping quietly to myself.

"Annie." Jarvis says my name without turning his eyes from the road.

"Sorry," I say. "I know I'm being bad company today."

"Don't apologize. Jeez, don't even worry about that." He shakes his big head at the windshield in front of him. "Listen. I'm just going to mention this one more time, and then I'll leave you alone about it. You gotta get Darlene back into rehab."

He is right, I know. "She's been through it twice. We've all been through it twice."

"Sometimes that's what it takes. Besides, that was just detox. You got to get her in to a place they do dual diagnosis. Treat the whole problem."

"She's not mentally ill, Jarvis. Drug abuse is the whole problem."

"Maybe," he says, though he is not convinced. "But more than seventy percent of people with a substance abuse problem also have a mental illness."

"Don't quote numbers to me, Jarvis!" My voice is harsher, shriller than I intended. "Don't treat me like some idiotic, ass-addled neophyte desperately in need of your wise counsel! I've been around this block before and I know all the statistics. I'm telling you, Darlene is an addict. Period. That's all there is to it."

Jarvis turns his head to look at me, but I cannot look back at him. I can only stare out the window at the white dashes down the middle of the turnpike as they flash by and disappear under the van.

"Who the hell was that?" he says finally.

"What?"

"I've known you over twenty years and I've never seen you snap like that."

"I'm sorry. I didn't mean to snap—"

"I'm not looking for you to apologize. I'm a big boy, you might've noticed. I can take it. But you—I don't know that side of you. Must be one deep nerve I just hit."

"No." My head is shaking of its own volition. "No nerve. I mean, I just want to focus on the real issue, which is breaking the addiction. Darlene has a mean streak in her, but that's an emotional flaw, not mental illness."

"Uh huh."

Damn him.

"I'm hungry," Jarvis says as he steers the van onto a service road leading to a large rest area. "You?"

I am not, but I understand that Jarvis has an almost Pavlovian response to the fast food Golden Arches; he cannot pass them by without sampling their goods. He parks the van and we walk together across the parking lot toward the large gray building that houses restaurants and restrooms.

"So anyway, I know of a good place," Jarvis says. "Good success rate. Think about it." His long legs carry him quickly for such a large man and I have to trot to keep pace. "And that's the last I'm going to say about it. Really."

We reach the entrance and Jarvis pulls open the door for me. "But if I can be of any help," he is saying, and I cannot help but smile to myself at the knowledge that Jarvis will be utterly unable to keep his pledge to not mention it again. His heart is simply too big and I know that he considers me a friend. And so I forgive this friend.

It is bustling with people inside the building, and I look around for the restrooms. A paper McDonald's bag falls to the floor nearby, and I glance at the person who dropped it. She is a woman about my own age, somewhat plump and with hair not quite as gone-over-to-the-gray-side as my own. It is only when I feel her eyes on me and look back into hers that my heart stalls in my chest. A prickly clamminess crawls over my skin. These eyes staring back at me are the same eyes that shared in my adolescent angst and laughed at my jokes and sympathized and conspired with and comforted me. These are Pam's eyes, and as I look at this woman's face, although it is fleshier and sadder, I see that it is Pam's face. I also see that she has most definitely recognized me. And I am terrified.

We stare, across ten feet and thirty-seven years, and I feel as though we are trapped in our own bubble and the world is moving indifferently around us. She does not move and I am unable to. Somewhere underneath the fear, buried way deep inside the many layers I have built up over the decades, something flickers in the cold darkness of my false self. A tiny flame that is pain, longing.

Why is she here? After all this time? In this place? If she approaches me, do I acknowledge her? As my brain fumbles with these questions, Pam moves. She picks up her fallen food bag and walks forward, toward me. I am still frozen in my spot, even as I sense Jarvis looking at me, asking what is wrong. Pam ducks her head, stares at her feet, moves past me and out the door and she is gone. Still, I am unable to move.

Pamela Mercurio, whose South Dakota license bore the name Monica Patterson, sat in her pickup truck and waited. She had moved the truck so that she had a good view of the rest stop entrance. The engine was running, and the new pink Red Sox hat she'd purchased inside was pulled low over her face.

That had definitely been Lucinda in there. Even if she hadn't been sure, the woman's reaction confirmed it. She had definitely recognized Pam, and she was definitely not happy about it. Well, likewise to you, bitch.

When they were teenagers, Pam had been sure they would be best friends forever. Lucinda had been her savior when she'd moved to town at fourteen, shy and gawky and still wearing braces. Her first months of ninth grade had been agony until the beautiful, blonde Lucinda Whittendon had taken her under her eminently popular wing and given her a place to belong. And they'd grown to be close, inseparable, tied-at-the-hip best friends. Beautiful and exciting, Lucinda could have chosen anyone for a best friend. Pam had been grateful at first, and then thrilled, and then incapable of imagining life without her friend. So when Lucinda went off to the University of Massachusetts at Amherst, Pam followed. She would have gone anywhere, done anything for Lucinda. And she did.

"Pam, we could make such a difference," Lucinda had said one afternoon over banana splits. "In fact, we don't really have a choice. This is a criminal war. And by just going along, living our cozy little lives, we are complicit in the crime. Every day we sit here doing nothing, hundreds more innocent Vietnamese people are murdered by our invading army. How can you live with those deaths on your conscience?"

Pam sucked whipped cream off a maraschino cherry. "That's not fair and you know it. We are doing something. We go to all the demonstrations and sit-ins, we sign the petitions, we speak out. We're doing everything we can legally do."

Lucinda smacked her palm against the table sharply. "Legally. Right. But let me ask you something. If an invading army marched into Boston or New York or Chicago and started murdering people in the street, wouldn't we do anything—everything we could—to stop them, legal or not? So why is it different just because the victims are on the other side of the world? It's—it shouldn't be!" She pulled a strand of hair from the top of her head and wound it tightly around her middle finger. "I'm not explaining it well," she said, exasperated. "Can you just come to the meeting tonight and listen? That's all I'm asking. Just come and listen."

"You're explaining it fine," Pam said. "I get it. It's just that they seem so extreme, those guys."

"My God, Pam! Where have you been these last few years? Extreme is exactly what's needed right now. This country is extremely screwed up, or haven't you noticed? Aren't you sick of scanning casualty reports for names of guys you know? Aren't you sick of watching our friends march off in a uniform they never wanted to wear to murder women and children. And then wondering if they're ever coming back?"

Pam set her spoon gently in her bowl, lifted her face to look at her friend. "Nothing," she said, "will bring Ray back, Lucinda. Nothing you or me or anyone does will ever bring him back."

Lucinda gaped, eyes watering, at Pam for a long moment. "My brother," she said quietly, "was supposed to be an architect. He was supposed to marry Sue Ellen Barker and have kids and a dog and a picket fence. He wasn't supposed to die in a miserable jungle on the other side of the world. And no, he's never coming back. But there are other guys like him being sent over there every day to die in that jungle." She twisted the strand of hair around her finger tighter. "Do you know what he said to me when he hugged me goodbye?" She waited for Pam to shrug a no. "Nothing. I wished him good luck and I said I would miss him, and I waited for my big brother to say something to me. He was always saying something, giving me advice I didn't want. But that day, he said nothing. And I looked at him, waiting, and his face…he was scared. Ray. Scared. He's never been scared of anything in his life. But that day, he was so scared he couldn't even talk."

And then Lucinda had said please, and smiled her prom queen smile, and Pam knew she would go to the meeting with her friend the next night. If only she hadn't gone. How many countless things would have been different over the last few decades? If only she'd been able to resist Lucinda's smile.

The older, gray-haired Lucinda emerged from the building and Pam hunched down in her seat. The big black man was still with her, and together they walked toward the parking lot. As much as Pam hated to admit it, Lucinda still had that prom queen way about her. Even with the lines in her face and the white in her hair, which was short now, the elegance and grace that had made her so popular was unmistakable as her still-slender body ambled across the lot.

Pam eased her truck forward as Lucinda and her large friend rounded the corner of the building, keeping them in her sight. They weaved their way between parked cars and finally stopped at a large blue van with white letters stenciled on its side. Pam maneu-vered her truck so that she could read the lettering. Food Recovery of Greater Springfield. *Springfield*! Lucinda was in Springfield? Just forty-odd miles from where they'd grown up in Dunlee Mill? Pam craned her neck and watched as the blue van pulled out of its parking space. The prom queen had come home. Shouldn't be so surprising, but it was.

The blue van rolled across the parking lot toward the ramp to the highway. Its path would take it right past Pam's truck. Pam watched motionlessly for an instant, then rolled down her window and snatched the cap off her head. She stared at the van as it approached, leaned her head out the window and waited to see Lucinda's face behind the van's windshield. It was there, staring back at her as the van slid by, a naked fear marking her pretty features. Pam smiled. Very satisfying.

CHAPTER 7

Catherine closed the door to the hospital room behind her slowly. He didn't know. The disappointment was overwhelming, crushing. Despite her best efforts, she had allowed high hopes to overwhelm good sense and believed that the man in the hospital bed would know where she could find Lucinda. But he did not. He hadn't seen any of them since the day of the robbery, he'd said.

"Murder," she'd corrected him, with a cold look.

His eyelids closed briefly in a silent nod. "Murder," he acknowledged.

Catherine's eyes wandered over the dying man curiously. She had never seen a murderer in person before. She would have expected a person much different from regular human beings. A hardness, an exposed callousness like the rough shell of a crustacean. But this man seemed weak and frail and defenseless. Abandoned by God as he died. Pity welled up in her before she could stop it and she turned to leave. She did not want to feel pity for this man.

She stopped at the door and turned back toward him. "There's something I always wondered...needed to know," she faltered. "Who actually shot the security guard?"

A monitor on the wall beeped a steady, monotonous rhythm. "We all did," he said. "We're all guilty."

Catherine shook her head in frustration. "I know. I know you're all guilty. But who actually pulled the trigger? I know it wasn't you or Pamela; you were both outside the building. And the other man who was shot, his gun had never been fired, the police said. So it was either that third man, Gordon Blackwell, or it was…Lucinda." She took a deep, silent breath and exhaled slowly. "I need to know. Who it was."

The man on the bed turned uncomfortably through the many tubes hooked up to him toward Catherine. "I don't know," he said, his voice raw. "They didn't talk about it."

"I don't believe you." She said it more as a challenge than because she knew it to be true. She was probing. Yet she could not escape the feeling that she had just barely ducked under the proverbial bullet whizzing straight at her heart.

Pam stopped abruptly outside the hospital room door. Someone was in there. It was probably just a nurse or someone, but to be sure, she stood down the hall, ready to duck around the corner. She chewed anxiously on a fingernail. God! If this wasn't nerve-wracking enough.

Michael is sick, she reminded herself again. Really sick. Not to mention thirty-seven years older. Cut off all that thick, shaggy dark hair, and make it short and gray. Maybe add a few pounds to his body and face. Maybe a lot of pounds like she'd added to herself. He wasn't going to look twenty anymore, she knew that. But he would still be handsome. He must be.

She'd thought so the instant she saw him. Stretched out across a couch and coffee table, his body was long and athletic. Thoroughly relaxed, yet ready to spring into action at any time. Although she'd allowed Lucinda to talk her into going to the meeting, she was uncomfortable being there until Michael had looked up at her and grinned a heart-melting grin.

"Outta sight," she'd seen him say to himself, and she'd known it was meant for her. He waved to her to come sit next to him.

"Hi," she breathed, settling onto the couch next to him.

His smile was friendly, welcoming. "Never saw you before. First time here?"

Pam's head bobbed up and down. "My friend Lucinda talked me into coming."

"Good. We need more chicks in this organization." His eyes roamed over her face. "Especially ones like you."

Pam felt the heat rise in her face and knew it to be turning a sweaty pink. She looked down into her lap.

"Oh, you embarrass easily," he laughed. "I'm sorry. I just couldn't help myself. What's your name?"

"Pam."

"Real big welcome to you, Pam." He reached for her hand and shook it formally. "I'm Michael."

Her hand felt warm, lovely, comfortably at home wrapped inside his, and Pam smiled now, all these years later, at the memory of it.

Down the hall, someone was leaving Michael's room. An old woman. Who looked oddly familiar, although Pam couldn't see her entire face. She was crying, it seemed, her hands folded and pressed against her mouth. Then she took a deep, loud breath and shuffled down the hall away from Pam, toward the elevators.

Pam watched her go, breathed in heavily herself, and walked timidly toward the door of Michael's room. It was time. She pushed the door open, peeked inside. A gasp escaped her before she could contain it. The man on the bed couldn't possibly be Michael. He turned toward the sound of her and stared. Pam looked into the man's face and felt the pull of tears behind her eyes. It was him.

She stepped into the room and over to the bed. He looked so...

small. His bones pressed through papery, mottled skin, and the wonderful thick hair she had buried her fingers in so many times had withered into no more than a few wisps of gray. His eyes peered out at her from deep sockets ringed with sallow bruises.

"Michael." Her voice was no more than a feeble whisper.

Michael's eyes stayed still and focused on her face for so long without flinching that she began to believe he could not see. Finally, he spoke, and she could hear that his disease had ravaged his smooth and mellow voice as well as the rest of him.

"Pam?" he said in a harsh rasp. "Oh my God. Pam? Really?"

Pam nodded, squeezing the tears back. "Really."

Michael reached a bony hand out toward Pam, and she took it and pressed it between both of her own. "Pam," he croaked, "you shouldn't have come. I think they're watching my visitors to see if any of you show up." Dampness seeped out from between his own lids. "I'm so sorry. You're going to get caught now."

Pam smiled down at him. "I figured they might be watching. I knew I might get caught. It's okay." She squeezed his cold and bony hand, lifted it and pressed it to her face. "It's worth it."

He shook his head, a sad, feeble smile playing across his face. "God, Pam."

"I just mean," she continued, "it doesn't matter where I spend the end of my life. I've got nothing. Never really did, all these years."

"I know how that goes," he breathed heavily.

Pam studied his face closely. "What about—has Lucinda been here?"

"Lucinda?" Michael's eyes widened. "No. But her mother was in here just before you came in. Wanting to know where she is. Do you know?"

Pam looked away, avoiding his gaze. "No, I...I kind of thought you might."

"No. You're the first one of us I've seen since we split up in Utica."

She turned back toward him. "Seriously? I kind of thought...I always wondered, you know, all this time. Why didn't you meet me in Cleveland like we planned?" She stared down at their hands, still intertwined. "I waited…"

Michael's eyes narrowed, the anguish in them radiating darkly. "I'm…so…sorry. I just—when our pictures hit the news I just panicked, I guess. I thought that if they'd gotten you, it might be a trap, or something. I just—I was scared, Pam. I'm sorry."

Pam's head bobbed, her chest shook with little sobs. "I was scared too. I thought you had been caught. I kept watching the news…and then I thought…. You broke my heart, Michael." She wiped at her eyes with the back of her hand. "For the second time."

"Pam—."

"Just tell me one thing," she said. "Did you…did you love Lucinda?

Michael gazed sadly at Pam, looking through her. "No," he said finally. "No, I didn't. That was just…a mistake. I loved you, Pam."

Pam smirked up at the ceiling, dropped Michael's hand. Did he know what a piss-poor liar he was? Love? It was the days of free love. And he was twenty and believed it all really was free. But now he is 57 and smart enough to know better, and so he reaches for the better answer, the kinder answer. Give him credit for being kind.

"I miss those days," she said. "Don't you?"

"I used to. For a long time. Now I just feel ashamed."

"You shouldn't. You didn't shoot anyone. And neither did I. We have nothing to feel ashamed about, Michael. We were trying to do some good in the world. It's the last time I ever felt I did anything important."

"We were cowards, Pam. All of us. In just about every way."

Pam looked down at this withered old man who was no longer Michael. A dying man she did not know. "I'm going to go now. It was good to see you, Michael. I've missed you."

"Pam. I…thank you for coming. For taking the risk."

She waved a hand at him. "I told you. I got nothing to risk. The last good thing I had was you."

CHAPTER 8

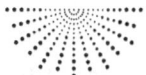

I have always wondered what became of Pam. More than any of them, and despite the fact that she hated me at the time we split up, I have missed her friendship more than anything save my own family over the past three and a half decades. It was with Pam that I tasted my first beer and coughed over my first cigarette. It was to Pam that I entrusted the secret of my first real crush on a boy, and on Pam's comforting shoulders that I later cried over him. It was with Pam that I shared all the giddy joys and earth-shattering anxieties of adolescence, and Pam who took the blood (actually beer) oath with me to be friends forever. During what would turn out to be my final years as Lucinda Whittendon, I felt closer to Pam than anyone in the world, my family included.

And so it was Pam that I lured into joining the Soldiers of Democracy with me to fight society's injustices. It was Pam I convinced to join the operation in New York. She didn't want to come. She was afraid, I could see. I did not—could not—let her know that I, too, was afraid.

We were nineteen. Children still, although it is only much later that I realized that. We knew we were in the right; we were the country's only hope to save itself from the corrupt and violent path down which it was headed. Individually, we may have been children, but together we were a revolutionary force that would change the world. We had moral justice on our side; we could not back away from this.

At the time, I was sure that Pam was persuaded by my ability to exude so much confidence in what Soldiers was doing. Years later, I realized that my closest friend must obviously have seen past my false bravado and into the soul of the frightened little girl I truly was. And that, I believe now, is the real reason she came with me.

That, and Michael. Pam was smitten with him the moment she met him. And I, to my older and wiser regret, used that.

We were at another meeting, our third or fourth, and Gordon was expounding on the plan for New York, trolling for recruits. Pam had dressed with extra care that night. She wore her favorite lavender and fuchsia striped bellbottoms and a filmy lavender blouse with a boldly dipping v-neckline. Her normally wavy brown hair fell in tight curls over her shoulders. When we arrived, Michael was across the room, his long body ranging over his favorite couch and coffee table as usual. I watched Pam as she spotted him, her face bright with excitement. Too shy to approach, she waited for him to notice her.

"Go sit with him," I nudged her. "I told you, he thinks you're really cool."

"I still don't think I believe you."

"His exact words were, 'really groovy and totally digs what we're talking about.'" Groovy, he had in fact said; the last part was my own embellishment, although I believed it to be true. "He's waving to you! Go!"

"Come with me," Pam grabbed my hand and pulled me across the crowded room.

Michael was pulling on a lumpy, hand-rolled cigarette as we approached. "Hi," Pam smiled shyly.

He exhaled a burst of gray into the already smoky room. "Hey, Pam. Reefer?" he offered.

"Okay," Pam agreed, accepting the half-smoked joint from him.

His eyes roamed over her appreciatively. "Bitchin' threads."

"Oh," she breathed, looking down at her clothes as though she had no idea what she was wearing. "Thanks."

"Hey, Michael," I waved at him from behind Pam.

"Hey, Lucy." I preferred not to be called Lucy, and Pam flashed a grin at me.

"She doesn't really like Lucy," Pam said apologetically.

Michael nodded. "I dig. Too redheaded dingbatty?"

"Definitely."

"Okay, everybody," a voice pierced through the noisy room. Gordon Blackwell, in jeans, a black shirt, and even blacker hair falling loosely down his back, stood in the center, arms raised. "Let's get started. We've got a lot to talk about."

"Here, squeeze in, you two," Michael said. But there were other people on the couch and only squeezing room for one of us.

"You sit, Pam," I said. "I got the floor."

She smiled gratefully at me and pressed herself in beside Michael. Pam passed the reefer to me and I watched Gordon pontificate for a while, his black mustache bobbing up and down on his lip as he spoke. He was a strikingly handsome man, one who demanded attention and spoke eloquently and persuasively. Yet there was something about him that seemed not real to me. Artificial. Like a hunk of beach glass polished smooth to look like a gem.

"There are no innocents in this war!" Gordon shouted into the hushed room. "Those who blithely accept the peace and privilege of their lives while ignoring the violence their country perpetrates on innocents are just as guilty of the violence themselves. Those who allow the large corporations of the Establishment to profit from the deaths of innocents have spilled the blood of babies themselves. Those who quietly submit while the government sends our own young men off to kill and be killed have murdered those men —men who should have had their whole lives before them.

"It's our generation that's going to the killing fields, not the old men in suits who decided to send them. All of us in this room know someone who has gone to Vietnam and not come back. Your best friend, maybe. Your cousin. Your brother. They had no say in the matter. No choice. It's a free country, people say. Well, it wasn't free for those dead kids."

Of course I thought of Ray, and the terror in his silent face the day he shipped out. The day he went off to die. Surely Pam would see the wisdom of Gordon's words. Who could not?

"Who gets to decide," Gordon's voice filled the room, "that it's acceptable to squander our future, our lives for the imperialist ambitions of a few old men in Washington? Who decides that we will die so the rich can get richer? The Establishment. The government and the big corporations of the Establishment are sending our generation out to die so they can profit.

"We can't bring back the dead. And we can't save those kids who are shipping out tomorrow or even next week. But we can save those on the list to ship out next month. If we act now. How? By bringing the war home. The violence can't be ignored when it's right here at home. We," he spread his arms wide to encompass the entire room, "those of us who strive for peace, will not be ignored any longer!"

Looking around the room, I could see that everyone felt, as I did, that they were in the presence of a profound truth. We were called, all of us, to serve our country by exposing the truth and ushering in a new era. What a privilege! And a responsibility.

I glanced back at Pam and Michael. His arm was around the back of the couch, his hand resting just above her shoulder. She was squashed tightly between Michael and the boy on the other side of her. She must have been uncomfortable, but when she smiled at me I knew this was the happiest she had ever been. I grinned back and felt a warm rush inside. She deserved this.

I always imagined that Pam and Michael were living a happy life together all these years. They had made plans to meet somewhere after we all split up, I knew, and I felt vicariously content to believe they were together all this time. Excruciatingly lonely at times, but happy for my friend. And as I built a life with Charlie, and I imagined Pam and Michael together, I often thought about our beer oath to be friends forever, to live near each other and do things as a foursome with our husbands, who would also be best friends, of course. If I had known how to find Pam in those early days, I would have done so. For many years I felt a great aching hole that was her absence. Then I felt mostly regret that our friendship had to end, and remorse at the way it ended. Lately, I had not thought much about her at all, except fleetingly when I drove past her old house on the way to my mother's.

Now, after seeing Pam at a rest stop on the Mass. Pike, the ache has returned. Yet I am also afraid. I cannot believe it is a coincidence that I saw her for the first time in 37 years just days after Michael confessed. I also do not believe that they have been together all this time, at least not recently. If they were together and Pam did not intend to turn herself in with Michael, she would have left the country, or at least the state, before he confessed. The rest stop I saw her at was on the eastbound side of the pike, so she was heading toward Boston and Michael, not away. So she is going to see him. She must realize how unwise that would be. She must know she will likely be arrested. Yet still she goes.

It is the look on Pam's face today that frightens me. It was either fear or anger, and I do not know which I should hope for. Could she still be angry after so much time, or was she simply terrified at the sight of me as I was at the sight of her? Either way, Pam will likely be arrested. And she has seen me, in Massachusetts, in the FROGS van. If she chooses to talk to the police, and either fear or anger may make her choose to, it will not be difficult for them to find me. After 37 years, it is ending. First Michael, then Pam, and I will be next. I can feel the frigid knot of terror inside that has been dormant for more than three decades twisting and squirming, sending icy tendrils throughout my body. I can run. If I leave right now, I could probably evade the police. Again. But I will have lost this second life, this life I have come to love, in many ways more than the first. I can stay and be arrested or I can run and hide. Either way, Charlie and Amber and everyone else in my second life will know what I am, and this life will have ended. I do not know if I have the strength to begin a third life. I am not at all certain I have a right to.

CHAPTER 9

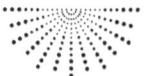

I think that maybe Pam will not talk. I think also, that maybe I am
deceiving myself. If it was simply a matter of forgiving me for
stealing her away from her family, leading her into a tragic mistake
and robbing her of the rest of her life, I would be more confident
that she would not wish to expose me. I am shamefully aware,
however, that it is not that simple. So I am prepared to be exposed.
I will not run. If running would save Charlie and Amber from the
truth, I would do so. Running will only save me, however, and I do
not deserve to be saved. So I will stay, and I will wait for the news
of Pam's arrest, and I will live with the cold knot of fear inside me
for the remainder of Annie Pulkowski's life. For if the police arrive
at my door, this life will be over and I will resume my former existence as Lucinda the killer. I will no longer have Charlie and
Amber. They will not want the counterfeit Annie.

Opening the door to my house, I am welcomed by the fragrant
aroma of dinner and the distant, delicate clinking of pans on the
stove. Charlie is in the kitchen. I peek my head in and watch him
sprinkle some spice into a pan on the stove with a flourish. Maestro
conducting the symphony. "Hey," he says, looking up from the
large stir-fry. "How was your day?"

"Long." I step over to receive my welcome home kiss and wrap my arms around him. I settle my head on his shoulder and savor the warmth of his body through his thin cotton shirt. I do not let go.

"Everything all right?" he asks.

"I'm just really tired," I say, holding him as though it is the last hug I will ever share with him. Perhaps it is.

"You sure?" he says, pulling back and holding my face between his hands. His eyes hold concern, and I force from my mind the image of that solicitude morphing into disgust and dismay.

I rub a hand over his chest. "I'm sure," I say, summoning a smile. "I just need to be home with you two. Where's Amber?"

"In her room." He kisses the tip of my nose and grins mischievously. "And she's got a little surprise in there with her."

I wait for an explanation, but none is coming, so I walk up the stairs toward Amber's room, the cool spot on the tip of my nose fading way too quickly. The door to her room is open and I hear voices inside. Amber is lying on her bed, side by side with her mother. They are belly-down, heads propped on hands, looking at a book together.

Amber hears me at the door and swings her blonde ponytail around. "Hey Nonny."

Darlene pushes herself up more slowly and sits, facing me. "Hi, Mom." Her hair is pulled back off her face and fastened with a barrette. Her face is clear of makeup, her fingernails are trimmed and free of their usual blue-black polish. A single gold stud rests in each earlobe. I have not seen my daughter looking like this for years.

"Darlene," I say. It is all I can come up with at the moment.

"I was just showing Mom the pictures of all the plays I've been in," Amber says. "She's going to come to the next one. Right?" She peers up at Darlene.

"Right," Darlene agrees with a smile. "June seventeenth. I'm holding the day."

I walk cautiously into the room. "That would be really nice." They both look up at me and I can see the resemblance in their faces that had long been hidden underneath Darlene's trampy façade. The swelling in her lip has gone down, and she has skillfully masked the bruise under her eye with a small amount of makeup. "You look good," I tell her. "Wholesome."

"Clean," she smiles.

"Yes."

"She's staying for dinner," Amber says. "Grampa said it was okay."

"Sure," I nod. "Of course it's okay." I do not forget Jarvis' words from this morning, but at this moment I cannot help but feel joy that my daughter has returned to us. I only hope that it is not now my turn to leave in disgrace.

Charlie has already set an extra place at the table and is humming an old Byrds song as he serves up his creation onto individual plates. We sit around the table as a complete family for the first time in many years, and I think that if I will have to be going off to jail soon I am fortunate to have had this moment.

"This is really good, Grampa," Amber says as she scoops up food from her plate.

"Delicious," I agree. I look at Darlene and know that Charlie is doing the same.

"It's really great," Darlene says. "I haven't eaten like this in a long time." She holds a forkful in front of her and looks across the table at Charlie. "Thank you. Really."

"You're welcome," Charlie beams. "I'm glad everyone likes it. I tried a little something different this time. I julienned the vegetables in a mandoline instead of by hand, and also acidulated the coulis a bit."

"I have, like, no idea what that means," Amber says, "but it's great."

"Mmm," Darlene agrees through a full mouth. "What she said."

Charlie finishes chewing a mouthful and swallows. "Well," he says, "the coulis is—"

"Wait, wait," I cut him off with a wink. "Don't tell them your secrets. It adds to your mystique."

Charlie laughs, wide-eyed at me. "Mystique? I have no mystique. You have mystique, but I am completely lacking in anything resembling mystique."

I have mystique? For years I have strived to be as common and un-mysterious as possible. "I have no mystique," I say. "Really. No mystique."

"For once, I'm happy to agree with you Mom," Darlene says. "There's no mystique in you. What you see is what you get."

"Aw, come on," Charlie says. "You don't see it? Amber? You see it?"

Amber rolls her eyes upward. "All grownups have mystique. But that's just because they, like, never tell us anything."

This provokes a chuckle amongst the three grownups, and I am grateful to Amber for the change in focus. And grateful, also, to have this family here together, like a real family. Like a happy family.

It is later, while Charlie is serving up seconds, that Darlene has something more substantial to say. She twists her napkin between her fingers, takes a sip of water. "I um," she says, "I've been doing a lot of thinking. And, first of all, I want to thank you. You, Mom, for coming to get me the other night, and Charlie, for the great meal, and both of you, for taking care of Amber all these years. That's really—I'm really grateful. Thank you."

"Oh, you're so welcome, honey," Charlie says, but Darlene holds up a hand to stop him.

"Please. Let me finish." She takes another sip of her water, dribbles some down her chin and wipes it away with the twisted napkin. "I'm really determined to stay clean this time. And sober. I want to get my life back. I know I've made a mess of things these past few—many years. But I'm going to get it back. And so, I've decided, that what I want, really need, is to have Amber back."

I am so stunned I am unable to open my mouth, much less speak, and I am not even certain I have heard her correctly. Charlie has stopped serving and Amber has stopped chewing and there is utter silence in the room.

Darlene looks around the table uncomfortably. She stretches an arm out and rubs her daughter's back. "Wouldn't you like that, honey?"

Amber looks from her mother to me to Charlie, unsure what to do. There is a tiny glimmer of hope in her eyes, I can see.

"Like I said," Darlene is continuing, "I'm really grateful to you for taking care of her when I couldn't. But now I can. I'm ready to be a mother."

When I speak, my voice comes out as a growl, and I do not care. "You have been clean for all of about five days and now you think you are able to be a responsible mother? Do you know how ludicrous you sound?"

"You don't think I can stay clean," Darlene says it as an accusation, which I find equally ludicrous.

"I think you have never been able to stay clean before and you need to prove that you can do it permanently before you can be trusted to be a parent."

"I *am* a parent. I *am* a mother. Amber is my daughter, not yours. And I know I can be a good mother to her. Better than you ever were to me. At least I have a beating heart." Regret crosses her face instantly. "I'm sorry. I take that back."

But she cannot take it back. How can she not realize that?

"To be honest," Darlene levels her stare at me, "I need Amber. I think that if I have her, if I know I have the responsibility of taking care of her, then that will actually help me stay clean. It'll be my motivation, you know?"

The utter selfishness of this enrages me. "Have you even thought about Amber? Or is she just some motivational tool? What happens if it's not enough motivation and you relapse again? It's never been enough motivation for you before. You have to prove beforehand that you're capable of doing this! What happens to her when you fall into a drugged-up stupor again? You haven't even thought about *her* wellbeing, only your own, which only proves—"

"Annie! Annie, stop. Calm down, honey." Charlie's hand is on my shoulder. His gaze is calm, reassuring. "Relax, honey." To

Darlene he says, "No. The answer is no. After you've been clean for a full year, then we'll talk about it. Until then, there's no sense in discussing it."

Darlene lifts her head defiantly and glares at Charlie. She purses her lips together, places her hands flat on the table in front of her, her chin thrusting forward, signaling a spike in temper. "Not to be…hurtful, or difficult, or anything," she says, "but you're not even a blood relation to her. Or me. You don't have any right to make decisions for us."

Charlie is frozen, his face a mask of pain and rage seething under the surface. I cannot fathom how my own child could cause such pain to a man who loved her so deeply her entire life.

"He is your *father*!" I do not even attempt to contain my fury. "He has raised you since you were born! He took care of me while I was pregnant with you. And then when you turned out to be such an irresponsible low-life, he raised Amber since she was a baby. He is the best father you could have ever hoped for. How could you treat him this way? Hurt him like that? He doesn't deserve that after everything he's done for you."

Darlene sighs loudly. "I'm not trying to hurt him, I said that. I just want to make it clear that I have a legal right to my daughter. And neither of you actually do." She turns to Amber and says, "Charlie is a good man, but he's not your real Grampa, you know." Darlene is oblivious to the sadness on Amber's face and turns back to me. "And that brings me to something else. If I'm going to get my life back on track, I need to know the truth about my life. I need to know who my real father is. I have a right to know that. You lied to me for years, both of you," she includes Charlie in this, "and then you refused to tell me the truth. Well I won't accept that any more. I don't care how painful a story it is, you don't have a right to keep that from me."

She is correct, unfortunately, about that. She does have the right to know who her father is and I do not have the right to keep that from her. Yet I will. I cannot tell her, and all of them, that her father is now lying in a hospital bed in Boston, expected to die at any time. She has the right to know this, and would perhaps wish to see him before he dies. Michael, too, has a right to know his daughter before he dies. But I must deny both of them those rights. I cannot tell my daughter the truth, so I tell her the lie I told Charlie thirty-seven years ago. It is a familiar place for me; trapped in an old lie.

"His name was Joseph Carter, and he was my stepfather. I have no idea how to find him or if he's even still alive." I look her straight in the eyes as I speak, as though this will convince her that this is the truth. "I wish you had not made me tell you in front of Amber." These words ring with truthfulness and I am glad I have said them.

Darlene returns my gaze, and I believe I discern a subtle softening in her eyes. She nods her head silently. "That is bad," she says. "I'm sorry."

I recognize now, that softness. It is pity, and it fills me with shame. *Do not pity me. I do not deserve it.*

"God, Mom. I'm really sorry," Darlene says again. "I really am. I always thought you were so squeaky clean."

"It wasn't your mother's fault," Charlie snaps. "She is squeaky clean, as you say. She didn't do anything wrong."

"No. No, of course not. I only meant, I always thought she couldn't understand...stuff, you know." She turns back to me. "That you'd never experienced anything bad or difficult."

I can feel the tears threatening to spill and I swallow hard before speaking. "Well you were wrong." And that is more true than any of them know.

The sympathy in Darlene's face and voice chafes at me because I do not deserve it and because it emanates from one who has sunk so low. I cannot bear to be in the same room with it, and I push my chair away from the table. "I need some space," I tell them all, and then I leave them and escape into the cool, uninquisitive night.

The door closed quietly behind Annie, and Charlie dropped into her empty chair. He propped his head in his hands, pressed hard on his temples, and scowled at the woman across the table. "You know," he said, "you really have a mean streak in you, Darlene. Where does that come from? We didn't raise you to be like that."

Darlene rolled her eyes upward. "Maybe it comes from being raised on lies," she said. "Besides, who knew she even had feelings?"

"My God," he said. "Nothing's ever your fault, is it? You don't take responsibility for anything. You're trying to convince us you're fit to be a mother by attacking your own?"

Darlene watched her hands flex against each other, then looked up at Amber. She ran a hand down the girl's ponytail, sliding the blonde hair easily through her fingers. "You're right," she said finally. "But I don't mean to be mean. I just don't know how to be…sensitive sometimes."

"Same thing." Charlie was unsympathetic.

"Should I go after her?"

"I think your mother's had enough of the magical Darlene touch tonight," he said. "If you've had enough to eat, you should probably go."

Darlene looked down at her full plate, her untouched second helping. "Right. Okay." She turned to Amber and wrapped her arms around her. "Goodbye, sweetie. I'll call you tomorrow, okay? Maybe you could come over after school."

Amber squeezed her mother tightly. "I have rehearsal tomorrow until six," she said, disappointed.

"Okay," Darlene said, a forced cheeriness in her voice, "well, maybe the next day, then. I'll call you." She stood and walked around the table to Charlie, leaned down and pecked him on the cheek. "Bye, Charlie. Thanks for dinner." She walked quickly across the living room, stopped and slid into a denim jacket hanging on a peg, then pulled open the door.

"You know, Darlene," Charlie said from across the room, "I really thought this time was going to be different."

Darlene turned to face him, studied him seriously. "It is."

She turned her back to him, walked out the door and was gone. Charlie and Amber sat, across the table from each other, in the harsh, empty silence. Charlie smiled awkwardly at her, then stood and began clearing plates from the table. Amber picked up her own plate and glass and followed him into the kitchen. They worked together wordlessly, Amber emptying leftover food into the trash, Charlie loading plates into the dishwasher.

"Grampa," Amber's voice broke the stillness. "I know Mom's technically right, but it feels like you're my real Grampa to me."

Charlie stopped, frozen over the dishwasher, and leaned heavily on the counter. He sniffled damply and swallowed the pang swelling in his throat. "It feels like it to me too, honey."

CHAPTER 10

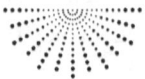

My pocketbook is heavy with the few thin sheets of paper it holds. They are a burden, these commonplace, mass-printed, simple pages I carry, and my legs trudge with difficulty over the sidewalk under their ominous weight.

My lunchtime appointment has taken longer than I anticipated and I am now late getting back to FROGS. I have not told Jarvis where I was going, although I believe he would be supportive and may even be able to offer some helpful advice. So why do I not tell him? Perhaps because I cannot shake the feeling that I am sneaking around doing something underhanded. That should not be an unknown feeling for me, yet it is somehow foreign and troubling. Over the years, I have grown to believe my own fabricated identity. Being Annie no longer feels like a lie.

Up ahead of me, a heavy man in red high-top sneakers shuffles gracelessly atop the sidewalk. It is Sean, heading to FROGS to donate his daily half sandwich. I can see the brown paper bag wadded up between chubby fingers. He ambles slowly, and I will overtake him in seconds. I do not wish to talk to Sean today. I have much to think about—important things that could impact many people I care deeply about, and I am just not, frankly, in the mood to talk to Sean at the moment. But when am I ever?

"Hi Sean," I say loudly as I pull astride of him. "I thought that was you."

His eyes dart nervously in my direction, then back down to watch his red shoes plop one after another in front of him. He stops abruptly, lifts his head and offers a shy smile. "Oh. Hey. Hi Mrs. Pulkowski." He shifts uncomfortably on his feet. "Hi."

"You on your way to the center?"

He nods. "Tuna today. I got tuna today." He holds up the paper bag and grins, revealing a thin strand of tuna wedged between his front teeth.

"That's great, Sean. Thank you. Tuna is always popular."

"Is it? Should I bring tuna every day? Would that be better? Maybe I should bring tuna every day if it's the most popular. If that's what people like."

"We're grateful for anything you bring, Sean. Really. Everything is appreciated."

Sean blinks, ducks his head and walks faster. "I can bring tuna every day. I could do it. My mom could make tuna every day."

I should have just walked on by; he would not even have noticed me, and I would already be sitting at my desk. Alone.

"I don't want her to be mad at me all the time." Sean stops abruptly and looks at me with pleading eyes. "I don't want her to be mad."

"Your mother? Why would she be mad?"

"She only gives me tuna when she's mad at me. I hate tuna. She gives it to me when she's mad at me." His eyes glisten damply. "I don't want her to be mad at me every day."

"No. No, of course not." How has a simple hello turned into this disturbing emotional familiarity? "Why does she get mad at you?"

"Sometimes I forget to bring her stuff she asks for. Sometimes I embarrass her in front of her friends. Different stuff." He twists the paper bag in his hand fiercely, heedless of the fate of the hapless sandwich inside. "I try not to embarrass her. But I don't always know what's the right thing to do. I told her I don't mean to be stupid. But I'm always gonna be, she says."

Sean turns suddenly and hurries away from me toward the FROGS door, and as I watch, I feel only anger toward him. *No, no, no! You cannot choose me to confide in, to tell your terrible little secrets. I do not have the capacity to accommodate your hidden truths; there is no room in here for you. I am filled up!* These words scream in my head, a silent thunder that terrorizes only me.

Inside the office, the air is stuffy compared to the brisk spring breezes outside. I feel as though I may throw up. Sean is explaining to Lindsey that he cannot bring tuna every day, despite it being the most popular sandwich among the underfed. Unless, of course, she felt it was really very important, and then he could, in fact, bring tuna every day.

I make my way to my desk, avoiding any eyes that may be turned in my direction. My head feels as though it has been cracked open by the thunderbolt of my own silent voice, and I lay the two cleaved halves in my hands. Perhaps I can press them back together. I feel Jarvis' presence before he speaks, and the improbable wish that he will just go away floats through both pieces of my brain like cognitive flotsam.

It is a gentle touch on my shoulder that comes first, and I am surprised. As caring as he can be, Jarvis does not make physical contact with people. It is as though he knows that his size can be imposing and wishes not to intimidate people further with a touch. He lets his kind words make contact with those in need.

When I lift my head, I see Jarvis' face above me. It is concerned, but not shocked, the massive rift down the middle of my head evidently not visible from the outside. This is good.

"What is it?" he asks, quietly so no one else will hear.

"Nothing. Just a headache."

His big hand slips off my shoulder. "Annie. Let me help you. If it seems overwhelming—"

"I'm okay, Jarvis! I'm handling it, everything. Everything's fine."

"Yeah. Fine. That's why you're snapping like a rubber band all the time."

"Please, just…leave me. Alone."

He nods, and in his eyes lingers the same solicitous compassion he bestows on all his needy cases, and it embarrasses me. I am not a needy case. I am not homeless or hungry, indigent or handicapped. Do not pity me, Jarvis. And do not help me.

He probes sausage-like fingers into his chest pocket and pulls out a small white card. "This is a good place," he says, dropping the card on the desk in front of me. "It's what she needs."

I stare at the card, its words blurring into fuzzy gray, and I know Jarvis has walked away. For now.

I am eager for Amber to leave. She sits here at the dinner table, chatting happily, telling us about her day and her friends and her plans, not at all the brooding, uncommunicative teenager she has every right to be at her age. It is one of the things I love and appreciate most about her. I cherish her warmth and openness, and her trust in Charlie and me. It is truly the joy of my life.

Since Charlie and I raised her, I believe we deserve much of the credit for the wonderful person Amber has become. We did not do well with Darlene. We have, in some sadly redemptive way, got it right with Amber.

Yet I wish her to go. I need to talk with Charlie alone, to tell him of my meeting today. To tell him of my plan. And when she finally does leave, to her room to do homework, I find myself unsure as to how to begin. Surely, props will help. So I fetch the papers from my purse and place them in his hands.

"What's this?" he asks.

"I met with a lawyer today," I tell him. "I think we should formally adopt Amber."

He looks from the papers to me, shock and pain crossing his eyes. "How can you give up on Darlene just when she's really showing some effort?" *What kind of mother are you?* is on his face, though he kindly does not articulate the words.

"I'm not. It's just—we need to protect Amber."

"Amber's in a pretty good place right now. As good as it can be. But you drag this family through a custody battle—because you know Darlene won't agree to this willingly—and that could be devastating to Amber."

"I know. That's true. But if she's pulled out of here to live with Darlene, that will be even more devastating."

"Darlene can't just *pull* her out. Amber would have to want to go. And we'd have to agree."

"Not necessarily, Charlie. She's the biological and legal mother of Amber. We've only got Amber because Darlene just left her here for the last thirteen years. And if she really does try to take her back like she's threatening, we have no legal standing."

"Still, she has to know she can't just waltz in here and take her. We could take her to court and make her convince a judge she was competent, which I think she would have a hard time doing right now."

"Right now, yes. Maybe. But at some point...." I know I must say it, although it will hurt him. "Charlie, Darlene had a valid point the other night. About you not having legal rights when it came to Amber. If it came down to a judge deciding between her biological mother and you...."

"So, what? Are you leaving me?" He smiles, teasing, burying the pain.

"No." I say much too quickly, and I must stop and turn away from him. "Of course not. But you know what I'm saying. What if something happens to me?" *Like I end up in jail.*

There is no answer from him, nothing except the sound of him dropping into a chair. "I can't figure it out," he says finally.

I turn and face him. "What?"

"We've been through all this with Darlene before. A number of times. As bad as it got, it never made you so frantic before. Why the panic this time?"

"Because she's talking about taking Amber this time."

"She's talked about that before."

"That was always just talk. It's different this time."

He shakes his head slowly, his fingers absently flipping an unused spoon over on the tablecloth. "I don't know that it is any different this time. For her. But it is for you. And that's what I don't get."

I do not know how to answer this in a way that sounds like the truth but is not the truth, and so I do not say anything. I would like to run and hide and pretend that I never started this conversation.

"I don't know, Annie," Charlie says, staring at the table. "Where's the concern for Darlene? You do this to her, and it could devastate her. Make her feel like she has nothing to live for, and give up entirely. I guess that's what's different this time. I agree that Amber needs to be protected, but you seem so ready to sacrifice Darlene to do it." His pale cobalt eyes do not waver, boring into me. "I just can't do that. She's our daughter. Yes, she's got a lot of problems, and yes, she's caused us a lot of pain, but my god, Annie. She's our *daughter*."

I want to tell him. I want to tell him that I am terrified of the havoc wreaked upon this family when I am sent off to jail in disgrace. When all my words and actions over the years will be dismissed because they issued from an evil criminal. Amber will need Charlie's strength and guidance to make sense of what happened; he will need her love and sweet innocence to ease his pain. They will need to cling to each other, put me behind them, and move on. There will be no useful place for Darlene's hysteria in the aftermath of my shame; it will only be more destructive in an already shattered family. I do not wish to sacrifice my daughter, but the sad truth is that I am not at all sure she is salvageable. Charlie and Amber most certainly are, and I will do anything to ensure that they are saved.

There are tears in my eyes now and I turn so Charlie can see them, so he does not think I am some monster that does not love her daughter. "I have done everything, for 36 years, everything I could do for her. You can't believe I want to sacrifice her now. I can't even believe you used that word."

"It was a poor choice of word," he says with a sigh. "I'm just struggling to understand why all of a sudden you want to drag this family through what will be a very difficult and very ugly fight. It doesn't seem as though you've thought through just how traumatic that would be for both Darlene and Amber. And me. And you."

"You know me better than that. Of course I've thought it through."

Charlie concedes a nod. "And you still think it should be done?"

"I do," I answer slowly. "I think it's crucial that you especially have a legal right to Amber's guardianship in case Darlene challenges it and I'm no longer around. No matter how ugly it gets, it's worth it to make sure Amber has a stable, normal home." I try to smile at him. "I really think it's necessary."

Charlie continues to watch me after I have stopped speaking. Then he nods his head, stacks the dirty plates from the table and stands to take them into the kitchen. In the doorway, he stops, turns back to me. "I don't," he whispers. "I can't do it."

CHAPTER 11

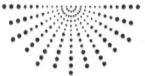

Dinner in front of the television was not the way Catherine was raised, which was ridiculous to even contemplate since television did not yet exist during Catherine's childhood. But the concept was the same. It was shameful, really, and she would be just mortified if someone were to walk in and find her so engaged. But Sam was no longer here with her to partake in a proper dinner, involving linen napkins, correct place settings, perhaps a glass of wine. And conversation. Glorious, under-appreciated, civilizing conversation.

There was no sense sitting alone at a table, staring across at an empty chair; she had to be practical about things after all. The evening news was informative, often stimulating, and it made some good old highfalutin' noise in this god-awfully quiet house! But still, if anyone were to find out, she would simply die of shame.

Truth be told, she was watching for news of Lucinda these days, though it was a truth that could not, in fact, be told. Even the few old neighbors who knew the truth of Catherine's daughter wouldn't dare discuss it with her. Oh, she'd seen their stares in recent days, since the story broke anew, and she knew none of them had the courage to approach her about it. Whether she was appreciative of, or angered by, their cowardice, she had not yet decided.

She stretched out a hand to stroke the pink and green embroidered letterbox that had sat on the top shelf of the coat closet for years, and now sat next to her on the couch. Her ghost box. And then the television showed her what she waited for: the black and white photos of Lucinda and the other four spread across the screen. Something was happening. Maybe they'd found her. The hope was almost too great to bear. And then what? Then she watched her daughter be taken off to jail. Forever. At least she'd know where she was, could see her face. What did her once beautiful girl look like now?

But they had not found her. They had found her victims.

"I never really knew my dad," an attractive middle-aged woman with blonde hair was saying. "I was six when he was killed, and of course at that age, you don't really understand why your dad could go off to work one day just like any other day and not come back." She smiled briefly. "He was a great father, from what I remember. I wish I'd known him better."

A young female reporter flashed onto the screen. "Michelle Varna's sister, Rachel Chelnick, an attorney in Ludlow, Vermont, was only three when their father was killed. But she hasn't given up hope that justice will one day be served. Another, different middle-aged woman in a stylish suit and glasses looked sternly into the camera. "My father was murdered when he was just 32 years old, just for doing his job. We never thought any of those responsible would ever be caught and brought to justice. We never thought our family would find peace. And now, with one of the killers dying in a hospital, never to pay his debt to society or to our family, well, it's just very unsatisfying. We are hoping, though, that the renewed interest in this case will prompt officials to reopen it and make a concerted effort to track down those others—there are three others still out there—who are responsible for murdering my father."

The reporter's voice returned over an image of a small, one-story house on a dirt lot. "Robert Dechesney's widow, Angela Dechesney, was just twenty-eight with three young children when her husband was killed. She now lives alone in this house in

Kelsey, New York. She declined to speak to reporters for this story." The camera zoomed in on the open door of the little house, the weary face of a woman peeking out. She squinted, shook her head and waved a hand at the camera, turning away. The door of the house, its yellow paint peeling off to reveal a mossy green beneath, closed slowly, pressed tight to its frame from the inside.

Catherine stared at the screen long after the story ended. She contemplated the face of the woman who had lost her husband 37 years ago. Sam had been gone just five months. Did that woman love her husband as Catherine had loved Sam? It was impossible to tell from her face now, this many years later. How much love could be left after all this time?

How fortunate she would be, she thought, fingering the embroidered ghost box, if she did not truly know.

Pam chewed her bacon cheeseburger slowly as she examined her own face in black and white on the television screen above the bar. She glanced at the bartender and the one other customer across the bar, but neither seemed interested in either the TV or Pam. Lucky for her she looked nothing like the skinny nineteen-year-old from 37 years earlier.

Her eyes roamed over the tiny room. Frayed and dingy sports posters hung on naked brick walls, and an ancient jukebox lurked in the corner with a hand lettered, "Out of order," sign taped to it. Not much in the way of décor, and the food was greasy, but considering she had half-expected to be sitting in jail by now, not so bad. And, not to be overly optimistic, but if the cops didn't grab her as she left the hospital, they must not have been watching the room, and so don't know who she is or what she looks like. They had no way to find her now. She smiled. Home free. Unless they were watching her to see if she led them to anyone else. Which is exactly what she would do.

Pam looked back to the TV screen where an unknown woman

was talking. "…never thought our family would find peace," she was saying. It was the daughter of the guard who was killed. Must be. The guy had three little kids at the time. And here was one of them, all grown up, whining about a life without peace. She had no idea.

There was no sadness in the woman's voice that Pam could see, rather a steady anger as she continued to speak. "…will prompt officials to reopen it and make a concerted effort to track down those others—there are three others still out there—who are responsible for murdering my father."

She was wrong about that too. There were only two people who were responsible for her father's death. Two people who brought loaded guns—despite a unanimous agreement not to—into the bank and shot them at a human being. Two people who ended this woman's father's life and ruined so many more. And yes, those two people deserved to pay for all of those crimes. Pam could only deliver one of the two, but that one was the most deceitful, treacherous one, and the most deserving of punishment.

On the TV screen appeared an older woman, saying nothing, shutting a door behind her. It was the wife. There, in her eyes, was the sadness, the pain, that had been missing from the other woman's face. Pam turned away. *Don't. Don't blame me. I didn't shoot anyone.* She picked up a French fry, then dropped it. *But still. I am sorry.*

I cannot bear to watch them, and yet I am having difficulty turning away. These children who grew up without their father seem to speak directly to me. They are blaming me, as they should, and challenging me to do the right thing and come forward. They do not understand that there no longer is a right thing. That, while coming forward was clearly the one right thing to do three decades ago, now it will cause excruciating pain to other innocent people.

New pain on top of old. More victims in addition to the original sufferers. Can that be right?

I can see their father, as I have always seen him, as he falls to the ground. I remember Robert Dechesney more vividly, perhaps, than do his own children. Certainly more intimately. For I watched the life slither out of him through the bloody hole in his neck. I watched as his entire existence, all that he had ever done and said and wished for, all that he ever was, culminate in one final instant of being, before withering away into nothingness. What could be more intimate than that?

Angela Dechesney's final gaze was directed at me. Paranoia on my part, perhaps, but I do not believe so. She knows I am watching, looking for her, to catch a glimpse of her after all these years. And she is right. Now I wonder; is she searching for me?

My hand is burning and I smell the sharp smoke of a just-fired gun. I look, and there is nothing there in my empty palm of course. Yet the pain does not abate. It is so hot, hotter than I remember the gun being, and I rub at it fiercely. There is a loud bang in the kitchen and my heart leaps in my chest, even as I realize it is just Charlie dropping a pot.

They have left the television screen, these victims of mine, and so have released me. I am free to go. I must wash my hand of whatever is on it that is burning me. In the bathroom, I run cool water over my palm, but the pain will not go. Charlie is calling me. Dinner is ready, he says. Just as soon as I wash up, I tell him. I rub soap into a thick lather over my hands. I turn the cool water colder. But the pain will not go.

CHAPTER 12

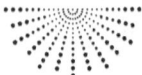

"You didn't even say nothing," Bobby Dechesney flapped his arms like a petulant child. His red flannel shirt hung open over a black Guns N' Roses t-shirt stretched over a paunchy belly. Dingy blue jeans, faded and frayed, slung low beneath his gut, the tattered hems trailing along the ground. "They should of interviewed me. I would of said something."

Angela sat on a faded orange and green plaid couch, her finger pulling at a ragged hole in the fabric. Her long gray hair fell over her shoulders as she turned to look up at her son. "What would you have said? You were just a baby."

"I could of said what Michelle said. I wished I'd a known him better." He flicked the TV off and tossed the remote onto the coffee table where it clattered and skidded onto the floor. Annoyance colored his dull gray eyes. "You all got to be on TV and I didn't."

Angela stared silently at the enormous, now-vacant television screen. The TV, Bobby's most recent irresponsible and extravagant purchase, gleamed shiny and new against the shabby surroundings of the living room.

"Meanwhile," Bobby said, "I hope that guy in the hospital fries in jail."

"He's going to die before he ever gets to jail."

Bobby blinked. "Good."

The electronic jangle of the phone sounded from the open doorway to the kitchen.

"Would you get that, Bobby?"

"No," he snapped. "It's gonna be Michelle or Rachel calling to brag about being on TV."

Angela's eyes closed briefly as she took in a silent breath. "Please, honey. My back's been hurting all day."

Bobby grumbled his way into the kitchen, snatched the receiver from its cradle and snarled into it, "Hold on," then delivered it to his mother.

"Hello," Angela said.

Michelle's voice came through. "What's with him?"

"Oh. Nothing. Just being…"

"Bobby."

Angela shot a glance at her son. "Right."

"What?" Bobby hovered over his mother. "What's she saying?"

"Hey," Michelle said, "we looked good on TV!"

"Well," Angela conceded, "you did."

"You looked fine, Mom, for the two seconds you were on. Hey, Rachel did great, don't you think? She was so…smart and tough."

"A little too tough. But that's a lawyer for you."

"What's wrong?"

"Nothing," Angela sighed. "I just wish she hadn't been quite so hard-nosed about it. It's not her fault; I don't blame her. I just…I really wish they hadn't come looking for us."

"But it's a good thing," Michelle said. "Isn't it? Maybe now they'll reopen the case and start looking for those people again."

"Exactly."

The line was silent for a brief instant. "I don't get it, Mom. Isn't that what you want? What you've always wanted?"

"No. Yes. I did. But now…now I just wish they would leave it alone. It's ancient history. Just let it die."

"Well, I have to say this is not what I expected. I thought you'd be happy. I mean, I know it's painful, but I really thought you wanted the closure."

"I do. I want the closure. But this, all this attention can cause problems too."

"How? What problems? A few reporters poking around? Who cares? It's worth it, isn't it, if finally, after all this time, they can catch Dad's killers?"

"Just…never mind. It doesn't matter. I don't," Angela hesitated, "I don't know what I want, honey."

"Well I want them caught, Mom. I want the closure," Michelle's voice was hard. "And I know Rachel does too. And she's going to push for it."

Angela let her eyes fall shut. "I know," she said. "It doesn't matter now. It's probably too late anyway."

"Too late for what? What are you talking about?"

"Nothing, honey. Nothing."

"What's too late?" Bobby demanded.

Angela pressed her lips together. "You know what honey?" she said into the phone. "I've got to go. I'll talk to you later."

"Yeah, okay. Mom," Michelle said, "this is important to me. Really important."

"I know. It is to me too." She smiled faintly. "Good bye honey."

"So?" Bobby persisted as she hung up the phone. "What's too late?"

Angela scowled. "Nothing, Bobby. Just let it go."

"What? It some kind of secret, or something?"

"Yes," she nodded, exhaling heavily. "It's a secret."

CHAPTER 13

Everything Gordon said always made sense. Patently obvious, indisputable, unambiguous, factually-substantiated sense. That the white Establishment did not or could not see the truth of what he and others like him spoke of was evidence of their moral and ethical depravity. How could one not see the murder of innocents in their own land as wrong? How could one see the deaths of thousands of American young men—boys, some of them—to serve the imperialist ambitions of the wealthy ruling class as anything but wrong? Only if one chose to. Our country was sick. And we were the only ones able to see it through fresh eyes and recognize the sickness. So it was up to us to cure it.

"The Federal One Bank," Gordon told us over burgers at a diner across the street from the bank on 51st Street, "with branches all over the country, is one of the American corporations most entrenched in the Establishment. They have grown fat and happy with no regard for the repercussions of their actions. They are the epitome of the corrupt Establishment. It is only fitting that their ill-gotten gains be rescinded from them, and be redirected to finance the revolution of morality that this country needs and will face."

We sat, the five of us, squeezed into a red vinyl booth next to a somewhat grimy window. "Lucinda and Pam," Gordon continued, "you'll do the initial reconnaissance. You'll be checking for number and position of security guards, exits, and basic layout of the interior. I want details. The more, the better. Michael and Jimmy, you two are in charge of procuring a getaway car."

It struck me, as I listened to Gordon issue commands, that he spoke more like a general in the military, an elite member of the Establishment, than he would likely prefer. I wondered if he was aware of it.

Michael sucked hard on his cigarette, eyeing Gordon as he exhaled a column of gray smoke. "What are you in charge of? Besides us?"

Gordon flicked his eyes toward Michael without turning his head. "Weapons."

"Whoa, what weapons?" Michael's voice was edgy, tense. "Nobody ever mentioned weapons. We're supposed to be nonviolent, remember?"

Gordon's eyes closed briefly, his lips pressed together. "They're just to scare the employees into giving us what we want without a hassle. Did you think they would just hand over the money because we asked?"

Michael ignored the condescension in Gordon's voice. "So they won't be loaded. Right?"

Gordon lifted his cheeseburger, took a bite and chewed.

"No. No way, man," Michael said, stabbing his cigarette out in a metal ashtray. "I'm out if you're planning to go in there with loaded guns."

"Right on, Michael," Pam agreed. "I'm splitting too if anyone can get hurt. That's not what we're supposed to be about, man. We're about peace. *Stopping* the violence."

Pam looked at me to support her position. I could see plainly that this turn of conversation frightened her. "We are about peace and stopping the violence," I said. "But we're also in a war. This is a revolution! And there are times in revolution when extreme measures have to be taken."

"Lucinda!" Pam said. "Stop spouting that stuff and think about what could really happen. If we shoot innocent people, we're no better than the Establishment fuzz that we hate so much!"

When a truth is spoken, at the right moment, in the right place, it fills entirely the very space in which it exists. Any gracelessness in the words do not matter; their veracity holds all the power. Five pairs of eyes stared wordlessly at the truth strung out between us.

"She's right," I said finally. "We can't let ourselves become like the enemy."

Gordon looked around the table as Jimmy nodded his agreement, silently as usual. "Absolutely right," Gordon agreed. "We're a peace movement. The guns can't be loaded. It would undermine everything we stand for." He slipped a cigarette into his mouth and lit it. "I'm glad we're all in agreement."

We were the good guys. The conscience of a nation engaged in unconscionable acts. We were going to set America back on the right path, because the entrenched Establishment was too corrupt or blind or greedy or unenlightened to be trusted with the nation's wellbeing. We were saving America. Saving her very soul. She would thank us one day.

There is no engraved thank-you note on its way to me. No sugar-tongued expression of gratitude for my contributions to society. There has been, I think, some acknowledgement, by some people, that the radical protests of the 60s were instrumental in bringing positive change to this country. Dismissed as we were at the time, our fervent dedication to creating a better world forced open eyes and minds, and eventually doors for many under-appreciated, under-acknowledged segments of the population. We are a more tolerant, fair-minded people today, although we are far from having completed the journey.

Many of my contemporaries who protested and demonstrated in the face of harsh and abusive law enforcement may rightfully feel good about their contributions to the conscience of their country. And why should they not?

It was so clearly the right thing to do, to fight against the bloated, avaricious, imperialistic, materialistic and racist ruling power. We were so pure of spirit, if impetuous and judgment-impaired in our execution. Immature, perhaps, and certainly naïve. But oh, how I wish the world could have seen into my heart at the time, could see into it still. I wished only to save lives, to end the madness, the senseless killing. It was not wrong to fight for that. It was not wrong!

Lately, even before Michael appeared on the news, I have felt the stirrings of Lucinda in the debate over today's war in Iraq. There are so many similarities to Vietnam. Lucinda yearns to be out there in the streets with the other people of conscience, protesting against this illegal war of an arrogant president. But she has trapped herself inside Annie, and so cannot go. Annie is no protester.

CHAPTER 14

What to do? Now that she was here, standing outside the Food Recovery of Greater Springfield office, which was ridiculously easy to find, Pam was thoroughly befuddled as to what to do next. Wait, she supposed, for Lucinda to come in or go out, verifying that this was where she worked. And then?

The original plan had been to turn both herself and Lucinda in to the police. It was tiring, hiding from your past. Exhausting, this work of not being who you are. And after 37 years, utterly boring. An entire lifetime wasted, just hiding. She had had quite enough of it. On the other, more sensible hand, there was certain to be no shortage of monotony in prison, and even the monotony of South Dakota farmland was preferable to that. If just barely.

And besides, and even more to the point, she hadn't killed anyone. She didn't deserve to rot in jail. Not like her dear old cheating, lying, boyfriend-stealing, murdering ex-best friend Lucinda. Now there was a guilty person. How could she live with herself all these years? Pam shivered through a warm breeze. No decent, moral person could have.

What kind of life had Lucinda lived? Toiling in the mud, breaking her back in a sloppy field for years upon endless years?

Pathetically alone, wondering why the love of your life abandoned you? Why your best friend betrayed you? She brushed away an errant tear before it got started. Wondering if they were together somewhere, laughing at you?

I must be going now. Jarvis is talking and talking about procedures and systems and the finer points of food storage, and many other things that I already know but he apparently believes I need to hear again. What I really need is to be going now.

"You're not even listening to me, are you?" Jarvis' head is cocked sideways, his eyebrows raised high.

"I am," I say, and it is only sort of a lie. "Enough to know it's all stuff I already know."

He presses his lips together but cannot keep the words inside. "You're on your own for the next three days, Annie. With just her to help you."

Lindsey, well aware that she is the "her" in question, shakes her head silently at her desk.

"We will do just fine, Jarvis." I am suddenly irritated by his lack of confidence in both of us. "Lindsey and I are more competent than you like to give us credit for."

"I have all the confidence in the world in you, Annie. I just know you've been kind of distracted lately."

I feel a burning in my chest and I force a smile to press down the anger. Jarvis has not told me where he is going for the next three days and I have respected his privacy by not asking. I often wish he would accord me the same consideration. "I am still able to do my job," I say quietly. "You just go and enjoy your three days of leisure."

Jarvis is looking at me as though we have never met. He opens his mouth to speak, shuts it abruptly and walks away.

I should perhaps apologize, yet I am uncertain as to what, precisely, it is I have done. And really, I must be going.

Darlene was planning to pick Amber up at school today and spend the afternoon with her. Some good old-fashioned mother-daughter quality time. It would make me feel all warm and fuzzy if it were not for the nausea churned up by the mere thought of Amber in that dank, rancid hole Darlene calls an apartment.

It is only a few minutes' drive from the FROGS office and I am just swinging by after work, saving Darlene the trouble of driving Amber home. I may be a little earlier than we had agreed on. Perhaps an hour. Or more. Darlene will no doubt be furious and accuse me of checking up on them. On her.

I pack up my belongings into my macramé pocketbook and fish out the car keys, which feel pleasantly cool in my hand. There is a little red patch on my right palm where I had tried to wash away the burning sensation last night. I may have rubbed too hard because it is raw now, and tender to the touch.

"Good night, Annie," Lindsey says as I walk to the door. "See you tomorrow."

I turn and offer her a sincere, if distracted smile. "See you tomorrow." Jarvis has disappeared into the tiny closet he refers to as his office where he keeps a second, private desk and not much else.

Outside, the air is warm and slightly hazy, and the sweater I just put on inside is now oppressively heavy. I squint and hold up my hand as a shield against the sun, which is low in the sky, shimmering radiantly as it sinks into the horizon. It is as I am crossing the street against traffic that I see her, silhouetted against the orange sky-glow like some mythical demon. She has come to haunt me, to steal my life, and the very sight of her seems to pull the breath from my lungs and the blood from my veins.

She stands there, watching. For what?

I have stopped dead in the middle of the street, and the blare of a car horn startles me into moving. I should move away, back the way I came, but I do not. I continue forward, bringing myself to within a few feet of where she stands. I am not surprised she is here. Some part of me was prepared for it. Even, possibly, hoping for it.

She is so much different than she once was. Older. Heavier. Sadder. Yet she is the same. She is the best friend of my youth and the one person who truly knows me. There can be no barriers, no pretensions with her. I cannot hide my truth from her. All those years of lies and deceptions relinquish their pernicious grip on me and I am falling open. Open and free. What a delicious, liberating, indulgent relief.

"Pam," I say, and the warble in my voice betrays the parallel tremor in my heart.

She stares at me and I struggle to read her face. I see both anger and sorrow, perhaps because it is what I expect to see. I take a step closer. And now can truly see her. Deep inside the fleshy middle-aged face, I can discern the sweet, bubbly nineteen-year-old I once loved like a sister. Does she know that I love her still?

Confusion and uncertainty muddy her dark eyes. She is surprised; by what, I do not know.

"Pam," I say again, but I do not know if she heard me, or even if I actually spoke aloud.

There is a softening in her eyes, a kind of wonder, doubt. My hand reaches out toward her and I see something in her shift, contort, and then there is no mistaking the fury that overtakes her face. "Don't you dare," she hisses. Her eyes flash something between rage and repugnance, and she backs away from me as though I am a contagion. She turns her back to me and walks, then runs down the sidewalk, arms flailing gracelessly. I watch her until the water in my eyes blurs her image and she is gone.

The aloneness that I am left with is more empty, more hollow than any I have known. With Charlie, and everyone else in Annie's life, I am alone in my truth. I cannot let anyone in with me; I must keep them out with my grand charade. Pam, I can let in. She is already in; she does not know the fiction that is Annie. And now she has walked away.

She could have forgiven me, perhaps, for dragging her into a misguided and mishandled act that turned us into fugitives and destroyed our lives. She could forgive this, I think, because she knows this was not my intention. For her or myself. But the theft of Michael she cannot forgive. And I have no defense. Except youth and stupidity, and I have used that one so often that it is entirely used up.

I did not think about it in terms of Pam at the time, and that, of course, is why I made the wrong choice. And why she has every reason to be angry with me. At the time, however, it did not feel like a choice.

We were floating in a dreamy fog of euphoria, teetering in a stupor induced by some illicit substance I cannot recall. I felt happy and light, a little off-balance and giddy. When Michael kissed me, it seemed funny, like a joke. We made a little game of stripping off each other's clothing, both of us giggling like children. We were playing. Just playing. I was on top of him when Pam came into the room, and my sensation that we were playing an innocent game was so strong that I was happy to see her. *Come in!* I wanted to shout. *Come play with us.*

The look on her face confused me and I did not understand why she ran out of the room and did not stay and play with us. She is my best friend. Why won't she stay with us?

Afterwards, I knew enough to feel guilty, shameful. But not real, true compunction. No real empathy for what effect my actions had on Pam. I could blame it on the drugs. I was high and did not know what I was doing. But I cannot hide the truth of me from myself, regardless of how adept I have become at hiding it from others.

There is no one here at Darlene's apartment. The door is locked; the windows are dark. It is empty, lifeless. I do not know if I am happy that Amber is not here in this cockroach-infested dump, or worried about what other place Darlene may have taken her.

There is a part of me, an intuition, which tells me I should be worrying about myself. I have always done so, to the exclusion of others, and that is why I find myself deeply entombed in the middle age of a counterfeit person. I realize now that sometime, somewhere during this ersatz life, that impulse for self-preservation has left me. Not merely transformed or matured, in that I worry more about Amber now than myself, but vanished completely. Evaporated into the ether. No trace left. And I wonder what that says about a person who no longer possesses the fundamental human instinct to survive.

CHAPTER 15

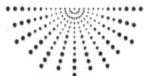

"So your plan was just to show up and knock on the door?" Charlie is dicing onions and does not look up at me.

"Pretty much."

"Even though it would be totally obvious that you were just checking up on her?" There is a sharpness in his voice that is completely out of place coming from him. Very un-Charlie-like.

"Why does that surprise you? I've checked up on her before." I decide to press the point he already knows. "And so have you."

He aims his blue eye-arrows at me and I look away, ashamed. "When I was worried about her."

"So I was worried about her."

"You were worried about Amber. Not," he says quickly, "that you shouldn't be. But there was no concern for Darlene. You were just trying to catch her in the act."

Now I am angry. "How is it exactly that you are able to read my mind and tell me that I have no concern for my daughter?"

Charlie's shoulders slump and he puts the knife down. He wipes his hand on a blue-striped towel and finally lifts his head to face me. "I know," he says deliberately, "you love Darlene. I'm not questioning that. But these last couple of weeks…I don't know." He flings the towel lightly on the counter and settles himself into a chair at the table. His normally cheery face wears a shroud of weariness that shames me further. "You've been different lately. I don't know exactly how to describe it. There's an edge to you, I guess. A hardness. And that's definitely," he says softly, "not my Annie."

A shy smile flickers briefly over his face, and I am overcome with such overwhelming adoration, sullied by bitter regret for what I have done to this sweet, good man. That is Lucinda, I wish to tell him, but cannot. She is here and I cannot make her leave. She will ruin us, you and me, yet I cannot make her leave us alone.

He is watching me, waiting for me to speak, but my brain is flustered and miserable and unable to come up with an acceptable lie. So I say nothing, and thus am lying just the same.

A haze of disappointment dims his face, and after a long, expectant silence, his voice fills the awful quiet. "You've always been quiet. Introspective. But lately, it seems like you're in your own little world. Someplace you don't want me. You're—it *feels* like you're deliberately keeping me out."

"I'm not," I say quickly, because I fervently want it to be true. "I'm not keeping you out. There's nothing to keep you out of." I still do not have a good lie but I must say something. "I don't have any explanation for what you're sensing. I don't feel like I'm keeping you out and I don't feel like I have an edge, as you called it. Maybe…I know I'm maybe reacting more intensely to Darlene than before. Because I just sense that her mindset is different now." Perhaps that will do. Perhaps he will find that believable.

But he is not buying this sham story. He is shaking his head. His hands cover his face for a moment, then slide down slowly, as though they could wipe away the melancholy. "Annie. I feel stupid for saying this because it seems ridiculous, sort of. But I just can't stop thinking about it." He lifts his eyes and holds them on me, unblinking. "Are you," his voice warbles so very slightly, "having an affair?"

Oh! Oh my god. Is this heartache I feel? Or relief? Anguish that I have caused this man I love so dearly to suffer such pain? Or elation that I have succeeded in deceiving him once again? And how terrible a person does that make me if I feel both?

"Charlie. Sweetheart." I am hesitant to approach him, as though he is a stranger. But when I get to him, I throw my arms around his neck in an unselfconscious hug. I am crying when I say, "I would laugh if you weren't in such obvious pain. I love you with all my heart. You know that. There is nothing—and no one—that could ever tempt me away from you." I kiss him. In the dimple first, then on the mouth. "It really is one of your more ridiculous notions."

He has let me kiss him, but does not kiss me back. "It's a problem that I even thought it," he says. "Something's wrong if the thought even occurs to me." He holds me back, his steady blue gaze on me. "Something is wrong."

"I don't," I stutter, "know what. I don't know what's wrong."

Charlie nods, stands up, and walks away, over to the counter. He picks up his knife and chops listlessly at the onion.

"I love you so much, Charlie."

His chopping hand keeps its steady, monotonous rhythm. "I believe you."

I do not know what he is thinking. But I know I will not be able to convince him tonight that everything is all right. It is because of her. Charlie is worried about another man when the problem between us is another woman. Lucinda is here. She cannot be so conciliatory and nurturing as Annie. She does not possess the capacity to ease someone else's pain. She is a causer of pain. *It is the other woman in the room who is the problem, Charlie. Not me.*

I am walking out of the room when Charlie's voice stops me. "Darlene called before. She was taking Amber to an early movie and then for a bite to eat," he says to the onion. "That's why they weren't there when you stopped by." He trades in the chopped onion for a green pepper and slices into that. "I said it was okay."

Okay? He said it was okay? Rage swells hot in my chest until I am saturated, drenched by it. He made this decision without consulting me? And then, when I was worrying, and wondering where they were, he does not tell me about it? He was toying with me! The fury has filled me up and will spew out if I open my mouth, and so I do not. I just leave, the steady thump of a knife blade on a chopping board the only sound.

CHAPTER 16

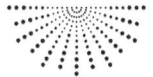

"My guardian angel!" Darlene laughed with obvious delight as she opened the door. "Come in, come in."

Carrying a large cardboard box, Charlie stepped into the oddly-shadowed living room with faded green wallpaper and continued into the narrow kitchen where he set the box down on a yellow Formica counter. Turning, he caught her quick kiss on his cheek and held her closely a moment longer. "Hi sweetheart," he smiled, sliding a stray wisp of hair from her face. "You look terrific."

Darlene grinned happily, revealing for a brief moment the bright young girl she had once been. "Thanks. I feel terrific."

"So," Charlie said, reaching into the box, "we've got all the usual stuff. Eight—no ten—individually wrapped servings of veggie lasagna for the freezer. Turkey chili packets—six of those. Oh, and a special treat; trout, caught by the chef himself, with butter-lemon sauce. Some apples and plums that looked good. And," he brought his hands out with a flourish, holding an array of brightly colored miniature fruits.

"Marzipan!" Darlene shouted, throwing her arms around Charlie in a tight squeeze. "Charlie, you are the best!"

He smiled weakly at the sound of his name, but held on tightly to her, savoring the hug.

"So," he said, releasing her, "how was your night with Amber?"

"Great," Darlene examined a little almond candy in the shape of a banana. "Didn't—what did Amber say about it?"

"She said you had a nice time."

"We did. We really did. She's such an amazing kid. So smart. Funny. And smart, not just intelligent, you know? But really savvy about things, people."

"I know."

"Of course you do. You and Mom have done a really great job with her. Really, really awesome. I'm really grateful." She paused. "And I'm mad at myself for missing so much of her life. I've made a mess of things; I know it. And I'm going to fix it."

"Good." Charlie pressed his lips together in a noncommittal grin.

"You don't believe me. You don't think I can do it."

"You're wrong. I know you can do it and that makes me wonder why you haven't before."

Darlene's eyes flashed in anger, her chin thrust pugnaciously forward. "Well—" She closed her mouth, settling her lips into an acquiescent smile. "I don't know what I was going to say. I don't have a good answer."

"That's the first time you ever admitted anything like that. I think it's a good sign."

"Yeah? I guess so." Darlene grinned. "Thanks Charlie. It's nice to know someone else has faith in me. Mom certainly doesn't."

"She does. She's just...well we've all been round this before, Darlene. It takes a lot out of her and she's tired, I think."

Darlene smirked, unconvinced. "You know what I think? Honestly? I think she doesn't want me to succeed so she can keep Amber."

Charlie's face showed nothing, but he processed this for a long moment.

"Damn. I didn't really want to be right about that one."

"You're not right."

"Yeah, I wish. But the fact is, she loves Amber in a way she never loved me."

"God no, Darlene. She adores you. And always has. That's why it breaks her heart every time you damage yourself and your life with the drugs and everything."

"Yeah," Darlene dismissed this with a shrug. "Whatever. You know what? Let's just not even talk about her and ruin our visit."

Charlie shook his head, sighed heavily. "At the risk of ruining our visit, she and I both think you should go back into rehab.

"Rehab is for addicts."

"That's right."

"I'm not an addict, Charlie." Irritation laced her voice. She breathed in deeply. "I'm sorry. I haven't given you much reason to believe otherwise. But I've never been really, clinically addicted. I don't need the stuff. I've just been indulgent."

"Putting aside the fact that the patient is not usually the best one to make the diagnosis, we're supposed to believe that now, all of a sudden, you no longer feel the need to be indulgent?"

She faced him, met his gaze. "Yes. Because now I'm scared."

Dread flickered in his eyes. "The night you called us?"

Her head inclined in a slow nod.

He swallowed, winced. "Something really terrible happened to you, didn't it?"

She looked away, unable to meet his eyes. "My awakening, you might call it. But now, everything's going great. All according to plan."

"According to plan?"

"My plan," she said airily. "To get my life back. I've asked for more hours at the salon, doing other stuff besides manicures so I can work up to stylist. I think Cara's going to give them to me. I'm sure she is. They can use the help right now. I was almost finished with my schooling, so I could be done in a few months. I haven't had a drink or—anything else in thirteen days, which I know is not so much, but I feel good. Not like it's difficult or a struggle or anything. I can do this. I know I can."

"That's more than half the battle, I guess."

"The only thing left is getting Amber back."

"You never really had her, you know." A pained look of regret crossed his face as he uttered the words.

"I know."

"I think," he said carefully, "we all want what's best for Amber. And that means a stable home environment. Stable implies no dramatic changes over a significant period of time. So I think you need to be patient. Work on healing yourself, fixing your own life. Before you try to take on someone else's life." He grinned. "A teenager's, no less. It doesn't get any more difficult than that."

Darlene shrugged, smiled sheepishly. "I timed that badly, didn't I?"

"I really want you to be with her, Darlene. I think it would be great for Amber to be with her mother. But only if you can be a strong, positive influence in her life. Your best chance at success is to get your own life in order first so you can better deal with whatever comes up in hers. Be a good role model."

"I will. And it will happen sooner than you think."

"I hope so." Charlie slid his arm around her shoulders and squeezed.

She allowed herself to be held, slipping her hand behind his back and relaxing into the embrace. "Sooner than a year. Way sooner."

For a half hour longer, Charlie puttered about the apartment, helping her load the freezer, tightening the washer on the leaky bathroom faucet, adjusting the hinge on a cabinet door that wouldn't close properly. After he'd left, Darlene rummaged through the fresh fruit left in the cardboard box, poked around in the carton of marzipan, and peeked under the foil wrapping of the packets in the freezer. Finally, in a square hunk of foil labeled veggie lasagna, she found what she was looking for. A thick sheaf of twenty-dollar bills, folded in half. She grinned at how Charlie must have enjoyed the pun: cold cash. Someday, hopefully soon, she would not need his charity. Maybe then she would get some respect from both of them.

CHAPTER 17

Today is the day Annie Pulkowski dies. The police will come through the FROGS door that Pam has directed them to, looking for Lucinda. They will find her. She will spring to life in a whirlwind of dissolving fantasy, landing her house of guilt on poor Annie, like Dorothy flattening the wicked witch. Except today, the wicked kills the good.

What a relief! Yes. Appalling as it is to admit, even inside the private space of my own head, it will be a delicious relief, like a cool drink on a parched throat. It takes a great deal of effort to keep Annie alive. It has been many years, and I am tired now. I do not even think I will miss her. Yet I know two people who will, and I am filled up again with grief and shame.

Perhaps that is why I continued to hide the truth from Charlie last night. He will know the truth today. Annie will be gone and he will hate Lucinda. And Annie too, for lying to him all these years. This illusion I cling to with my obstinate grasp is shifting under me, disappearing like sand between my toes when a wave washes it away. Yet I continue to hide in Annie's life for however many precious moments she has left.

The door to FROGS opens and I freeze, the bloody muscle in

my chest jolts to a stop, waiting, just waiting, until it is safe to pump again. A damp sheen of sweat erupts all over my body and I am cold and hot at once. It is a young man, come to sign up to be a volunteer. That is all.

The telephone rings and Jarvis answers it. He listens intently— did he just glance at me? Jarvis mumbles a few words occasionally. I am so quiet; I must hear what he is saying. I cannot breathe; the inhaling and exhaling of air will be too loud, will not allow me to hear what he says. Dizziness swirls in my head; I do not know if it is terror or a lack of oxygen.

I rub at the growing rash on my palm. It swells larger, redder, each day. How old hat of me! How derivative and uninspired to have grown Lady Macbeth's spot on my trigger hand. How utterly unoriginal!

The phone rings and the door opens dozens of times today, and each time I brace myself for the accusation that will be thrown at me. The name I must answer to. Yes, I am Lucinda Whittendon. Yes, I am guilty of being her. Jarvis and Lindsey will look at me with shock and disbelief that I will not see because I will not look at them. I will not know them. Lucinda does not know Jarvis and Lindsey.

Yet the end of the day arrives and Annie still lives.

I am not prepared for this. I cannot go home because Amber is at her play rehearsal, and so Charlie and I will be alone in the house. We have not spoken in any real way since last night, and I cannot bear the chasm that yawns between us like a black hole. I want everything to be all right between us again, but the only way to get there is via another lie. It is not that I cannot think of a lie; I have become very adept at that. It is, frankly, what is the point? Annie has only a few hours, maybe days, left. Perhaps it will be easier for him if he is angry and disappointed with her when she dies. Perhaps it will not hurt him so much.

I call Charlie and volunteer to pick up Amber at rehearsal. He says okay, and not much else. Despite my acceptance of Annie's imminent demise, her heart shudders with pain at the coldness in his words. She will miss him.

It is too early to pick up Amber. So I linger in the office, I run a few unnecessary errands, and still I am early. The school auditorium has been darkened slightly, except for the stage, which glows brightly with the lithe forms of adolescents play-acting. I take a seat near the back, and watch for the shining, redemptive light of my life to appear.

She materializes as though by divine miracle, surging on stage as a dervish of light and energy. Her essence draws attention to her form at the expense of the others, who now seem dim and lackluster by comparison. I am supremely aware that this is almost surely my own personal bias. But I have only a few hours to live; I will indulge myself in one last fantasy.

Amber wears low-slung blue jeans and a lacy purple top that hangs from spaghetti straps and reveals a large expanse of belly. A costume, apparently, as such clothing is not permitted in school. She is confident and comfortable—more than comfortable on stage. She feeds on it, draws life from the act of performing for others. It occurs to me that she is not so different on stage from how she is in her every day. Life, in many ways for her, is one enormous theater production. What character will I play today? What will I make my audience believe in this situation? I make this observation with no judgment attached; I am undoubtedly more guilty of it than she.

The rehearsal runs a few minutes late, and I wait for Amber near the main door to the school.

"Hey, Nonny," she says brightly, zipping up a green hooded sweatshirt. "I thought Grampa was picking me up today."

"I had some extra time, so I told him I'd get you. It gave me a chance to see you in action." I hold the door open for her and follow her out into the parking lot.

"You were watching? So you saw Molly Bonardino as Rizzo." She rolls her eyes upward in an expression of derision. "Totally miscast."

"I take it that's the role you wanted?"

"Not so much wanted, just better suited for it." She winked at me. "I'm just thinking of what's best for the show, Nonny. It's all for the good of the show."

"Your selflessness is inspiring, my dear."

"I prefer to think of it as dedication," she says seriously. "So anyway, what'd you think?"

"You were magnificent."

"You always say that."

"It's always true."

We have arrived at the car and Amber climbs into the front seat next to me. As she slides the seat belt across her chest, it pulls her sweatshirt open slightly, exposing a bit of purple lace.

"What shirt are you wearing?"

"Oh, I don't know. Just something I found in the back of my drawer."

"Let me see it."

She lifts her eyebrows in surprise and pulls the sweatshirt open a little with her hand.

It is the same shirt she wore on stage. I am sure of it. "Unzip your sweatshirt."

"What? Why?"

"I want to see your shirt."

Perhaps I am imagining it, but her face appears to redden. She slides the zipper down slowly, pulling it open at the top, but keeping it closed at bottom, as though I am some idiot who will not realize what she is doing.

"Amber! Show me the goddam shirt!"

Her eyes are big. I have frightened her with my outburst. *I have frightened myself too, sweetheart.* I watch her pull the sweatshirt open to reveal the skimpy purple item I believed was a costume.

"Where did you get that?"

"I don't know. I've had it a long time."

"Don't lie to me. That's a new shirt. Where did you get it? And more importantly, why are you wearing it to school? It's against the rules."

"I didn't. I mean, well, I did. But I wore my sweatshirt over it."

"Really? So if I contact the school, talk to your teachers, no one will have seen you without the sweatshirt?"

"Nope. I wore my sweatshirt the whole—well, Mrs. Griffin might've seen, for a little while, but I was hot and so I just took it off—"

"Amber! You're babbling. Because you're lying."

"I'm not lying!"

"Where did you get it?"

"I told you, it's old."

"That's a lie, too. I know all your clothes." She is glaring at me, which only serves to make my rage spin out of control. "Where did you get that shirt? I want the truth!"

She whispers her answer. "Mom bought it for me."

This, I realize, is why I am so furious. It is what I expected, what I feared. "Last night?"

She inclines her head in a yes, just barely.

"When I asked you what else you did besides the movie and dinner, you said nothing."

"I forgot—"

"*Stop lying to me!*" I pound my fists against the steering wheel and the horn blares, and I pound again and again. *"I will not have you lying to me! I will not let your mother do this to us! I will not be lied to! I will not! Do you get that? I will not!"*

Amber is frozen, and the worst horror is that I can see on her face what this has done to her perception of me. *I take it back!* I want to cry. *It was not me who said that.*

I believe she knows that to be true, for she is looking at me as though she does not know me.

CHAPTER 18

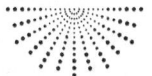

My god, it was humiliating. Angela Dechesney stood at the end of the driveway and scowled at her small, drab home. It had been such a cute little bungalow when she had first moved here with the children all those years ago. When had it gotten so dingy and rundown? The bright yellow paint she'd put on to add some cheer to their existence was now peeling badly. There was a crack in the front window from the errant ball thrown by a neighborhood child last year—no, it was more than a year. My god, that small child was almost a teenager now. A shutter on the same window that had been slightly loose some years back now hung at an odd angle, ready to fall off altogether. There was no lawn to speak of anymore; just weeds and dirt. It was a shambles. And it—and she—had been on TV for everyone to see! My god she could just die of embarrassment.

Bobby was supposed to maintain the place as part of their agreement. The one that said he didn't have to pay rent if he maintained the place. Angela frowned. She had been too easy on him and he had turned into a lazy bum. How had she allowed that to happen? The girls had turned out fine. Michelle taught fourth grade and was married to a nice man and had two beautiful children. And

Rachel—who would ever have dreamed it—was a lawyer! Although her tiny practice was still struggling financially, she was a lawyer! Respectable, educated, ambitious. All the things Bobby wasn't. Angela shifted her heavy purse from one sore shoulder to the other. He was her baby. Like any mother, she'd wanted to take care of her baby, to do things for him. And now he did practically nothing.

She tugged open the rusted metal mailbox—even that was looking like crap. A few envelopes lay inside and she glanced through them as she walked to the front door. No bills, so you have to be thankful for that. But would there be...yes. A plain white envelope with a typed label and no return address. Postmarked in Massachusetts. Every month for the past thirty or so odd years, one of these envelopes would appear in her mailbox. Sometimes they were postmarked in Connecticut, even New York once in a while. Always loaded with cash. It was one of *them*, she knew. It had to be. Trying to buy a little forgiveness. Or peace of mind, maybe. Whatever. It was good to get the cash.

She folded the thick envelope in half and tucked it into the pocket of her skirt. Had to hide it from Bobby. Once, she'd made the mistake of opening the monthly envelope in front of him and he'd snatched the cash from her hands. Blown it all in one night buying rounds for everyone at the bar. She'd made up some story about someone paying her back a loan so he wouldn't know the money came every month. The truth was, she'd come to depend on it. Without it, the bills just wouldn't all get paid.

Inside the house, Bobby sat in a straight-backed wooden chair cleaning his hunting rifle, which was pretty much the only thing he did maintain. His fleshy fingers worked deftly along the gleaming metal.

"Hey Ma," he smiled, glancing up briefly. "Me and Dean are going hunting out by the ledge tomorrow."

"What about work?"

He grinned. "Feeling a cold coming on. Bad cold. Wicked bad cold."

"How many times you think you can get away with that?"

The glee in Bobby's eyes withered into resentment and he turned back to cleaning his rifle with a low grunt. "Goddam federal case just to wanna have a little fun around here."

Angela watched her son continue to buff the dark metal shiny in strained silence. And what would happen if and when he got fired for slacking off so much? She clutched the envelope of cash in her pocket. Could she count on anymore of these? Or was this the last anonymous monthly guilt payment? Now that the story was in the news again, and maybe cops getting involved again, would the guilty benefactor get scared and dry up?

She'd kept this monthly secret from all of them. At first they'd been young children of course, but even as they grew, and there were opportunities—obligations, even—to tell them, she'd kept it from them. Deliberately. And keeping it from Bobby was completely justifiable, frankly. He was greedy and lazy and could not handle money responsibly, and had proven as much the one time he did discover the cash. But keeping it from the girls was another matter. One that she could not feel quite so righteous about. Rachel and Michelle wanted closure and justice. They wanted their father's killers found and punished. And this monthly envelope was —maybe—a clue to finding one of them. The postmarks, all from the northeast, and overwhelmingly from Massachusetts, could possibly provide some clue for the authorities to follow. Maybe. Or maybe it was not enough to go on. Angela shrugged. She really had no idea. But she did not want to take that chance. She couldn't afford to take that chance. It wasn't a choice, really.

CHAPTER 19

It had been there for hours already. Well, maybe an hour. Catherine glanced at her watch. Thirty-five minutes anyway. The point was, really, that it didn't belong there. She peeked out through the pink lace curtains again. No one in this neighborhood owned a car like that, and no one had any visitors who had a car like that, that she could remember. And the biggest point was that it had been parked across the street from her house for, let's call it an hour, and the driver was sitting in it the whole time! *That* was the point, really.

The electronic wail of the telephone sounded from the next room and Catherine turned to go to it, then stopped. The last time the phone rang, which was yesterday afternoon, there was a newspaper reporter on the other end. How did she feel, the young man wanted to know, seeing her daughter's victims speaking out about their loss? *How did she feel?* Did she know where Lucinda was now? Off the record, of course. Any contact with her at all in the last 37 years? So, nothing? No comment at all, Mrs. Whittendon?

Must have been six, seven rings by now. Call it ten. Catherine stood, listening to the phone and knew she was incapable of ignoring it, despite the journalistic risks involved.

"I'm coming, I'm coming already," she snapped at the relentlessly persistent instrument. "Hold onto your bloomin' drawers, you insufferable noisemaker." Unhurriedly, she shuffled to pick up the receiver. She cleared her throat, and when she spoke into the mouthpiece, her voice was melodious and lilting. "Hello."

"Hey, Mom." Colin's voice was serious.

"Hi sweetheart," she smiled her relief. "Nice to hear from you. How's everyone?"

"Fine. Everyone's fine. Mom. I've been watching...I'm sure you've seen all the news coverage, the interviews with the family members. There's a big interest again in finding Lucinda and the rest of them."

Catherine nodded silently, the receiver firmly against her ear, until Colin continued.

"Mom. I think you should give them the letter."

"What?"

"I really think you should turn it over to the police. It could be of help."

"Help how?" Catherine's voice was hoarse but sharp.

"Mom, come on. You should have turned it in years ago."

"It won't do any good now. It's too old. Outdated."

Colin's loud sigh was audible through the receiver, and Catherine could see the exasperation that would be lining his face. "So fine, then there's no reason not to turn it over."

"It's all I have left."

"Then give them a copy. But Mom, it's the right thing to do. You have to do it."

"No. No I don't. Colin, she's my daughter. If she were your child, if she were Vanessa—"

"Don't!" he hissed. "How can you even mention them in the same sentence? Vanessa is a wonderful human being, kind and goodhearted and—"

"So was your sister! You used to love her so much; I don't know why you've turned on her."

"You don't? You're not serious! I was a kid. I looked up to my older sister. I didn't know what she was."

"She was my child. She is my child. You can understand that, can't you?"

The silence was long, uncomfortable. "Yes," he said finally. "I can. But I still think it's the right thing to do. And it'll help you find closure for yourself Mom. If they can find her, well, you'll finally know where she is. You'll be able to see her. Talk to her, if you want."

Catherine snorted. "That's a rather abrupt change in tactics. You just want her to be punished."

"She deserves to be punished. You can't argue with that. And it really will help you find closure. Anyway, just think about it. Just give it some real consideration, okay?"

"Goodbye, Colin. I forgive you."

She set the receiver back in its cradle, only hearing his protestations from a distance. She did forgive him. It was painful and disappointing how easily he dismissed his sister, who he *did* love, despite what he says now. But she understood. He took a lot of abuse from other kids when it happened, from his friends' parents, from teachers. It had not been easy for him, and the resentment still simmered inside him, that was obvious.

Her ghost box sat on the table where she'd left it. The pink and green threads, arrayed in orderly little stitches over the large wooden box, had frayed only slightly over their long and sedentary life. But the colors had dimmed, faded ghosts of the vibrancy they once flaunted. Catherine's hand shuddered and hesitated over the lid of the box, steeling herself for yet another visit with the ghosts who dwelled inside. At first, this box had sheltered photos of Ray, his dog tags, the official letter from the army confirming his death in combat, and various newspaper articles about his life and his death. Later, she had added photos and news articles of Lucinda when she had disappeared, and most recently, the same for Sam when he passed on. All of her precious, beloved ghosts. Might they be together in God's heaven too?

Certainly Ray and Sam would be, those two good and decent men. Lucinda however, if she really did what they said she did....

Catherine lifted the lid slowly and pulled out the yellowed envelope on top. The ancient letter she'd read dozens of times in the last few weeks. The postmark was faded, barely legible, but Catherine knew well what it read. July 14, 1982. San Francisco. There was no need to remove the letter inside; Catherine knew every word. But it was nice to see the handwriting, to run her fingers over the page. This letter said, I am not quite a ghost. Not real, but not altogether gone, either. She spread it out over her lap, and allowed herself to sink into the profound pleasure imparted by this solid, non-ephemeral, distinctly un-ghostlike sliver of a life.

Dear Mom and Dad and Colley,

Yes, it is me. I wish I knew if you were happy or horrified to hear from me. Since I cannot know this, I will allow myself to believe that you are happy and are still reading.

I am so sorry for what I have done to our family. That is the first, and main reason I am writing to you. I have regretted what I did from the moment it happened, and I am so sorry to have put you all through the shame and humiliation of being my family. My actions were no reflection on you, I'm sure you all know that. They weren't even a reflection on the real me. I know I have to pay the price, and I am paying it. I'm just sorry all of you do, too.

I miss you all so much! I cried myself to sleep, and then again when I woke each day, for so many years because of the ache of missing you all. Remember how hard it was when we lost Ray? Remember how much it hurt just to breathe? Well, magnify that a million times more for the way I feel at having lost all of you. Not just three times more, because there are three of you. But you three were all I had. You three were everything to me. I lost my everything. I don't know if you can imagine that. The ache goes so deep, it is me. The ache is what I have become.

I don't know if you feel the same sense of loss over me as you felt for Ray. It can't be the same, I know, because I've shamed the whole family. But I hope—at least part of me hopes you miss me at least a little bit. But part of me doesn't want you to feel the pain, or to worry. And that is why I'm writing to you now.

I want you to know that I'm doing okay. I've actually managed to make a nice life for myself. I'm married to a wonderful man, and we have a beautiful daughter. Yes, that's right—you're grandparents, Mom and Dad! Your granddaughter is just perfection—you would love her. She's got a real spunk to her— just like her grandmother. She even juts out her chin when she's angry just the way you do, Mom. It's like I have a little piece of you with me, which is comforting most of the time. I'm so sorry she will never know you all, never have you as her family.

And my husband is such a kind, giving, wonderful man (much like my father!). He doesn't know about my past—he is too good to know. I don't know why I had the good fortune to find him, and I know I don't deserve him, but he has helped me make a normal —even good—life for myself. You would love him, I'm sure of that.

I'm sending you this from San Francisco, where we are taking our first real family vacation ever. We're having a wonderful time, but one of the best things about this trip is that it affords me an opportunity to send you this letter, something I've been wanting to do from that very first day thirteen years ago. Call me paranoid, but I didn't want to risk sending you something from the town, or even the state, where I'm living. Probably the police are not looking for me any longer, or watching your mail, but like I said, I'm a little bit paranoid. I've had to be, I guess, to survive this long.

I could write forever! I could just go on and on, because it makes me feel like I am talking to you, although I'll never hear a response. I don't know when I'll have the chance to write to you again—hopefully not another thirteen years. But I honestly don't know. I think of you all every single day. I love you and miss you all every single day. I guess that's the real reason I'm sending you this. I want you to know how much I love you all. Colley, you must be all grown up into a handsome man by now. How I wish I could see you! How I wish I could see and touch you all. Just one quick hug would be more of a joy for me than you could imagine.

   All my love forever,
   Lucinda

Catherine smiled at the yellowed paper with the faded ink. She no longer cried when she read these last words from her only daughter. There was joy here on this page. Lucinda was happy. She had a good life. Colin was wrong to want to take that from her. Wrong to want her punished more than she already had been. She folded the letter carefully, slid it into its envelope, and tucked it back safely into its embroidered crypt with the other ghosts. *You are safe in there my girl.*

When Colin called, she had been doing something important. Oh, yes. The car across the street. She bustled back to the window and peered out. Still there. Looking very much out of place. In point of fact, it was quite some favor to even call it a car. It was more of a truck, actually. A dirty pickup truck. This was most certainly not a pickup truck sort of neighborhood.

Pam shifted her hefty bulk on the sticky vinyl seat of the old truck. Lucinda's house was so much more compelling than her own had been. It was unchanged, for one thing. Same white clapboard siding and black shutters, same cozy little backyard nestled up to untouched wooded acres of land. She and Lucinda had wandered those woods often, telling secrets, sneaking beer or boys. Or both. The weeping willow tree still cascaded gracefully over its patch of the front yard, although both the tree and the patch were larger. The mailbox still said Whittendon. They were still there.

Unlike at her own home, which had been painted a revolting shade of mint green and had a clumsy little addition slapped onto one side of the living room. Plastic children's toys littered the yard and her mother's favorite purple rhododendron was gone, replaced by a sandpit for what looked like a horseshoe game. And the mailbox. Not that she'd actually expected to see the small white box that her mother had let her paint with rainbows and peace symbols as consolation for having to move to a new town. It was just that she had never seen anything else there on that post. The new mailbox, big and black, had crooked gold peel-off letters that spelled, "DePalma." No artistry. No character. No life.

Pam stared at the Whittendon home across the street, the heat rising in her chest. Lucinda worked just thirty miles from here; surely she sees her family on a regular basis. How was it that the murdering man-stealer got everything back, and the gullible dupe with the good intentions got nothing? For 37 years she'd lived a hard life alone, halfway across the country from those she loved. All because of Lucinda. Yet Lucinda had managed to get her life back. Her family. Her home. And, it seemed likely, Michael, despite his denial. Lucinda had even managed to get part of Pam's life for her own.

The door to the house opened. An old woman stepped out. Mrs. Whittendon. She was slower, stooped, and a little heavier, but definitely recognizable as Lucinda's mother. She should have recognized her right away at the hospital. Mrs. Whittendon must have been delivering some message from Lucinda to Michael so her daughter wouldn't be caught. Her own mother would have done the same, no doubt. Her own mother loved her, would have protected her. If she'd still had her.

Pam choked back a knot of anxiety as Mrs. Whittendon walked directly toward the truck. She'd once known this woman very well; had hung around her house for hours on end; had called her Mom, as though she were just another Whittendon sister. Pam felt the word rise up in her throat. Mom. She swallowed it, and it left her aching. Would this second mom, the only one left, recognize her?

Catherine stopped at the end of her driveway and shouted across the street. "You have been loitering here all day. This is a nice neighborhood. You can't just park your car and sit there for hours. Move along, or I will call the police."

Pam peered, frozen, at this face from long ago. *Don't you know me?* Maybe she knew where Pam's family had gone. *I could use a hug, Mom.* Had Lucinda told her mother she'd seen Pam recently?

"Are you a reporter?" Mrs. Whittendon accused. "What are you watching for? I have rights, you know. You can't just stalk me."

Pam blinked. "I—I'm not stalking you," she stammered. "I'm not a reporter."

The old woman squinted at her, and her shuffling feet brought her into the narrow road, closer. Then her eyes grew big, her hand clapped to her mouth. "Pamela?"

"No." Once again, the fear was bigger than the truth.

Catherine stepped to within a few feet of the truck, the beginning of a smile on her face. "Pamela."

CHAPTER 20

They are talking about me. I cannot hear them, but I know it to be true. They have much to discuss. Amber is frightened and befuddled as to why her mild-mannered Nonny exploded into frenzied paroxysms of rage over a shirt. Charlie will ostensibly attempt to rationalize Annie's behavior (or will he?), but privately is perplexed and disturbed by the recent changes in his normally restrained and considerate wife.

I need my coffee. But I am afraid to walk into the kitchen and face them. Frightened of their accusing stares and awkward silence and the enormous emotional distance engulfing such a small room. Behold the depths to which I have sunk. Charlie and Amber are my sanctuary, my comfort zone. And I am terrified of them. But I really do need my coffee.

"Good morning," I say as I enter the room.

Charlie puts down his spatula and turns to me. "Good morning," he says, but does not proffer the customary nose-tip kiss.

Amber brings her plate from the table to the sink. "I'm late," she mumbles. "Gotta go."

"Bye sweetheart," Charlie says, kissing the top of her head.

Amber tosses a glance at me, furtive and quick, but enough for me to see the anxiety in her eyes. I am ashamed.

"Have a great day," I say, but even this master of deception cannot imbue the words with the upbeat enthusiasm they should contain. My voice sounds desperate, hopeful, and I wish immediately that I had just settled for "goodbye."

She murmurs a "'bye," in my direction, and then she is gone.

And now I am really in trouble. Charlie wishes to talk. Wishes, is perhaps more optimistic than accurate. Charlie *needs* to talk.

"Amber wants to live with Darlene."

Difficult, I was expecting. This thunderbolt leaves me breathless.

"I said, no," he continues. "At least not right now. But the fact that she's asking, right now, this morning, has got to make you ask why she's so eager to leave all of a sudden." He folds his arms across his chest. "Or maybe it doesn't."

"Don't look at me like you're waiting for some big confession." I am suddenly irritated by his attitude. "I lost my temper. I know she told you. It happens. It's not a big deal. She's just being thirteen and overreacting."

"Maybe. But since when is it a crime for a kid to accept a gift from her mother?"

"Her crime was lying! She deliberately hid that shirt from me, and then when I asked her about it, she lied. I wasn't mad about the shirt; I was mad because she deliberately deceived me."

Charlie nods, lifts his ocean blue eyes to mine. "Yeah. That can be maddening."

"Maybe," I say, launching my offense-as-defense, "she's just been spending too much time over there. I mean, you letting them go off on an extended evening the other day, dinner *and* a movie, didn't help. I would never have agreed to that, which, you should have asked me, by the way, instead of going behind my back. They're spending way too much time together. This is all part of Darlene's plot to get Amber. You're playing right into her hands when you allow them to stay out so long whenever she wants."

Awestruck. It is the only word to describe Charlie's reaction, and I am confused by this. Have I said something so astounding?

Charlie blinks and rubs his hands over his face. He takes a few slow, measured steps to the table and eases himself gingerly into a chair. "Who are you?"

The question catches me off guard and while my heart petrifies into a solid block in my chest, Annie and Lucinda dance a spirited tango in my head.

"Do you hear yourself?" Charlie is saying. "A *plot*? Going behind your back? You're paranoid. You're temperamental. You're withdrawn and distant. You're not anybody I recognize."

"I don't know—"

"And don't tell me you don't know what's wrong!" Charlie's voice explodes in the little room. "God, Annie! Don't treat me like I'm some stranger. Or some idiot. I know you. And I know there's something wrong, something troubling you, and it bothers me that you won't tell me. It *hurts* me." He thumps his chest with an open palm. "I don't know what you expect from me. Do you expect me not to care that you're hiding—deliberately deceiving—me? I don't...I just don't know what to do."

"Charlie. I'm not deceiving—"

His hands slap loudly on the table. He stands abruptly and strides toward the doorway.

"Charlie."

He stops, turns. There is more sadness in his face than I have ever seen. "This is a sham conversation that we keep repeating over and over. I'm not playing anymore."

He is walking away and I no longer have to wonder just how excruciating it will be to lose him. Down the hall, the bedroom door closes. Not an enraged slam, spewing fury and contempt, but a dawdling click of weary torment, as though he is giving me time to speak up and win him back.

And that is my choice, I see. I can go to him, tell him the truth —the real truth of me—and then turn myself into the police. And Annie will be gone forever. I can stay silent, and live my last few days, or hours or minutes, with Charlie cold and distant toward me. Or I can go to him and tell him something that will bring him back to me, and we can spend Annie's last days together, in love, as we once were.

"Charlie." I would say his name softly.

He would turn toward me, waiting.

"I—I didn't want to tell you until I was sure. Because I didn't want you to worry." I offer a weak smile. "But I sure messed that up. I guess the stress of it all—"

"What?" he interrupts. "Just tell me."

I open my duplicitous mouth and the lie falls out with terrible ease. "I...may...have cancer."

"Oh my god." He comes to me and wraps his arms around me in the most deliciously wonderful embrace of my life. "Sweetheart. You should have told me. You shouldn't have to go through this alone. Honey, that's what I'm here for." He cradles my face in his hands and kisses it everywhere. "Tell me everything. What kind? When will you know for sure? Oh my god," he stops and probes my skull with his solicitous blue eyes. "That's why you've been so worried about me having custody if you weren't here. Oh sweetheart, I wish you'd told me," he says, folding me up in his lovingly protective embrace.

And I know it is brilliant. This lie I have told, just one more in so long a line of falsehoods, is brilliant. It explains everything, all my odd behavior, and accomplishes the goal of making Charlie love me again and take care of me for my last few days. It is so warm in here in this hug. I hold him and cry on him, breathing the musky smell of his skin, feeling his breath on my hair. It will be worse when he finds out the truth, but the future be damned! It is damned anyway, regardless of what I do now. And it is worth it to me to gain a loving end to Annie's final days.

Yes, it is truly brilliant. And terrible. More evil than the murder on my conscience because it is premeditated harm on the most benevolent and cherished of souls.

And so I stand here, alone in my kitchen, savoring the conversation and the caresses we will never have. My most brilliant lie in my long and lucrative career of deception will never be told. I simply cannot do it to him.

I do not delude myself that this makes me a good person. Goodness is far more than refraining from evil. Yet evil requires only the slightest error in judgment, the smallest misstep off the path of good. The coffee that I so craved just moments ago sits untouched in its pot, a steaming lesson in true yearning as I contemplate the lost embraces of the man in my bedroom.

I have decided not to run this morning. Or any morning. Annie runs to stay healthy so she may have a long and productive life with her family and in her job. Lucinda cares nothing for any of that.

Charlie is lost to me. He was mine for 37 years longer than I deserved him, so I have no right to lament it. Yet I do. Early on, after he had rescued me, I spent every day believing it must be my last with him. My shining white knight who became my armor. How long could my good fortune possibly last?

He had been harboring me for three months, and I already both needed him and loved him, although I had confessed to neither because I was unsure of his feelings. He was so kind; perhaps all the affection he showed me was just compassion for a needy soul. I still am completely unsure which came first, the need or the love, but there can be no doubt my life would have been tragically different without him. I knew this even at the time.

It was December 1, 1969, and we sat together in the living room of his apartment on the old couch covered with the faded batik-print throw. The screen of the television set was small, and the black-and-white picture grainy, but we were riveted to the images there. Old men in suits hovered over a large glass barrel filled with small plastic balls. Death balls. Each one of these innocuous-looking globes contained a date—a birth date. They would be drawn randomly, arbitrarily condemning young men to service in Vietnam. Death balls.

Charlie, whose draft deferment for college would end when he graduated the following spring, fidgeted anxiously.

"What's the holdup?" he said, bounding up for the twentieth time in ten minutes. "Why don't they just get started already?"

I wanted desperately to say something comforting or helpful or insightful. Anything at all. But the fear had taken hold of me as well, and my entire being felt numb at the prospect of losing another loved one to the rapacious vacuum of Vietnam. Charlie did not know I had lived this nightmare before, when Ray had been drafted.

I ran my hand pensively over my growing baby-bump, which was just beginning to make my clothing uncomfortably tight. The thought of losing Charlie filled me with dread. There were 366 death balls. One for every day of the year, including February 29. The first third of the birthdates drawn, or up to number 122, would definitely be drafted; the last third would definitely not be. One evil death ball in there contained September 15, Charlie's birthday. Let it be particularly heavy, I thought, so it will sink to the bottom. Or slippery, so it will elude the grasp of a groping hand. *Please don't take him from me.*

Charlie was against the war, but not in the fervent, activist, desperate way that I was. Or the way I had been, before I adopted this introverted victim persona who had more immediate personal worries than to be out protesting a distant war. I struggled with it, my instinct to rail against Nixon and the other warmongers. It was perhaps the most difficult part of my assimilation into being Annie.

The telephone jangled, and we both knew immediately it was his mother. Again.

"Hello," Charlie answered, his voice calm for her. "Hi Mom." He listened patiently to this woman who had two sons of draft eligible age. "I don't know why they haven't started, yet. I know you are, Mom, thanks. I'm praying for me too. Nate too, yeah, of course I am."

"Charlie!" I interrupted. "They're starting!"

"Mom, they're starting. Talk to you later. Yeah, love you too."

He came and sat next to me, but he was not still. I could virtually see the adrenaline coursing through his body, twitching in his thin legs, vibrating through his narrow torso, buzzing in his skull. Finally, the adrenaline won and he bolted up off the couch and stood, glaring warily at the television. I stood alongside him, reached and took his hand in mine. I do not believe he even noticed.

On the screen, a gray-haired man with thick black-rimmed glasses reached his hand into the big glass barrel to select the first ill-fated birthday. He read the date aloud, and each syllable seemed to take an eternity to utter. "Sep…tem…ber…four…teenth."

Charlie's hand clenched tightly around mine, crushing it, and our collectively held breath burst out, our hearts galloping. "Oh my god," Charlie murmured, his face ashen.

Tears began to seep from my eyes before I knew they had formed, and I hugged him tightly.

"Oh my god," he said again, wrapping his arms around me. "My god, that was close."

We stood together, smiling and crying until the phone rang. "Hi Mom," he answered, flashing me a weak grin.

After the first dozen or so dates had been drawn, we relaxed enough to sit back down. The danger was far from over; September 15 could be drawn at any time. When the 29th date was drawn, Charlie sunk into a dark funk; it was the birthday of his roommate sophomore year. When November 2 was drawn in the 34th place, I remembered sadly Andy Fellsworth, my prom date from high school who now was definitely going to the war. I wished, for a brief moment, that I remembered the birthdates of the rest of my male friends from Dunlee Mill, until I realized this process was far less painful not knowing. Many of the boys we both knew would be going to Vietnam and making the return trip under the shroud of an American flag. The killing and the dying had been continuing for so many years, yet we had not yet grown numb to it. The terrible weight of this evening's events made it fresh once again.

When we passed the one hundredth place with neither Charlie's nor Nate's birthdays being drawn, Charlie and I breathed a sigh of uneasy relief. So far, so good; number 122 was getting hearteningly close. The bottom third was home free; they would never have to go. Those stuck in the middle were stuck with uncertainty, an easy choice over the certainty of going.

One after another, various younger people thrust a hand into the barrel. One inch this way or the other, and one young man could continue on his life while another would be pulled from it, suited up and armed. Shipped off to a steamy, bug-infested jungle where he would have to make the daily choice to kill a stranger or allow the stranger to kill him. Could it be called a choice when there were no options?

Number 110 was pulled and we were still safe. Number 112, and there were only ten more until the relative comfort zone of the middle third. And then number 113 was the exploding bombshell, the potential death sentence. September 15 selected as the 113th draft number. I stared in disbelief, I cried, I held onto Charlie as though I could keep him there with me forever.

Charlie was quiet. Eerily calm. The phone rang, of course, and he talked to his mother. She too, was crying, I could tell. How did this war continue when there seemed no one left who believed in it?

I lost my big brother, my friend and protector, to this war. I lost the rest of my family and all my friends—my whole life—to my efforts to end this war. I simply could not lose Charlie to this war. He was my second chance. My only chance.

"You could go to Canada," I said. "You have to go. You can't go to this war."

He looked sadly at me. "I'm not going to Canada."

"Well you can't go to Vietnam! You can't go, for a cause you don't believe in, and shoot people. *Kill* people." *Careful, there.*

Lucinda creeping through. I softened my tone. "You know you can't."

"I can't just run off and let some other poor kid have to take my place, either."

It was slipping away from me; I could feel it. Charlie, and his goodness, and this whole new chance for a decent life. And, dare I hope it, his love. But you cannot lose what you never had. It was entirely possible, likely even, that Charlie did not feel about me as I felt about him. All of this, the shelter and the food and the help finding a job, and even the hugs and the kisses (for we had not progressed beyond that intimacy), all of it was just charity. I did not deserve this charity any more than I deserved a decent life, or, least of all, the love of such a good man. Yet I could not just let them slip away. And so I gathered up my courage and told my very first truth to Charlie.

"Charlie. Maybe this is the wrong thing to say. Or the wrong time to say it. Maybe it will ruin everything. But I don't see how things can get much worse now. So anyway, I know that you may not feel…you're just being nice to me, I know that. But I have to tell you. I've fallen in love with you. And not just because you've been so nice to me. Even if I wasn't so pathetically needy, well, you're just the most wonderful person, and my feelings are real. And I guess I'm just telling you because, well, it's the truth, and I just need you to know."

Some truths are much harder to speak than the worst lies, and this one shook me to the core, so great was my fear and desperation at what might be his response. He saw me shudder and tremble, and once again bestowed his kindness on me. He took my hand, pressed it between his own.

His voice was soft, pure. "I love you too, Annie. I just thought, after all you've been through, we should keep things simple. For now."

Perhaps it was more charity, but I wanted so badly to believe it. "Then, if you do, stay with me. Don't go." I smiled weakly through my tears. "Please."

He leaned in, over my face, pressed his lips gently against mine, and lingered there a moment. "I would do anything to stay with you. But I can't cheat."

So, even as he broke my heart, he made me love him more.

We did not talk much more that evening. We watched the rest of the lottery, Charlie noting when the birthdays of his friends were chosen. His brother Nate's birthday was selected at number 172; a number in limbo. Not safe, but not definitely doomed.

Eventually, over the coming weeks, we came up with an idea, almost a plan. If Charlie were to have minor dependents, and his absence would cause "extreme hardship" to those dependents, he could defer his military service. My baby (not to mention me) would certainly suffer extreme hardship in the absence of Charlie. Still, it was a huge responsibility for him to take on, and one I would never ask of him. But he was committed, he said, to both me and my baby, and if I could possibly believe he was not just trying to avoid the draft, he would be thrilled if I would consent to marry him. *Consent?* It was more than I ever could have hoped for. It was the true beginning to my life as Annie, and one of the happiest times of my life, in part because I realized how far in the other direction my life may have gone had I not found Charlie.

Although well into the middle third of the lottery, Nate was drafted late the following year. He never returned from Vietnam. This is something Charlie and I have in common; a beloved brother lost in a murderous Asian jungle. But Charlie does not know that.

Could I have survived without Charlie? Perhaps, but I did not even ask the question at the time. I knew that I needed him. Annie has had almost four decades to grow into a real person, her own person. Yet the truth, that I alone know, is that Annie came into being the moment I met Charlie. So the question becomes, can Annie exist without Charlie? And does she want to?

CHAPTER 21

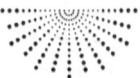

Does she want to? Finally, an easy question. I do not have to agonize or dissect or over-analyze this one. Every lie Annie has ever told was for the purpose of maintaining her happy life with Charlie. That life is clearly over now; it can not get any worse than this. Annie is already gone and Lucinda must confess herself so Charlie may mourn his wife. One deep, sanitizing breath, just for momentum, and I will go.

The hallway down to the bedroom stretches far ahead of me, yet it is not long enough. I will not be able to watch him as he comprehends what I tell him. It is cowardly, I know, but Lucinda is lacking in virtues such as bravery and honor.

The bedroom door is open, and I am surprised and momentarily confused. I did not hear him come out and the house is eerily quiet. He is gone, out the side door to the driveway, apparently. And then I hear it, muffled and distant; a car starting outside. I look out in time to see Charlie's gold Taurus backing slowly down the driveway.

Is this my convenient reprieve? Am I off the proverbial jagged hook until I see him again this evening? I am tempted only for an instant, out of habit, I think, so conditioned is Annie to grasping at anything that will further her grand illusion. But Annie has lost her grasp on everything, and Lucinda must set Charlie free.

Annie has left clothes draped over a chair, and I change into them as quickly as I can. I use her toothbrush and her hairbrush; I grab her car keys and head for the door. I will go directly to Charlie's studio and drop my wicked, exploding words on him, destroying his world. I will tell him I know how inadequate any apology might be, so I will spare him that insult. I also will not say goodbye; he never knew Lucinda and so will not care about her absence. I would love one last hug from him, but he will certainly not allow that.

Perhaps I could get a hug from Amber, if I stopped at her school before going to the police station, although she is angry with me too. Maybe Darlene. Could I possibly entice a hug from my daughter? The miserable truth of Annie's life is that after 37 years, no one will be sorry to see her go.

My hand is on the doorknob, but I am not quite ready to pull the door open and this world down. I will not be back here. Ever. How very different this is from the moment Annie sprung to life all those years ago. There was no time to think, no time to mull over consequences or mourn the loss of Lucinda.

Hanging on the living room wall is a framed photograph of Annie with Darlene and Amber, the three generations smiling and happy to be together. I must have this. I lift it off its hook, dust the glass with my sleeve, and slip it into my purse. There is one other thing I must have before I go. Back down the hall in the bedroom, I take the picture from my dresser and hold it a moment. It is Charlie and me, the day we were married. We are standing under a flowering arbor, arms wrapped around one another, the private laugh between us frozen forever on our faces. The bump that is Darlene is barely visible under the many flowing layers of clothing I wore. I put this in my purse with the other sliver of Annie's life. Now I can leave this place.

Annie's Prius waits for me in the driveway. As I approach it from the house, someone else approaches from the road. I am hoping it is Charlie and I see that it is Pam. A strange relief and joy rush over me. *Maybe you will give me a hug.*

She is staring at me and I realize I must be staring back, and it seems so very quiet. "Hi," I say, although I am nervous and my voice is feeble and reedy. "I'm glad you came back."

"Are you?"

She speaks in clipped tones through pinched lips. There is anger in her still, although it is different from the last time we met outside the FROGS office. "Yes," I say. "Really. It's been so long, and there's so much I want to ask you. Do you," I offer a smile, "want to come in? Have some coffee?"

And so I am back in this house that I had just left for the last time. It is strangely unsettling because I am here with Pam, who no more belongs here than does Lucinda. The two of us are intruders, trespassing in Annie and Charlie's home.

Pam wanders around the living room, touching furniture and picking up knickknacks. She stops at the wall of family photos for a long time, examining each one closely. She speaks, finally, to the wall and does not face me. "So are you A or C Pulkowski?"

She has been reading my mailbox. "A," I reply. "Annie."

She spins to look at me, nodding. "So that was C leaving a few minutes before you."

"Yes. Charlie." The sound of his name from my mouth sounds incongruous and reproachful, as though I no longer have the right to speak it.

"Annie, huh?" she mumbles dubiously.

"I wanted something bland and nondescript, and it was the first thing that popped into my head." A sudden melancholy infuses me. "I did not think I would be Annie forever."

Pam waves her arm about the room. "Annie seems to have done all right for herself."

"I was very lucky," I agree. "Meeting Charlie made all the difference in my life. I don't know why I was so lucky."

She says nothing to this, but I can see that she, too, is perplexed by my good fortune.

"How about you?" I ask. "Where have you been?"

"South Dakota."

"Really?" I am surprised by this, although I do not know what I was expecting.

She shrugs. "I got tired of worrying if people were looking at me funny, so I went someplace there weren't any people. Or, not many."

"Married?"

At this, she glares at me. "No. No, Lucinda, I spent my entire life alone, while you ended up with the husband and the kids, and the nice house, and it looks like even a grandkid. And you get to see your mother regularly, too. You have nice Sunday dinners together, do you? Everything's just perfect for you, isn't it?"

I do not know how to respond to this. "Pam," I say finally. "I'm sorry you've been alone. Really, I am. And I have been very lucky, and things have been good for me. But not perfect. I don't see my mother. She doesn't know I'm here. She has no idea where I am."

"You're lying," she turns away dismissively. "You live thirty miles away and you don't see each other?"

"No. I've always been too afraid to contact her."

"You're lying!" Pam shouts. "I talked to your mother! I know you see each other, so don't lie to me!"

I am stunned by this. "You talked to my mother?"

"Just yesterday."

Oh my god. "I can't believe you talked to her. How is she? What...what did she say?"

Pam's anger has turned to suspicion, maybe doubt, and I realize she has been testing me. "If you talked to her," I say, "you know I'm telling the truth. We haven't seen each other in all these years. Ever."

"That's what she said. I didn't believe her."

"What did you tell her? What did she say?" I am bursting with questions. "Did you tell her where I was?"

"No. I thought she knew. And then, what about Michael?" Pam looks around the room again. "I kind of thought you two might have been together all this time. But you had…how long have you been married?"

"Forever. Thirty-six years."

Pam's eyelids close tightly; there may be tears inside. She drops heavily onto the couch, then looks up at me. "I really thought you were with Michael all this time. I always thought that."

"Oh, god. Pam." I want to tell her I would never do such a thing to her, but she and I both know better. "I am so sorry for what I did back then. I hate myself for hurting you. But it was just…he never really loved me. It was you he loved. I always thought *you* two were together all these years. I hoped so. I am so, so sorry. You were my best friend. And I was such a jerk." I am sobbing now, but it is good, purifying, flushing out the corrosive sins lurking in my soul.

"It ruined my whole life, Lucinda. All this, that you have; Michael was my one chance at all this." Her face is red with fury and wet with tears, but the accusation that had clouded it has dissipated. "When he didn't show up where we were supposed to meet, I thought he had gone to meet you instead. But…"

"But he didn't," I say softly. "I haven't seen him, or talked to him, since that day we split up in Utica. I promise you that."

The grief is plain to see in Pam's face, but I do not know if she is mourning Michael and the life they never had, or the shattering of her conviction that I had taken him. Perhaps she does not know herself.

She rubs at her face with the heels of her hands. "Does your… Charlie know?"

I lower myself into the chair opposite where she sits on the couch. "No. I lied to him that first time all those years ago, and then, I was just kind of stuck in it. We both were. And the longer it goes on…how do you say, I've been lying to you for the past year? And then two years? And now 37 years?"

"So you're not so different from me," she seems pleased by this. "We've both lived a dishonest life—just hiding, covering up the truth, and lying every single day." She snorted softly. "And you've done it to people who love you. That's worse."

It was intended to hurt, and it does. "Yes," I acknowledge. "It is worse." I stare down at my hands. "But it's ending now, isn't it?"

"Is it?"

"Since this all came out again, Michael and then you showing up, and you seemed so angry…I thought you were going to turn me in."

She watches me, thinking about what to say. "So did I. I also thought you were living my life with Michael." She grabs a pillow from the couch and hugs it to her. "I went to see him. In the hospital. You know he feels nothing but shame about those days? And I…I'm more proud of those days than anything else in my life. We were fighting for a good, noble cause. We were about something. Something important and honorable. There was right and there was wrong, and we were on the side of right, Lucinda." She burrows her chin into the pillow. "And I haven't done a noble, honest thing since."

It is a blunt, unguarded truth and it stirs something inside me. There is, deep within, a fervor and a zeal only Lucinda has felt, and only she can acknowledge. And when Pam looks at me pleadingly and says, "Don't you miss those days, Lucinda?" I answer her with a truth that Annie would not dare utter.

"Yes," I whisper, afraid of my own voice. "Oh god, Pam. I really do. I miss us, and I miss our cause. I miss being right. And I miss who I used to be." I reach out to take her hand and squeeze it tightly. "I miss all of it."

CHAPTER 22

"Would you ever like to be famous someday?" I asked this question of Pam, not because I truly wondered about her answer, but because I wished to talk of it myself. It is, I think, why most questions are asked.

Pam stood near the white wooden desk in my bedroom, her slender body partially obscuring the giant poster of John, Paul, George and Ringo on the wall. She leaned over the turntable on the desk and carefully placed the needle on the spinning black disk. "Time for a little change of pace," she said, as Jefferson Airplane's explosive rage erupted into my little room. *When the truth is found, to be lies....* Pam came and flopped down on my bed with me, looking at the album cover in my lap. "Famous?" she said. "Like Diana Ross?"

I brushed my hand lightly over the wispy image of the singer. "She's so beautiful, isn't she? And everywhere she goes, people know her."

"You're already that kind of famous."

"Yeah, right," I said. "At big old Dunlee Mill High School. Doesn't really count."

"It counts," Pam insisted. "It's more than most people get." She swung her long brown curls behind her. "Most kids would kill to be you. Even for a day."

She was right, I knew, and it both pleased and embarrassed me. "You're just as well known as me at school," I said.

"Because I hang around with you. And that's," she said quickly, cutting off my protest, "plenty for me. Seriously. What do you want to be famous for?" she raised her eyebrows teasingly at me. "Do I need to point out that you can't sing?"

I shook my head and grinned. "Not necessary."

Pam pressed her lips together shyly. "I would like my name to be famous."

"You just said you didn't."

"I don't want to be famous, strangers recognizing me on the street famous. But I would like my name to be known. For having done something important. Something good, something that helps people.

"We could do something like that together," I said eagerly. "Maybe start a charity or something. To benefit needy children, maybe."

"Or people in Vietnam," Pam suggested, "who've suffered because of the war."

"Oh, Pam. That would be such a gas. We should do it. Let's do it!"

"Do what?" It was Colley's voice. He stood just inside the door looking at us.

"Colley!" I shouted. "Ever heard of knocking?"

"I did knock," he yelled back. "You didn't hear me." He lifted a hand in an awkward wave. "Hi Pam." I wondered if he knew how pink his cheeks turned every time he was in the vicinity of Pam.

"Hi Colley," Pam said brightly. "How you doing today?"

His head bobbed up and down. "Good."

"No baseball practice today?"

"No. I mean, yeah. A short one. It's over."

"Oh. Good. Are you the superstar of the team yet?"

Colley's eyes rolled up in his head in embarrassment. "No."

She smiled kindly. "Well, any day now."

"Colley," I interrupted this painful exchange. "What do you want?"

"Oh," he turned to me. "There's a letter. From Ray. Mom's reading it."

"Oh my god," I jumped up from my bed and followed Colley down the stairs to the kitchen. My mother stood there, a page of white paper fluttering in her shaking hands. She looked up as the three of us barged into the room, and I could see that her eyes were damp. "He sounds good," she said, feeble and unconvincing. "Here. I'll read it to you."

Dear Mom, Dad, Lucy and Colley,

God, I really miss you guys. Yes, even you, Colley. Don't get too comfortable in my room—it won't be yours for long.

So you know how they say everybody has a double somewhere in the world? Well I think I met mine. His name is Wally (Walford, but no way I'm calling him that), and he's from Tennessee. We're both nineteen, both have a younger brother and sister, and a girlfriend we're planning to marry when we get back, and all the guys say we look a lot alike. He's a real good guy (of course!). He's never been out of Tennessee—except for now, of course. So I invited him to come visit Massachusetts when we both get back to the real world.

And speaking of that, I was hoping I could put in a few requests for when I get home (just 72 more days! Is anyone else counting?). I've been kind of thinking up a homecoming meal. Actually, I have to admit it, I've been having dreams about your meatloaf, Mom. Really—actual dreams! I know I've said it before, but you just can't imagine the stuff they give us to eat. Doesn't even look like food. So anyway, the homecoming meal. Meatloaf. With mashed potatoes, of course. And I guess maybe that green bean casserole—I never realized I liked it until I was forced to eat army slop. I've also been dreaming about your pot roast. With dumplings. And the fried chicken too. I guess that's a lot for one meal, so if you can't do it all, I understand. I guess my priority would be the meat loaf. Maybe just a couple of pieces of chicken. And just one dumpling. I don't know, can you make just one dumpling? Whatever you can do, Mom, and it'll be heaven on earth for me.

It's been pretty good for us the past few weeks. Not much action at all, and believe me, no one is complaining. But even with nothing much going on, there are still guys who freeze up at any little noise. To be honest, I was kind of worried that I would be one of those guys when the bullets were flying, but I surprised myself. I actually get super aware and alert in bad situations. And tight. Really, really tight, like I'm ready to snap. They say that's the way to be. Hey, I made it this far, right? Just 72 more days of staying alert, and I'll be home before you know it. Better get cooking, Mom!

Love you all so much,
Ray

My mother smiled at the letter, dripping tears onto the thin paper.

"I'm happy to help with the cooking," Pam said, swiping a hand across her eyes.

"Thank you honey," my mother smiled, grabbing hold of Pam's hand. "We're going to need it."

"He loves those butterscotch brownies you make," I said to my friend.

Pam nodded, grinning. "I'll make a double batch. He sounds hungry."

I cried too that day, but only because I hated to see my mother so sad. I was still young enough to be optimistic, to have faith in the world that things would turn out all right, as they always had for me. Ray said he would be home before we knew it, and I believed him. My mother, however, was far wiser than my teenage self could ever credit her.

That is my last memory of everything being right in the

universe. The last memory I have of myself when I was not angry at the world, at circumstances, fate, the government, and God. That Lucinda was unconsumed by rage and righteous indignation, unsullied by a need for vengeance. I have not thought about that girl in many years. I can only barely remember her. Not enough to miss her.

CHAPTER 23

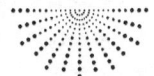

"You promised, Cara," Darlene said, chin out, cheeks flushed. "I need more hours."

"I said I'd try. I didn't promise." Cara counted out bills from the cash register and handed them to Darlene. "I'm sorry. That's all I can give you today."

Darlene's hands closed into tight fists at her sides. She looked into the enormous mirrors lining the wall of the little salon, watching herself closely. "Okay," she turned back to Cara. "What about tomorrow?"

"Tomorrow," Cara glanced down at the ledger book on her desk, "looks better, I think. Come in first thing, okay?"

Darlene nodded. "Yeah. Okay." She folded the bills in her hand and tucked them into the pocket of her pants. "Thanks. See you tomorrow."

Outside on the sidewalk, she inhaled deeply. *Relax.* The bus stop was four blocks away, and she started off at a brisk pace toward it, the whopping forty-two dollars not exactly enough to burn a hole in her pocket. Not even enough for a tiny little sizzle. But, whatever. Get over it. There would be more tomorrow.

One of these days, she would be able to tell Charlie she didn't need the 'secret' cash that he wrapped up with the food so neither of them would have to officially acknowledge the charity. *I'm all set, Charlie. Doing great. You don't have to subsidize me anymore.* And there will be real pride in his face, unpolluted by pity or disdain. Even her mother, remote, heartless machine that she was, would have to admit her daughter was not a screw-up anymore.

Up ahead on the left, a small green sign with white lettering stuck out from a weathered, red brick building. Smarfy's Pub. The old Darlene's usual hangout, before the new Darlene took charge and put both of them on the wagon. She had not set one resolute foot inside in over two weeks, since before that horrible night she thought she was going to die. And if she had gone to Smarfy's that night, instead of being lazy and going to the dive near the Laundromat, that terrifying night never would have happened. But then she wouldn't have been scared into getting clean and getting her life back. Maybe some mistakes happen for a reason.

She peeked in a window as she walked by. Keith was behind the bar, as usual. Jerry and Aaron and Rick perched in their regular spots on the other side. Patty was not there, but it was Thursday, and she worked on Thursdays. As Rick raised his glass to his lips, he tilted his head back to drain it, and his gaze fell on Darlene in the window. He squinted at her and she shrank back, guilt-ridden like some perverted peeping tom. She backed away from the window, then hurried past the building and down the street.

"Darlene!"

Turning, she saw Rick hurrying down the sidewalk toward her.

"Hey!" he called. "Where you going?"

She looked up into his face, angular and handsome, with a wavy frame of longish hair that was just beginning to turn gray. "Hey," she said. "I'm on my way home."

"Oh, no," he panted, jogging to a stop. "It's true."

"What?"

"There's a nasty rumor that you're going all AA on us," he grinned. "Please, say it isn't so."

"It isn't so," Darlene said flatly. "I don't need AA. I'm just not drinking anymore."

"No, no," he said with mock dismay. "You can't just abandon us. We all provide much needed validation for each other's drinking habits. One person going sober could disrupt the whole fabric of our co-dependency and lead to guilt, remorse, and eventually, proliferating sobriety."

Darlene blinked. "And you said that all with a straight face."

"Not bad, huh?" he laughed. "But seriously. You don't want to drink, whatever. But come hang with us. We miss you." He shrugged self-consciously. "I miss you."

I miss you too. Can't tell him that. "I really should get going."

"Come on," he said. "Just come say hello. I'll buy you the best water they got, or whatever you want."

He was just too damn good-looking. And after weeks of hard work, a few minutes of relaxation with friends would be so nice. But Smarfy's was just swarming with temptations.

"Five minutes," Rick said. "Just five minutes. Everyone wants to see you. And I gotta tell you, you really are looking great. Really, amazing."

Oh, don't do that. Darlene breathed deeply. "Just so we're clear," she said, "one glass of water, and then I'm going home. Alone."

"Yeah," he shrugged. "Sure. Whatever you want." He slipped an arm around her shoulders and steered her back toward the little bar. "The guys are going to be so glad to see you."

Steady and comforting, the pulse of Charlie's heart thumps gently in my ear, imbuing me with a blissful wellbeing and peace. My head rests on his chest, rising and falling with each of his breaths. We lie here, in our bed, together for the first time in a very long while. In one ear, I listen to the quiet non-sounds of a house asleep;

in the other, Charlie's blood and breath fill me up, his life nourishing my life.

I have done it. I have told my most terrible, most brilliant lie. I thought I had cancer, I told him, but received test results today that were negative. I am fine, and so very sorry that I put us all through this, but I was frightened. Yes, of course I know I can tell him anything, that he wants to share everything in my life with me, and I apologize for behaving so silly about it. Clearly, I wasn't myself. Very clearly. And this weird rash on my palm? No, not an indication of anything. Just a stress rash. I'm sure it will be clearing up very soon. It is always good to include a nugget of truth in one's lies.

He has forgiven me, of course, now that he knows the 'truth.' And, like all the other 'truths' I have told him over the years, he need never know this one is bogus. Since he will not know, this lie can never hurt him, and so it is not such a terrible lie after all. At least, that is what I tell myself.

Pam will not turn me in. She did not say so, but after our talk today, I am confident of it. She is my friend. We understand each other. We have lived different lives, but we are the same. And we could not hurt one another. That is what I tell myself.

I am bothered only by a discomfiting restlessness. Lucinda has been awakened, and will not slip quietly back into her secret lair in which she has hibernated all this time. She will go, eventually. Annie will make her go.

The sun had long since tucked itself down beneath the low edge of the earth, ceding its reign to the deep shadows of night. Yet here in the tangled network of streets trussing the city of Boston, the humid air was bright with the lights of street lamps and restaurants and car headlamps snaking their erratic, urgent paths through the city. Pam maneuvered her truck slowly, carefully into a left turn, and was immediately cut off by a silver Lexus. Had there always been so many lights? She had forgotten, after so many years, how very alive a big city could be, even this late at night. On the farm, in Shelton, South Dakota, night was dark, and people were at home, generally, preparing for a morning that came early.

Pam stomped hard on the brake as a young couple stepped off the curb and dashed across the street. It was unsettling here—and exhilarating. Anything could happen. You had to be alert and aware. There was danger here. And pain and anger. And heartbreak. And *oh god!* It all felt so good. It felt so good to feel.

Even the hatred. Especially the hatred. Hate could surprise you, take you off guard, force you to see things. She had been filled with the stuff when she had arrived at Lucinda's door. And it had been fun—yes fun!—to tease out the little snippets of Lucinda from that drab, empty shell of a person she called Annie. The glimpses of her ancient, trusted friend pulled on something within Pam and filled her with longing and nostalgia for the days when she had…people. Family, and real friends with whom she could have a real conversation. She blinked damply. Family. Her parents had been gone for years, according to Mrs. Whittendon. Gone, like everything else. Except Michael.

The Annie-shell, because it was empty of anything genuine in itself, had created an existence by collecting stuff. She gathered up people and things that made her seem like an authentic person. And all this stuff was important to the Annie-shell, because without them, there was just the emptiness.

The only real part of Lucinda that remained in the Annie-shell was the manipulator. The controller. She was still carefully directing the course of her life, still making decisions that shape other people's lives. And she had no right to do that. Never did.

Pam slid the truck into a metered parking spot along Charles Street and began the few blocks walk to Massachusetts General Hospital. *This is a waste of time, Pam. Michael will be dead within a few days.* But still, a few days was a few days. Thirty-seven years spreading manure in South Dakota; now *that* was a waste of time.

In the hospital lobby, Pam waited until the woman at the reception desk stepped into a back room before heading for the elevators. Maybe she wouldn't have been stopped, but the fewer questions the better. The women at the nurses' station on Michael's floor were busy and bustling and seemed not to notice or care about Pam's presence. She paused outside the door to his room, exhaled heavily. Pushing open the door, she hesitated; it was dark inside. He would be sleeping.

The rhythmic beeping and wheezing of monitoring devices infused the darkness with a kind of monotonous melody. A tenacious, insistent verification of life's existence, oblivious of its inherent desperation. Pam stepped inside gingerly, afraid to wake him, eager to see him. She hadn't believed Michael last time when he'd told her he'd loved her because she believed he'd forsaken her for Lucinda. She should have believed him. What they had was special, unique. It could transcend years and mistakes and regrets. Just for a few days. It was all they had left.

Pam walked slowly toward the near bed, allowing her eyes to adjust to the dark. She squinted at him, discerning his thin frame stretched out on the bed, and held out a tentative hand to touch an arm, maybe a shoulder. Did she dare touch him? Did she have that right?

He shifted suddenly and a bony hand shot out, grabbing hold of her outstretched arm.

"Ahhh!" she jumped back. "Oh my god," she breathed heavily. "Michael. It's me. Pam."

"Who?" the hand gripped tighter around her wrist, his skin and bones digging into her plump flesh.

"Pam," she repeated, wincing in pain. "I'm sorry if I—"

"You come to kill me. Nurse!" he shouted hoarsely, thrashing about on the bed. "Nurse! Nurse!" he pounded at the remote pager clipped to the side of the bed. "They come! They come to kill me!"

"Michael!" Pam tried to wrench her arm away from him. "What are you—"

A muted click and light flooded the room. Pam blinked and squinted in the brightness. The face staring up at Pam from the bed was pinched and vacant, with a feral light smoldering behind the eyes. And it was not Michael's.

"Who are you?" the voice came from behind her, and Pam turned to see a nurse in mint green surgical scrubs. "What are you doing in here?"

"She here to kill me!" screeched the man in the bed. "I told you they were coming. Call the police! I hold her till they get here." He twisted her arm in his grasp.

"Mr. Crenshaw," the nurse said calmly. "It's all right. Please let her go. Please." She pried his fingers from Pam's wrist and returned it to her. "It's not visiting hours," she said to Pam. "What are you doing in here?"

Pam rubbed at the red mark on her arm. "I—I was looking," she said, "I was looking for…for the man who was in here. Before. He um," she searched her brain for the alias Michael had used. "He was Steven Roberts."

Recognition, then a shadow crossed the woman's pretty face. "Are you a relative?"

"Why?" Pam felt a jolt in her chest. "What happened? Did… did he…oh god…did he die?"

"I'm very sorry," the nurse said. "It was peaceful. He was asleep."

Pam did not feel the strength bleed from her knees, but found herself suddenly on the floor, the blonde nurse hovering anxiously over her. She did not hear the woman's words, did not feel her touch, lifting her up and into a chair. She felt only a lightness in her head, the bed and tables and equipment in the room whizzing about her in a frantic, haphazard orbit.

Just a few days! That was all she'd wanted. Just a few goddam days! Was that too much to ask for? After all this time of just existing, of living a non-life, was it too presumptuous to request a few short days with the love of her life? Was that just too taxing for the universe, for fate, for whatever god existed, to grant one tiny little favor in an entire bleak lifetime?

Was she so terribly undeserving? She had long since stopped

expecting the world to be fair. But it was hard to overlook the fact that there were others, far less deserving than she, who had had a whole life filled with good luck and generous favors. Impossibly hard to overlook.

The emptiness inside so pervaded her, Pam could not even cry. There were no tears to spill, no heart that could ache or break. No soul to find meaning. There was simply nothing left. Absolute nothingness.

CHAPTER 24

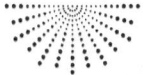

I weigh nothing. Not an ounce or a dram; nothing. The water is cool beneath me and floats me effortlessly. I do not bob and dip like a cork or a buoy, but drift smoothly on the surface of perfectly still waters. The tranquility suffuses my weightless body; I am the calm.

I contemplate this peacefulness with grateful devotion. I must not allow it to slip away. For beneath me, in the black depths of the water, swirls a danger. A sea serpent, a monster, a mythical, ethereal beast that waits for me. It has awakened from heavy slumber and thrashes about now with impatient, evil fervor. Think only of the peace. Do not allow the creature to catch the acrid scent of fear.

I feel it now. The soft rush of undercurrent against my back. The fiend has come closer, stalking me, and there is nowhere to hide. I am trapped here on my empty, peaceful sea. The sharp flick of a fin or a tail scratches my legs, and I am sinking. My wispy, light serenity dissipates into the air like dandelion seeds in a steady breeze. A stone of terror grows steadily in my breast, constricting my lungs and weighing me down. I cannot breathe. I cannot move. I cannot save myself. I cringe and stiffen, and await the final, deadly grasp.

Sweat has soaked my clothes and my hair, yet I am so relieved to open my eyes and find myself in my own bed, I welcome the real-life stickiness. Blue-gray light diffuses the room, telling me it is morning, and this too is a relief, as I do not wish to close my eyes again. The pillow beside me is empty; Charlie is already up. A cold shiver prickles over my skin, from the dampness, from the residual fright. Flinging aside the clammy sheet, I sit up and swing my legs off the bed. I will take a shower, wash away the sinister remnants of the night.

The hot, cleansing shower restores logic to my thinking. This crisis, this resurrection of Lucinda, should be over. Lucinda should be gone. So very badly I wish to believe this. Logic, however, tells me that there are still too many ends floating loosely, dangerously about. There is Pam, who I believe was as happy and relieved to have a long, heartfelt conversation with an old friend as was I. Yet there still lingers in her a resentment that I would be foolish to dismiss entirely. There is the police, who I had begun to believe were not actually working on this supposedly reopened case, until Pam informed me that they had, in fact, spoken to my mother. It was, it turns out, a wise decision to stay away from her house since Michael came forward. So reason dictates that I continue to be wary because this ordeal has not yet been unequivocally resolved. I cannot, however, prevent myself from hoping.

Dressing, alone here in my bedroom, I hear Charlie and Amber in the kitchen, the muted, comforting sounds of home. My home. I am home. Whatever place Lucinda had in the world has long since dissipated with her. I do, however, envy Pam for having spent time with my mother. And she welcomed Pam! Without apparent judgment or hostility. And she asked about me! About Lucinda. Can I believe she has forgiven me? It is as though a jagged void, a chafing question mark inside, has been filled with the hint of an answer. And that will have to be enough for Annie.

I stand outside the kitchen, watching them for a moment. Amber sees me first.

"Hey, Nonny," she says brightly.

"Good morning honey." I smile at her, and she comes to me and wraps her arms tightly around my waist.

"Morning, love," Charlie says and plants a kiss on the tip of my nose. The little dampness there brings a wetness to my eyes, so great is my happiness.

It is a welcome home, this hug and this kiss, as though the past weeks of tension and anger and distance were a long voyage from which I have returned. Perhaps it was.

"I can't sit with you this morning, unfortunately," Charlie says. "I've got an early shoot this morning, and I haven't showered yet. There are whole wheat cranberry scones on the table that even Amber approves of."

"They smell amazing," I say sincerely.

"They are pretty amazing," Amber confirms. "I gotta get going too," she says. "Math test first thing this morning."

"Well good luck, then," I say. "Have a great day."

"I will," she replies on her way out the door, and when she grins I see in the curve of her cheek, the wrinkles around her eyes, the sweet loveliness of a youthful, innocent Darlene. I have neglected my daughter these past weeks, so distracted was I with the tribulations of Lucinda and her potential exposure. Darlene needed me, to be firm about going into rehab, to help her formulate a real plan for her life, and I responded with a self-centered, obdurate callousness. But that was Lucinda. Now that Annie has returned, she will take care of her daughter.

The house is quiet after Amber closes the door, save for the distant rain of Charlie's shower. I break a corner from a scone and savor the sweet, spicy, still-warm morsel when I hear Amber scream from outside. It is terror-laced and shoots an eerie chill down my spine. I hesitate for only an instant before rushing out the door.

"Oh my god, oh my god," Amber is shaking, whimpering, backing away from something on the front lawn.

"What is it?" I have come up behind her, and now I see it

beside the wishing well. A human body, damp with morning dew, a waxy gray pallor to its skin. Bile rises in my throat. It is Pam.

"Oh my god, Nonny," Amber clings to me. "Is it…is she—?"

"Okay," I struggle to appear calm, despite the sickening sensation of blood draining from my own body. "Go inside and get the phone. Call 911. Okay?"

Amber nods. "Okay. Is she…?"

"Yes. Now go, honey."

She backs away, frightened but mesmerized by the only dead body she has ever seen. Amber disappears inside the house and I look more closely at my once-friend. Her eyes are closed, her face peaceful. She could be sleeping, if not for the grayness. Her hands are clasped neatly over her belly. Tucked inside her hands is a slip of white paper peeking out; this cannot be anything good. I squat quickly and tug on the paper, which sticks slightly and does not come easily. I dare not be caught reading it now, so I slip it into the pocket of my pants.

I must not cry. I can allow the horror and the revulsion to show, but not the grief. I cannot know this dead stranger on our lawn. I cannot know that this girl was painfully shy around boys but in private could do a pitch-perfect imitation of Mr. Calder, the straight-laced high school principal, and could belt out the lyrics to *Build Me Up Buttercup* with the dynamism of a rock star. This was a girl whose soft brown eyes filled with kindness when Bobby McDougal dumped me in tenth grade and sat mourning with me when news of Ray's death reached us. I can not know any of this. I can feel no personal sorrow at the loss of such a good soul.

Amber appears in the open doorway, telephone held up to her ear. Her eyes are red with fear and brimming tears. I go to her to hold her and comfort her, and find that I cling to her with my own needy desperation. Charlie emerges from the bedroom about the same time the Morrisville Police cruiser rolls into our driveway, and we go out in a group to meet it.

From the car steps Bob Sifert, a popular cop in town, and one of Charlie's fishing buddies. He carries a rounded paunch and a pockmarked face that is usually smiling as he greets and chats with residents. There is no smile today. The worst crimes committed in Morrisville are generally bicycle thefts and graffiti defacing public property. There has not been a dead body discovered in Morrisville during the almost thirty years Charlie and I have lived here.

"Morning folks," he says, approaching us. "Hey, Charlie. I thought this was your address. Annie," he nods at me. "Did someone here actually call in a…body?"

"Yeah, Bob," Charlie says. "Can you believe it?"

"It's over there," I tell them. "By the well."

The four of us walk over slowly, Amber and I the most reluctant of the group because we have seen this horror before.

Officer Sifert stops suddenly a few feet from Pam's body. He stares at her for a moment, then turns away abruptly, his hands clamped over his mouth. He is going to retch, I am sure of it, but then his body heaves with a few great gulps of air and he turns back to us. Charlie stands near Amber, the color gone from his face, eyes and mouth gaping at the corpse.

"So," Officer Sifert clears his throat, "who found her?"

Amber raises her hand hesitantly, her voice coming out in a whisper. "I did."

"You just came out of the house and saw her lying there, just like this?"

Amber nods.

"Did you touch the body?"

"No." She reaches out anxiously for Charlie's arm, which he wraps around her shoulders.

"Anybody touch the body?" he glances around at Charlie and me.

Charlie shakes his head. "No."

"No," I murmur quietly.

"Do you know her? Recognize her at all?"

"No. I've never seen her," Charlie says, his voice hoarse.

"Me neither," Amber says, looking directly at the officer, who then turns to me.

"No," I say. "I don't know her." *I am sorry, Pam.*

Officer Sifert turns back toward Pam's corpse. "All right. There doesn't seem to be any obvious cause of death. But there's a crime lab unit on its way from Springfield. I'm just going to stay and make sure the body is undisturbed until then. You folks, I'm sorry Charlie, but you're all going to have to stick around until they get here. You know, in case they got questions."

"Yeah," Charlie mumbles. "Sure."

Amber and I nod and murmur our agreement, transfixed by the colorless death among the blooming flowers in our yard. Lying there, amid the bright green grass and yellow lilies, Pam's gray body seems a part of the cold, wet earth. I rub my hands briskly over my arms, but the morning breeze is cool, and I cannot stop shivering. Why has she done this? I cannot fathom a reason, yet I am certain she has done it to herself.

"You know," Amber is saying hesitantly, "I thought...well...I don't know."

"What is it?" Officer Sifert asks.

"Well, I don't know, but I thought there was something...I thought she was like, holding something. In her hands. But...I don't know."

The police officer bends down low over Pam and peers under her dead hands without touching her. "I don't see anything. Did anyone else see something?" he looks at me and then Charlie.

"I just got out here the same time as you," Charlie says. He and the officer turn to me, the question on their faces.

"I—no. I didn't see anything. There was nothing." It has come out more stuttery-stammery than I would have liked.

"You're sure?"

"Well, yes. I definitely didn't see anything."

He glances around the yard and says to Amber. "Maybe it blew away. Are you positive you saw something?"

Amber looks shaken. "Yes. I think so. But no. I guess I'm not positive."

"It's okay, honey," I tell her. "It was a bad shock finding her. Anyone could get flustered, make a mistake."

She nods, gratefully, I think, and I do not believe Charlie is actually looking at me strangely. It is merely the shock of seeing a dead body that makes his face appear so bewildered. That is all.

"Thanks, Nonny." Amber tosses me a brief grin as she opens the car door in front of the two-story brick school building.

I have difficulty deciphering her face, but it seems the terror from earlier this morning has dissipated, replaced by a slightly unsettling exhilaration. "Are you sure you're okay to go to school?"

She nods agreeably. "Yeah. Like you said, it's probably best to keep busy."

Yes, and busy you will be, telling the hottest story in Morrisville Middle School in decades. "Okay," I attempt a smile. "See you tonight."

It is with some difficulty that I ease the car off of school grounds at a respectably slow pace. The little scrap of paper has been smoldering in my pocket, threatening to burn right through, since I took it from Pam's dead hands this morning, but the constant presence of the police, and Charlie, and Amber, has afforded me no opportunity to read it. I steer the car toward a small side street where I can pull over and read it alone, away from inquisitive eyes, a pounding urgency in conflict with dread at what it might say.

Amber's math test and Charlie's photo shoot did not happen as scheduled this morning, life necessarily giving way for the inconvenience of death. Both have been rescheduled, and Amber and Charlie will settle back into the mundane routine of their lives after this momentary—if acutely disturbing—blip. I will not.

This death means nothing to them, other than the fleeting jolt of macabre novelty, the transitory brush with deadness. It is a day they will not easily forget, but neither will it haunt their existence, or dance ghoulishly in their dreams. I will not be so fortunate.

Pam, who I lost so long ago, and believed I had regained yesterday has sucker punched me squarely in my falsified identity. I believed I knew her, that we were the same. That all the years and the terrible mistakes could be swept aside as we realized we were friends still. Yet she chose to end her life, just as we reconnected. And she chose to be found, dead, on my front lawn, deliberately directing police in my direction. Clearly, I do not know as much as I thought I did.

It is with no small amount of terror, then, that I reach for the note in my pocket.

CHAPTER 25

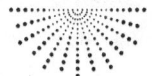

New York was hot that summer of 1969. The heavy, stifling air, sweat-till-your-socks-are-soggy kind of hot, but that was only part of it. Rhetoric and temperaments sizzled as well. I am sure there were thousands of bad decisions made that summer. Mine was only the worst of many.

The protest was small; no more than a few dozen people or so. Kids like me, mostly, with tie-dye shirts and hand-lettered peace signs. They were picketing on West 39th Street, in front of the offices of some company that apparently had ties to Vietnam. The details were murky, but it was a protest against the war and the Establishment, and so I had to be a part of it. Solidarity was imperative in a revolution. We people of conscience must stand, literally, side by side.

Gordon was with me and was not so much eager to join in as he was to find out what was going on. Perhaps he was looking for more recruits to expand his little kingdom of revolutionaries.

We joined the protesters marching on the sidewalk, slipping into the sloppy oval right behind a girl holding a sign that read, "Bartle Company Kills Innocents."

"Hey, man," the guy behind us said to Gordon. "Welcome to the cause. You too, sister." His light brown hair curled tightly in a large afro, a spherical frame to his long, angular face.

"What's your group here about?" Gordon asked, impatient, as usual, with frivolous and unproductive spoken greetings. Who are you, and are you compatible with my own credo, Gordon wanted to know when meeting someone. Anything else was superfluous. He soon had the young man and two women involved in an in-depth discussion of the peace-movement-according-to-Gordon Blackwell.

When the cops arrived, as they always did at peace marches, fulfilling the vital public need to rein in peace, I could feel palpable tendrils of the group's anxiety slithering in my own chest. We had to leave, the cops said; we were disturbing the peace.

"What peace?" shouted a girl in a green miniskirt. "There is no peace in this world; only war!"

"We're fighting *for* the peace!" yelled another.

"You're making noise and blocking the sidewalk. Now break it up!"

"Get out of here, pigs!"

"We don't recognize your authority!"

"You recognize this, you damned hippies?" The cop brandished his club, pushed at a protester with it.

"Don't touch me!" he swung at the cop, who blocked the blow with his club. Two other marchers came to the kid's aid, the three other cops joined in, and the chaos engulfed us all within seconds. Someone took hold of my arm, and I was dragged backward and out of the melee.

Gordon released me when we were across the street. "We can't get arrested now. We've got a job to do."

"Godammit!" I screamed, watching cops pummel unarmed kids shrieking in terror and pain. "It was a *peace* march! We were just *walking*!"

"Like they're some kind of farm animals that need to be put down," Gordon muttered through clenched teeth. "This is the way the pigs think of us. You see this, Lucinda? They treat us like we're animals. Not citizens."

"No," I agreed. "They wouldn't do this to guys in suits. How the hell do they get away with this shit?"

"This is exactly what we're going to be facing during our bank job. This kind of attitude." He slid a thumb and forefinger neatly along his dark mustache. "I've given more thought to the issue of our weapons. I think they should be loaded. The others don't understand like you do. Everything you said the other day about this being a war and we have to take drastic measures to fight the Establishment was right on." He fixed his black eyes on me. "It is a war. And in war, the weapons are loaded."

I shook my head to escape his gaze. "Pam was also right when she said if we shoot innocent people we're no better than the Establishment fuzz."

"There are no innocent people!" he barked. "I thought you, of all people, got that. The security guard in that bank is protecting the money of the greedy capitalist pigs. Any civilians that will be in there are giving that bank their money and their business, allowing them to grow even fatter. All of them, the tellers, the customers, even the guy who sweeps the floor are going along with the American fraud and depravity that is being perpetrated on the *real* innocents in the world, and all of them are complicit in the crime. Everyone is culpable!"

I did not answer.

"You know I'm right."

"Maybe," I said, flustered. "But we can't anyway. We'll lose both Pam and Michael. Maybe Jimmy too. And then we have no operation at all."

Gordon exhaled heavily. "Only if we tell them."

"What?"

He turned and walked slowly along the sidewalk, waiting for me to follow. "You know," he said as I pulled alongside, "Michael and Pam can make these high moral decisions, but they're not the ones going in there, risking their lives. That guard in that bank is going to have bullets in his gun. And he thinks of us as nothing more than animals to be put down, just like those cops back there."

He stopped and faced me again. "We have a right to protect ourselves, Lucinda. Our lives are the ones at risk."

And that, finally, was what convinced me. Not the righteousness of our cause, but the selfishness of my own survival. My life would be at risk. And Lucinda did not want to lose her life.

CHAPTER 26

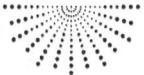

Catherine peered suspiciously at the shiny gold police badge. Looked real enough. She squinted at the photo on the ID card the man at the door held out to her, then inspected his face. Could be him.

"How," she said in her best formal voice, "may I help you?"

"I'd like to ask you a few questions, Mrs. Whittendon. About your daughter."

Catherine swallowed, and leveled a cold stare at the officer. "I haven't seen my daughter in 37 years, which I already told the other officer a couple of weeks ago. Nothing has changed in the last fourteen days." She scowled at him. This baby-faced boy hadn't even been born 37 years ago.

"I understand that, but new information has come to light, and we have to investigate it."

"Why?" Catherine demanded. "Why do you have to dredge up all this stuff again?"

"The family of the deceased wants closure. And…it's a murder investigation, Mrs. Whittendon. May I please come in and talk with you?"

"No," she said. "But I will come outside." She closed the door behind her and led the officer to the picnic table, now enjoying its afternoon shade. "You sit here," she said, directing him away from Sam's seat.

"Okay," he said, settling his slender frame into an old wooden chair. "Why don't we start with something else."

"What new information?"

"Excuse me?"

"You said you had new information," Catherine pressed her hands together anxiously. "What is it? Did that man in the hospital say anything?"

"He didn't, unfortunately. No. But he did receive some visitors, people not associated with his life in Cambridge. One of them matched your description."

Catherine blanched. "I have nothing to hide. I did go to see him, yes. I thought he might know where my daughter is. But he didn't. Or he said he didn't. He didn't tell me anything."

"Really?"

"Yes. Really. He said he didn't know, and I...I didn't have much choice but to believe him."

"You're sure? Because the other person who visited him was a woman in her fifties. Your daughter's age."

Catherine's heart spun in her chest. "Really? Officer..." she looked at the policeman's name tag for the first time. "Officer Nass, have you found her?"

"Not yet. But I was—"

"What was the description? Of that other visitor. What did she look like?"

He consulted a notepad. "About five-five, late fifties, heavy-set, short graying hair."

Catherine dropped her head in disappointment. "Pamela." The name was no more than an airy breath.

"What was that?"

She raised her eyes to him, this authority figure in uniform, and struggled unsuccessfully to hold back the truth. "That was Pamela Mercurio."

"So there really was a dead body on your front lawn?" Jarvis' eyes are big, his heavy arms folded across his chest. Both he and Lindsey have half-eaten lunches spread over their desks.

"What?" I make no attempt to hide my annoyance. "You think I would make something like that up?"

He ignores this question, and I am certain I would not have liked his answer. "Who was it?"

"I have no idea. None of us has ever seen her before." *That*, I made up.

Lindsey looks squeamishly at the bite of salad on her fork, then drops it. "Was there…blood, and stuff?"

"No. No blood or wounds. Police said it looked like a suicide."

Jarvis, whose appetite succumbs to no trauma, reaches for his sandwich. "Was there a note?" he asks, spreading his mouth wide for an enormous bite.

I feel heat in my face, although I know they cannot see the note folded in my pocket. "No note."

Jarvis' big head shakes as he finishes chewing. "That doesn't make much sense," he says, raising his bulk out of his chair. "When someone suicides, they're most often sending a message. They don't just pick a random yard to die in; they choose the location their body will be found. And they leave a note. Usually."

Shut up, Jarvis. Damned know-it-all. And stop—just STOP looking at me!

"That's some weird shit," Jarvis persists, refusing to shut up as requested. "Just doesn't add up. There's something else going on."

Officer Nass leaned across the table toward Catherine. "How do you know it was Pamela Mercurio and not your daughter? Or someone else altogether?"

Catherine looked away. "Lucinda is five-seven, not five-five."

The policeman raised his eyebrows. "I see. Mrs. Whittendon," he said, "have you seen Pamela Mercurio recently? Or ever, in the last 37 years?"

Catherine met his gaze. Could it really endanger Lucinda to tell him? Or even Pamela, who was no doubt long gone from Massachusetts by now? "She was here," she admitted softly. "Just a few days ago. She wouldn't tell me anything either. She had questions. Not answers."

"What questions did she have?"

"She wanted to know about her parents. Poor thing. Didn't even know they had died. All these years, wondering about them, and they'd been killed in an accident in '78." She raised somber eyes. "Poor girl was just crushed."

"Did she say where she'd been all this time? Or where she was going?"

"No."

"How did she get here? She must have driven a car. Can you give me a description of the car?"

Catherine blinked. That might be a little too much information. She probably shouldn't have told him this much, but enough was enough. "I didn't see it."

"And I assume you asked if she knew where your daughter was?"

Catherine stared at him coldly. "Officer Nass. If she had told me where Lucinda was, which she didn't, I would not tell you."

"Then you'd be impeding a murder investigation."

"I wish you would not put it that way. She is my daughter."

"Look, ma'am. I know this is difficult. I don't enjoy asking you all this stuff. But I was assigned to this case. I'm just doing my job."

And I am a mother. I'm just doing mine.

So the count is a hard three now. The legendary number three. Bears and little pigs and strikes until you're out. And deaths on my conscience.

I sit here at my desk, unable to think of anything else. Jarvis talks his booming talk on the telephone, his oak-trunk legs propped on his desk. Sean left moments ago after gracing Lindsey with half a peanut butter and cucumber sandwich, and Lindsey now works quietly at her own desk. All is as it should be out there in the world outside my head.

How quickly feelings of well-being can evaporate. Not so those of remorse, anxiety, or dread. Can it be only a few weeks ago that I lived Annie's comfortable life without anxiety? I have grown complacent over the years, expecting the peace will endure. Charlie saved me, and then the world left me alone. I should have known I would not be allowed to keep my peace forever.

Three lives have ended before their time, directly due to my actions. Robert Dechesney, the security guard who was just doing an honest job. Jimmy, who did not know the gun Gordon gave him was loaded, which is perhaps why he never fired it to defend himself, and who would not have ended up in jail to be beaten to death if we had not cajoled him into our ill-fated plan. And now Pam. My very best friend whose life I destroyed. On reflection, I enjoyed the peace and gifts of my life far longer than I deserved.

Now the world is coming after me. Pam, in her dead state, works against me. Michael does also, just by getting sick and bringing this whole thing from forgotten shadows into the light again. And Jarvis, unknowingly, simply because he needs to be helpful. And who else? Who else is hiding out there in the world who is coming after me? This is what frightens me.

Those who hold the truth and those who seek the truth threaten me. And what is my defense? I can shout, I can insist, *I am Annie!* But Annie, as I know too well, is a myth. Like Athena, sprung fully grown from the head of Zeus, Annie burst into being as an adult; no youth to rest upon, no experiences on which to lean. Now, with truth storming her wobbly foundation, Annie trips and falters; Athena stumbles.

Officer Nass hung his head, raked skinny fingers through blond hair. He looked up with a sigh. "So you're telling me you don't know where your daughter is, and Pamela Mercurio gave you no information about her own whereabouts or your daughter's?"

"That is correct."

Officer Nass looked sternly at Catherine. "Have you been in any contact, or received any communication from your daughter since 1969?"

Catherine shook her head slowly from side to side, the lying far easier when you don't speak.

The cop leaned back in his chair. "Mrs. Whittendon, that new information you were asking about. We received a call from someone saying you are in possession of a letter received from your daughter in 1982."

Catherine felt the blood drain from her face. *Colin!* How could he? "Someone," she snorted. "You mean my son."

The boy in uniform nodded. "Yes."

"What do you think such an old letter can tell you?"

"I don't know. But it's evidence, so we need it."

"Well, I don't have it. Anymore. I destroyed it. It was too painful, so I got rid of it."

"Mrs. Whittendon. We can get a search order. And if we find it then, you will be guilty of withholding evidence in a murder investigation."

Well done, Colin. You got both your sister and your mother with one phone call. Her head hung low with the weight of just how badly her family was broken.

It is later in the day, when I see the item in Jarvis' open newspaper, that I begin, possibly, to understand. A small article, near the bottom of page three, tells me that Michael died in the hospital yesterday morning. Perhaps Pam knew of this somehow. Perhaps Michael's end felt like her own end in some tragic way.

Pam blamed me for losing Michael; this I knew. I was not aware, however, how deeply she condemned—no, hated—me, until I read the slip of paper I found folded neatly in her dead fingers. Now, with Jarvis in his little closet-office and Lindsey out on an errand, I take it out to read it again. It is in blue ink, in her handwriting. An accusation, guilty verdict, and sentence, all in one.

Lucinda—

> *You did this to me. You took my trust and twisted it until it broke. Until I broke. You deserved to be punished more than I did, but somehow you ended up with the husband and family and the house with the picket fence, and I have nothing! Because of you.*
>
> *You can go on living in your nice little house with your nice little family, but now you'll always have this image of me here, dead on your lawn. I hope I haunt you the way you have haunted me.*

Pam, my best friend, the sweet, kind girl that I loved, despised me with such fervor that she spent her final moments of life devising a way to torment me. My anguish exceeds any words I could possibly utter.

CHAPTER 27

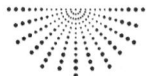

Charlie stepped out of the darkroom and blinked, allowing his eyes to adjust to the fluorescent lighting of the office. He rubbed his hands over his face and held them there, shutting out the fickle world that seemed to have turned on him lately. A dead body on the front yard? That kind of crazy stuff just doesn't happen to people. Normal people, anyway. Maybe, maybe, *maybe* he could have been gullible enough, or stupid enough to accept it as a freak coincidence because he so badly wanted the world to go back to normal. Maybe, if Annie hadn't grown a bizarre new personality over the past few weeks.

He eased himself into a chair, overcome suddenly by weariness. What had happened to his Annie? She had always been such a treasure. A lovely mix of steady, unflappable strength and tender vulnerability. She managed to need his nurturing, while being perfectly capable of taking care of herself, of going it alone. Smart and insightful, even when it was inconvenient, and so very self-aware. With an intense need to help, to ease pain or suffering in others.

Stretching forward, Charlie reached for the framed photograph on the desk in front of him; one of the best pictures he'd ever taken.

He wiped at the dust clouding the images with his hand. Taken long ago, it was of a young Annie and a tiny Darlene, at Darlene's first Fourth of July fireworks when she was about three.

A warm breeze blew through Chicago that night, and pedestrians crowded Navy Pier in search of a good spot to watch the show. Young couples strolled along, arms wrapped around each other, oblivious to all else. Families with babies in strollers and children skipping and running milled about. Darlene marched along beside Annie, her pudgy little hand tucked snugly inside her mother's, eyes big at the commotion around her.

Charlie gazed appreciatively at his young wife in her low-slung bell-bottomed blue jeans and peasant blouse. A soft blue velvet choker, the exact shade as her eyes, cradled her slender throat. A group of teenagers pushed past them and Annie nearly lost her grip on Darlene.

"Come here, sweetie," she said, hoisting her daughter up onto her hip.

"Want me to carry her?" Charlie offered.

Annie smiled at him. "Thanks, sweetheart. But I'm okay." She nodded at the large camera hung around his neck. "Besides, that would leave me to take pictures, and I don't think we want that."

"You're not so bad as you think," he grinned, leaning down to kiss the tip of her nose.

Annie pressed her face into Darlene's striped shirt briefly, rubbing her nose dry.

"Daddy take my picture!" Darlene shouted happily.

"You always want your picture taken, don't you?" Charlie teased, pursing his lips into her chubby cheek and kissing repeatedly.

"Yah!" Darlene giggled. "That tickles!"

"This is probably a good spot," Annie said. "What do you think?"

"Fine," Charlie replied, absently glancing around.

"Eww, look!" Darlene cried out, pointing a pudgy little finger.

Up ahead, a blond woman in a floral print skirt, not much older than Annie, labored to push a wheelchair through the dense crowd. A young boy, walking between her and the chair, pressed his palms against the back of the chair as though helping to push. In the chair sat a somber-faced man with longish brown hair. He wore a khaki US Army shirt decorated with medals and matching pants tied into a knot at the knee, where each leg abruptly ended. Alert, dark eyes darted about curiously.

"Mommy," Darlene whined, frightened, "he has no legs."

Annie stopped and put a hand over her daughter's mouth. "No, honey. Quiet." Her eyes misted as she gazed at the veteran. "That man," she said into her daughter's ear, "is a very, very brave man. He was so brave, he went to a dangerous place, even though he knew he could get hurt. He deserves our greatest respect—do you know what respect is?"

Darlene's little head shook timidly.

"We should think of him as one of the best and bravest men in the world. He's a soldier. And he was sent to a war that he probably didn't want to go to, and that's where he got hurt and lost his legs." Annie looked up and met Charlie's gaze. "Daddy's brother was a brave soldier too. Your Uncle Nate. And so…so were lots of people who you'll never know. But we must honor them."

Annie reached a hand out toward Charlie, who took it in his own, then slid an arm around her shoulders to embrace his family. He held them, and felt his own eyes beginning to tear. He buried his face in Annie's hair and clung to her. How lucky he'd been to find her. This amazing woman who had such empathy for Nate, a man she'd met only once when they'd gone to see him off. Or maybe her empathy was for Charlie, knowing how much he still mourned his brother. In any case, she was a treasure. His own private treasure.

Later that evening, when the fireworks began, Darlene clapped with glee at the spectacle. Charlie snapped only a few photos of the exploding light show in the sky before becoming captivated by the awe and delight in his daughter's face. He turned his lens on her, and Annie, still shy about being photographed, ducked her face into the nape of Darlene's neck as the shutter snapped.

Charlie smiled at the picture in his hands. This was why he loved photography—its ability to capture a single moment in time and preserve it for all of history. This photo preserved one of his favorite moments in his life. Against the black night sky, Darlene's sweet, innocent face lit up by fireworks and by her own joy, and the lovely profile of Annie, nestled lovingly against her daughter.

With an audible sigh, he leaned forward and carefully propped the frame back up in its place. That was one frozen moment from his life, real and precious. This also was a moment in his life. Unfortunately, also very real.

Charlie pressed a hand to his chest, a feeble attempt to quell the burning sensation that flared hot and insistent. Yesterday morning, after getting out of the shower, some noise or commotion or disturbance or *something* called to him from outside. He peeked out through the slats of the Venetian blinds and saw Annie out in the yard by the wishing well. Odd enough. But then she stooped, picked something up that he could not see, and tucked it into her pocket.

Only later, when he learned of the body, and that it was in the same spot near the well, did he wonder. Then when Amber remembered seeing something on the body that Annie denied was there… that was the moment the burning began in his chest. That was when the awful realization slapped him; maybe it wasn't the world that was turning on him. It was Annie.

He reached, hesitantly, for the telephone, tapped in a number, and waited.

"Morrisville Police," a brisk voice chirped through the line.

"Uh, yeah," Charlie said. "Is Bob Sifert in?"

"Who's calling?"

"Charlie Pulkowski."

After a short wait, Bob's upbeat greeting boomed in his ear. "Hey, Charlie. How you doing?"

"Fine, good, Bob. But I…I, you know, I keep thinking about… the body."

"Yeah, I hear you. It definitely freaks you out. I can't get it out of my head either. We might need another fishing trip to clear our heads, eh?"

"Yeah," Charlie chuckled unevenly. "Bob, I was wondering. Have you found out who she was yet?"

"Well, sort of. We found out who she isn't. We found a truck parked a few streets from your house with an empty bottle of sleeping pills on the seat and a South Dakota license with a photo that matches the victim. Trouble is, when we looked into the name on the license, we found that that person was already dead—for forty years."

"What? I don't get it."

"The name, and matching social security number, belong to a Monica Patterson, who was killed in 1966 at the age of seventeen. But then there's a job and income history for her starting in late 1969, which we assume is when the deceased woman took on her identity. So we know she's not Monica Patterson. But we don't yet know who she is."

Charlie felt a dizziness in his head, spreading slowly down as a prickly shiver along his spine. "You said late 1969?"

"When she adopted this new identity, yeah. Why? Does that ring any bells?"

"No," Charlie said hoarsely. "No bells."

CHAPTER 28

I need to see my mother. There it is. Fifty-six years old and I need my mommy. I stand here in the tiny, outdated FROGS bathroom, staring at my reflection in the scratched mirror over the sink. I have been here, in this same position, for ten minutes. She is old, this woman who stares back at me. I have never seen her before. She is tired, oh so worn out, and in a great deal of pain. This surprises me. I do not feel that I am in pain. I know that I am worried, and yes, tired. But the pain I do not feel, other than the rash on my palm which continues to spread and has developed tiny little blisters. I hide it from others as best I can, as it looks like some horrible and contagious disease. Be careful what you wish for, I know, but I cannot help thinking an honest malady would be kinder on my conscience, at least.

I did not realize just how much I depended on my secret visits to my mother. I believed they served me only sadness, the pain of longing, and that my need to continue visiting was some sort of masochistic addiction. I was mistaken. These past weeks without them have been like sailing unknown waters without an anchor. There are no plans to stop, and in fact it might be best to keep moving. But it is comforting to know the anchor is there in the event you need to take shelter from a storm. My visits to Lucinda's mother and her old house were Annie's anchor. By allowing Lucinda the occasional moments of remembered life, Annie was able to completely suppress her in her own life. The new real life.

And now I know who the woman in the mirror is. She is Lucinda. Annie is unable to continue without her anchor. So this old, tired, wounded woman will assume control. I cannot look at her any longer and I turn away. I must not let her win. Lucinda is of no use to Amber or Charlie. I must not allow her to prevail. I turn slightly, and eye her over my shoulder. *There is no place for you here.* She looks angry at this, but I do not care. "Go away," I say aloud, and my voice startles me in the tiny bathroom. I sound like a crazy person talking to myself in the mirror. I have been in here too long. Jarvis and Lindsey will think something is wrong.

Outside in the office, Lindsey glances furtively in my direction, and I can see in her face that she is troubled and frightened by the sight of Lucinda. Jarvis stands at the doorway, chatting with Harvey, the mail carrier. They are talking about Harvey's wife, Joanne, who recently had surgery for breast cancer. Jarvis was glad, he says, that they liked the surgeon he had recommended. And please, if there was anything else he could do to help, please let him know. Jarvis is too busy being Jarvis to notice me or my altered appearance. But that cannot last.

He says goodbye to Harvey and drops a stack of mail on Lindsey's desk to be sorted and distributed. "Annie," he says, walking toward my desk.

What?

As his eyes fall on my face, he blinks, startled. "Annie?" he says again.

"What!" My voice bristles, and it alarms me. "I just said what. What is it?"

Jarvis narrows his eyelids and peers at me suspiciously. "You tell me."

I take a deep breath because that is what you are supposed to do when you feel anger overtaking you. But I do not have time to count to ten, and I do not believe it will help anyway. "Jarvis," I say with a patience I do not feel, "you came to me wanting something. Now what the *hell* is it?"

His eyes widen and his head rolls slowly from side to side. "Never mind," he says, yet does not leave, as though he is waiting for me to say something further. But he does not wish to hear the cruel things I am thinking, and, through an extraordinary feat of effort and self-control, I manage to keep them inside my head. Congratulations to me.

I will ignore him. He may stand there as long as he wishes, and I may pretend he is not there. I reach for a stack of file folders and shuffle them about my desk, searching my memory for the task that needs doing. Finally, this man who is not really there walks away and into his own little closet-office. My head is clearer now, without him standing over me, and I am able, sort of, to focus on my work.

Lindsey slides her chair over to my desk and places a few envelopes on it. "Mail," she says shyly, and darts away again without looking at me. I feel a pang of guilt at this. I am Lindsey's only friend in this office, and now she is afraid of me.

I pick up the envelopes and glance through them. Two are invoices I have been expecting, but the third one is unfamiliar. My name and the FROGS address are typed on the front, but there is no return address. Curious, I slip a finger under the flap and peel it open. There is one piece of white paper inside. One line of writing on it, typed, just like the envelope. *I know what you did.*

A cold panic floods my body. The blood abandons my extremities, drains from my head, racing for the squalid pit in my stomach. The room spins and I believe my hands are shaking, although I cannot see them because the room seems also to have gone black.

I do not know how long I sit here before the darkness begins to lift. I can make out the outlines of my desk, and beyond it, Lindsey sitting at her own. My hands, when I can see them, still hold the piece of paper, gripped tightly so that it is crumpled on its edges. My eyes flit about the room anxiously. I cannot stay here. I must get out to somewhere I can breathe, somewhere I can think.

Lindsey dials the telephone, oblivious of me. Jarvis must still be in his office. I fold the note and its envelope hastily and cram both into my purse. I am halfway to the door when Jarvis' voice rumbles behind me.

"Annie. Where you going?"

I turn to face him, but continue to back up toward the door. "I'm sorry. I have to leave. Something…something has come up."

"Annie, wait. I need to talk to you."

"No," I shake my head. "Can't stay." I push open the door and am outside, where I am seized by an overpowering impulse to run.

"Annie!" Jarvis has followed me outside, and begins to trot down the sidewalk after me. "Just wait a minute."

Stop! Leave me alone! I am running hard now, and when I look back, Jarvis is already beginning to tire. Why does he follow me? Why can he not just leave me alone?

"Annie…" his voice fades away and I know he has stopped and is no longer chasing me. Yet I cannot stop. I run because it is all I can think of to do. Who has sent this note? Was it Pam, as just another means of inflicting punishment? If not her, then who? Who else is there who could know? Anyone who knows me may have figured it out, may have finally recognized me as the fugitive girl in the photo, but why the secretive note? What purpose is there to the note, other than to terrorize me?

I have no answers, only a constricting feeling of the world squeezing in on me from all directions. I am far away from the FROGS office and Jarvis now. Far away from his solicitous interference and all of his many questions. Yet I am still running.

I half expect to see Jarvis' car in my driveway, and I am prepared to drive right on past if it is. He has called my cell phone several times this afternoon, and I am sure he has called my home phone as well. I can only imagine what he has told Charlie and Amber.

It is becoming more and more difficult to hold onto Annie's life. I do not need to explain my behavior to Jarvis. I can tell him it is personal and none of his business and I wish him to drop the subject. But at what point in all this strange behavior of mine do I cease to be the Annie that everyone knows? Is it better that they think Annie has changed, gone crazy, weirded out, as the kids say? Or that she never was Annie in the first place?

I do not know the answer to that one. But if there is someone out there who knows this secret of my life, I will not have a choice. Lucinda will be revealed. And, as much as I try to deny it, I can feel the fates pressing in on me while Lucinda strains to get out. One way or another, she will have my life soon.

Jarvis is not here. At least, his car is not here. I pull into the driveway and park next to Charlie's gold Taurus. It will be much better for me to confess, rather than wait to be outed. Charlie and Amber will prefer to hear the truth from me, difficult as it will be, than from some stranger with a badge. I have always known this. I have always deluded myself—or perhaps been exceedingly opti-mistic—that it was a choice I would never have to make.

I hesitate outside the front door, as if the courage for what I am about to do can be gathered like flowers from the terra-cotta pots that crowd the porch. The door is unlocked. I enter quietly. The house is silent, although I can smell dinner cooking. Then, from around the corner, Amber comes bounding at me.

"Nonny!" she calls, throwing her arms around me. "Molly Bonardino broke her ankle!"

I peer down into my granddaughter's shining face, alive with exhilaration, and I am confused.

"So she can't do the play," Amber says, "so her part goes to the understudy who just happens to be your very favorite actress!" She dips low in a bow.

"Sweetheart, that's wonderful," I say. "Congratulations. Too bad about Molly—"

"So you're going to have to come early so you can get front row seats. And don't forget Mom is coming too. I want to see the three of you, my whole family, front and center."

"Of course. Of course we'll all be there. I can't wait." I smile my practiced sweet-grandmother-smile through this lie. *Sadly Amber, your grandmother is a felon and a fugitive and will likely be huddling on a hard metal cot in a cold prison cell during your performance. But thank you for the invitation. It is nice to be wanted.*

"I can't either. Oh my god, I'm like, so excited."

"I'm so excited for you," I say. *And I am terribly sorry to have to destroy your world, to reduce your "whole family" by a third. I know you need Annie. All I have is Lucinda.*

"Hey." It is Charlie's voice. He has come from the kitchen, wiping his hands on a towel. "Great news for our little superstar, isn't it?" His blue eyes are bright with pride as he grins at Amber.

I nod mechanically, watching him. "Sure is."

"So, you're kind of late," he says offhandedly. "Jarvis called looking for you. You weren't answering your cell phone."

"No, I…I was…the truth is…Jarvis and I had a bit of an argument. And I just didn't want to talk to him." And there it is. The lies just come too easily for me to make room for the truth. I want to tell them the truth. I need to tell them the truth. Yet I seem unable to speak anything but lies.

Charlie has not yet kissed me hello, and as I look at him, I want so desperately to hold him. I extricate myself from Amber and go to him, sliding my arm around his neck and pulling myself into him. "Hi," I say, but it sounds too much like a whimper. I lay my head on his shoulder and just rest myself on him.

"Hi," he says, and I wait for what seems a long time for his arms to slide around my back so I may feel loved. "So what was the fight about?"

I do not lift my head to look at him. I am too comfortable in here in this hug. It feels safe in here, even if it is not. I cannot give this up. "It was stupid," I say. "I really don't want to talk about it."

The silent pause lasts a bit too long before Charlie responds. "Right. Of course."

"If he calls again," I whisper in Charlie's ear, "tell him I'm not here."

"Sure," Charlie says. "Whatever you want."

It is late when I go to bed. Amber and Charlie have retired hours ago, but as fatigued as I am, worn down and worn out from the exertion of trying to sustain my no-longer-sustainable fake life, I am unable to sleep. It is simply too exhausting to maintain the outward appearance of calm, unflappable Annie while Lucinda thrashes about frantically inside me, and I can feel myself, my real self—whomever that might be—slipping away. Whoever I am, I cannot be Annie any longer. I simply do not have the energy.

I have stayed up, to just sit in my living room, my house that I have enjoyed and underappreciated all these years. It is quiet, but I can hear and feel all the life that has been lived here. I cannot fathom, or perhaps I do not wish to, what life will be like in this house after I am gone.

I am a coward. There is a truism for you, an inescapable surety. Death, taxes and my cowardice. It disgusts me to learn this about myself. Yet I am too weak and fearful and just too damned spineless to tell the people I love the truth they need to hear. I am even too cowardly to be here when they do find out. I cannot bear to see the revulsion in their eyes.

So I will leave. I will tuck my cowardly tail between my legs and run away. Tomorrow, after they leave for work and school. It will be easier for them to process the truth if I am not here. It will save them the difficulty of trying, perhaps, to be kind to me as they hide their disgust. I am helping them. Right, you contemptible coward.

With this decision made, I feel long-awaited sleep enveloping me. I go to Amber's room, as usual, for one last kiss before bed. She lies on her side, her blonde hair partially obscuring her face. Her breathing is soft and regular, tranquil and unsuspecting. A kiss will not be enough for this very last goodnight kiss. I settle lightly on the side of the bed so as not to wake her. This child, who has been allotted a sorely imperfect life, refuses to allow unfortunate circumstances to mar her own perfect person. Her invincible spirit, her inextinguishable quest for happiness in every act of every moment—all this I can see clearly in this placid face adrift in dreams.

I fold myself gently down over her, wrap my arms around her slender shoulders, rest my head on her chest. I hear her heart, her breath, strong and persistent. I feel her warmth and her very soul, and I do not try to stop the tears when they come. *I love you, my girl. You will need your strong spirit now. Do not let this change you, Amber. Do not let me ruin you. Forget me. Grow up happy and be the wonderful person you were meant to be. Just...forget me.*

CHAPTER 29

Juggling a paper cup of coffee and the bag from the bagel shop, Jarvis reached into a pocket for his big ring of keys. Annie was scheduled to have opened up an hour ago, and then later this morning would head on up to Chesterford for the weekly drop-off. He turned the key and pushed open the heavy glass FROGS door.

Jarvis squeezed through the narrow door to his cozy, as Annie called it, office. No note on his desk. He took a large gulp of coffee and set the bag of food on the desk. His breakfast—two onion bagels with cream cheese and a strawberry Danish for dessert— would have to wait.

Back out into the main office, he went straight to the answering machine on Lindsey's desk. One message. Had to be her. He pressed play, and listened to Annie's voice, feeble and thin, fill the room.

Um, hi. Jarvis. Or Lindsey, whoever gets this. I'm not going to be coming in today. I'm sorry. I'm just…I'm sick…not feeling well at all. One of you is going to have to go to Chesterford, sorry about that. So anyway, that's it. I did want to say, Jarvis, I'm sorry about…how I've been acting lately. All snippy and stuff to you. I…I know you're trying to help, and I'm sorry. You're...you're a good friend. Well, anyway. Bye.

Jarvis eased himself onto the edge of the desk, folded his big arms and rested them on the rounded shelf of his belly. "Sick, my ass," he said loudly to the empty room.

Sunlight sliced mercilessly through gaps in the window shade, infiltrated Darlene's closed eyelids and seared her quiescent brain. The pain lay dormant, unnoticed for a moment, until her shoulders twitched involuntarily and she sucked in a big heavy breath of air. Her lungs felt tight, constricted, as though unwilling to make room for the oxygen it needed.

"Ohh," she started to moan, but the sound reverberated in her head, pounding the inside of her skull.

First one eye, then the other broke the light crust of sleep and opened a crack, letting the light seep in a bit. The pillow below her face was wet with drool from her open mouth. Slowly, she rolled herself over onto her back and looked warily about the room. A dark wooden dresser that needed refinishing stood diminutively in the corner, next to a painted wicker hamper with clothes spilling over the top. Above both, a giant abstract poster covered most of the green and pink floral-papered wall. Darlene exhaled loudly. Her own room, thank god.

She turned her rock-heavy head to the clock on the nightstand. 11:43am. Shit. Goddammit! She was supposed to be at the salon at ten. Why hadn't they called her? Shit, shit, shit! The blinking red light on the answering machine said they had. Three times. *Oh, nice going, asshole.*

On her side, she pushed her unwilling legs over the side of the bed and looked at them hanging there, several inches off the floor. Legs were easy; the head would be much harder. Slowly, she pushed herself upright, eyes shut tight against the throbbing pain. Opening her eyes just a tiny crack to allow her to see, she shuffled unsteadily toward the bathroom. Just inside the doorway, she lifted her head…and screamed.

Sitting upright on the toilet, head slumped forward on his chest, was a man with thick black hair. Finer black hair covered much of his body, which she could see because he was naked, save for a pair of black socks.

"Oh my god," Darlene whimpered. "Oh my god oh my god oh my *god*!" She crept closer. "Who the hell is this?" she muttered, leaning down to peer into his face. "Hey. Wake up." She tapped timidly on his naked shoulder. "Wake up!" No response. "Oh, goddammit! I have to pee!" She poked harder, then gave him a firm push. "Come on!"

His body tilted to the side with her push, then continued tipping as if in slow motion, until finally he fell off, his head bumping loudly against the tiled wall. He lay there, wedged between the wall and the toilet at an awkward angle.

"Oh my god, *no*," Darlene wailed, her body shaking, eyes riveted on the lifeless body. She backed out of the little bathroom and ran frantically back to her bed, burying her face in the blankets. "No, this can't be happening," she sobbed deep, gulping breaths. "Please, please make this go away. This can't be happening to me," she whispered, tears running hotly down her cheeks. "Why is this happening to me?"

Several minutes later, exhausted, she lifted her head and looked warily around. "What am I going to do?" she asked the empty room. The apartment was so still, so apparently normal. Maybe she'd imagined it. With great exertion, Darlene stood and hesitantly, fearfully, tiptoed back toward the bathroom. She peeked in, irrationally hopeful that the body would be gone. *No*, god, still there! She bit hard on her fingertips. Forcing herself further into the tiny room, she reached over to the rusted metal vanity beneath the sink and yanked open one creaky drawer and then the other, pulling from it a large hand mirror. Pressing the mirror against the wall, she tried to slide it in front of the man's face, but the mirror was too big for the space. Darlene squeamishly put a hand to his stubbly chin and turned his face upward. She held the mirror up close to his face, waited a few seconds, then held it up to her own face to examine it. Very faint, barely discernible, a slightly foggy spot lay on the glass. She swiped a finger over it, leaving a clean mark. *Oh, thank god!*

Darlene sank slowly, weakly to the floor in relief, fresh tears brimming in her eyes. She hugged her arms tightly around her knees and looked back at the stranger slumped beside her. He was alive! She pressed her throbbing head between trembling hands. Now what?

Who will I be? I ask this of myself as I pack items in my suitcase. How many of Annie's belongings will I need? I cannot be Annie any longer. And I have not been able to be Lucinda for most of my life. So who will I be?

I will need a picture of Charlie and Amber and Darlene because I cannot be without them. Annie thinks I should turn myself in to the police. What horrible, sadistic person sent me that note? What do they want from me? Lucinda wants to see her mother one last time. I cannot leave without seeing Darlene, and in some ways that will be more difficult than saying goodbye to Charlie and Amber because I worry about what will become of her. She does not like me; perhaps her mother's disappearance will be good for her. How much money can I, should I, take from Charlie and Annie's account? I cannot keep all these thoughts straight or quiet or in any kind of order. They all seem equally trivial and crucially important at the same time.

I hugged Charlie and Amber too long this morning when I said goodbye. I could not help myself. Was everything okay, Charlie wanted to know? I am just not feeling myself, I told him. I do not even know who myself is, I wanted to tell him.

That is when he showed me the newspaper. "There's our dead woman," he said, and there indeed she was.

I took the paper from him and I could not stop my hands from shaking. The photograph was of Pam's driver's license from South Dakota with some fake name.

"You're shaking," Charlie said. "You sure you're okay?"

"It's just so disturbing, this woman dying on our front lawn."

"The name on her license is phony. The police are looking for help in identifying her. You sure you don't recognize her?"

"No. Of course not," I said, but I could not look him in the eye.

And now he is gone and I will never look into those eyes again. But I cannot think of that or I will break down and cry and fall to a million little pieces for someone to have to clean up. I must finish my packing and be gone, long before either of them returns home.

Pam's photo is in today's newspaper! This thought grips me with a fresh jolt of panic. How could I not have realized the significance of this before? Pam visited my mother in the last few days, so my mother will recognize the photo in the paper. The article said the police are looking for help identifying the woman, and my mother will wish to be helpful. Won't she? It mentions that the body was found on private property in Morrisville, my town. Will it occur to my mother that if she identifies Pam, she will be pointing the police in my direction? Or does she want me to be found?

I have never known the answer to that, and in this instance, it does not really matter. Once they know Pam's identity and her connection to Lucinda, how long will it take them to connect Lucinda to Annie? They may never connect those last two dots. Or they could be here, at my door, at any moment.

I must finish this packing now, then get to the bank, get to Darlene, then get away from here. The bank. If they have connected those last two damning dots, they could freeze our account, apprehend me at the bank. Perhaps I give them too much credit. Perhaps I give myself too much credit for being clever. The truth is I do not know and the worse truth is that I can no longer think. I cannot think!

I am racing and frantic, and this life I made and the life I left are whirling madly to and fro and into each other and I can no longer control either. With all this mad spinning, could not the eternal hands on the grand cosmic clock manage to turn a few simple revolutions backward? Could life not come with just one do-over?

I cannot claim I did not have time to think. There were so many instances, so many times and places where I could have changed everything. I did not even have to come to my rational, ethical senses on my own. Pam had arrived at hers.

Gordon was doing a final check of the weapons as we waited for Michael and Jimmy to arrive with the car at our safe house on East 7th Street. I leaned over him as he loaded the guns, alternately fascinated and frightened by the hard metallic clicks and thuds. He flicked a glance of irritation at me. "Go get Pam. They'll be here any minute."

I nodded and obeyed, climbing the stairs to look for Pam, who I found in one of the back rooms, sitting on the edge of a bed and staring off at nothing. Her wavy brown hair tumbled gracefully over her shoulders, her lovely profile was placid and still, hands resting easily in her lap. She was as if painted there, by one of the old masters who had managed to capture both her innocent beauty as well as her troubled thoughts. "Young Girl in Quiet Reflection," I named this painting in that serene, untouched moment before I spoke to it.

"Pam."

She turned at the sound of my voice, and in that brief instant I saw unguarded terror on her face before it hardened into disgust. She walked toward me, put a hand on the doorknob, and calmly closed the door in my face.

Oh, god. "Pam," I said through the door, "I'm sorry." Impatient, I pushed it open and went in, ignoring her look of startled annoyance. "Pam, I said I was sorry a million times. I'm sorry. I didn't mean to hurt you. There, a million and one."

"Just leave me alone."

I shook my head. "Time to go. Gordon wants us downstairs waiting for Michael and Jimmy."

She sank slowly back down onto the bed. "I'm not going."

"Excuse me?"

"I just can't do this. I'm scared. It feels wrong. And I...I just... I'm scared." She did not look at me, but addressed herself to the wall.

"No!" I allowed anger to carry my voice. "You can't just back out at the last minute. Everything's planned out. Everyone's got a job to do. You can't just desert us. We're depending on you."

She turned her face toward me as it twisted into a pained scowl. "I don't really give a damn."

Rage surged as a knob of bile in my throat. I was furious at her obvious fear, which I believed was just a kinder name for cowardice, considering the importance of our cause. I was angry that she would let us—me—down, and angry at her for being angry at me. And with that rage consuming me, I was able to justify any manipulation of her that I, in my eminent wisdom, deemed necessary. So I used, once again, her feelings for Michael to maneuver her into doing what I wished.

"Michael is depending on you too. Any change in the plan puts us all at risk. Including him."

She glared at me with a fury of her own, but I saw that I had strummed the correct chord. I watched the resolve in her face slowly soften and surrender, her fright swallowed in one gargantuan and painful gulp. And when she rose and walked past me out the door, she fired at me a look of pure loathing, so I would be sure to know it was not for me she was summoning her courage.

Downstairs, Gordon stood at the window with a large black knapsack over his shoulder. "They're here," he said as we approached. "Let's go." He held the door for Pam and me, then followed us outside. Michael's lanky frame leaned against the battered old white Pontiac Star Chief as he talked through the open front passenger window with Jimmy.

"All set?" Gordon said. "Where's the other car?"

"Fifty-fifth, near Ninth," Michael said. "Full tank of gas."

"Okay," Gordon nodded his approval. "Let's get this operation under way."

Michael climbed back into the driver's seat. Gordon went around to the passenger side door. "Jimmy, sit in back with the girls."

"Right," Jimmy agreed, as though he should have thought of that on his own. "Okay."

Michael wound his way expertly through the cramped little streets of the East Village to Third Avenue, where he turned right, to head uptown. Gordon unzipped his knapsack, turned in his seat to hand out supplies. "Bandanas," he muttered, tossing a green cloth to Jimmy and a red one to me. "Make sure they're tied tight; don't want them sliding down when we're in there. And," he said, reaching again into the bag, "your weapon, madam." He held a revolver by its barrel out to me. I reached out tentatively to take it from him, sharply aware that beside me, Pam was watching.

Its weight surprised me. It was a monster; so deathly cold, solid and real. It marked, with lethal finality, the end of our talking. This was no longer for us a discussion about right versus wrong, and us versus them, and truth and injustice. I looked at the gun in my hand and felt the same ruffle of terror I had seen in Pam earlier. And, oh my god, there were bullets in there!

I glanced up at Pam, who stared with unvarnished disapproval at the gun I held—and she did not even know about the ammunition inside. A misty sheen of sweat appeared on her upper lip; the fear had resurfaced, shrouding her face. Next to her, Jimmy's leg bounced up and down nervously as he held with both hands the gun Gordon had given him, as though it had the power to fire on its own. Michael drove silently, save for an occasional sigh emanating from deep in his chest. Even Gordon was uncharacteristically quiet, no longer issuing the usual commands and instructions. These faces that surrounded me, that had become so familiar over the past months, were closed to me and to each other on this terrible journey to the end of everything.

Toward our destination and our destiny we traveled, the five of us and the ghostlike silence that rode along with us, our foreboding and ill-tempered companion. An eerie, heavy dread pervaded the car, steeping each of us in its sinister chill. It was there, in that dark and somber moment, when evil crouched stolidly on our shoulders and goodness fluttered overhead, whispering faintly, tantalizingly within reach, that the choice waited to be made. Precisely then, words of logic and decency would have been heard through the righteous, overblown rhetoric that crammed each of our minds. I should have spoken. The horrific quiet was begging to be broken; my voice would have been a welcomed reprieve. The silence rang loudly in my ears, a shrill crescendo waiting for me to speak the words that would save us all. My heart stopped, then thumped ominously in my chest. *Say something!*

I have relived that moment many times over the years. That was my moment! That was my test. It was my opportunity to shake off evil's seductive grasp and reach for the gentle, modest grip of goodness. The choice was a conscious one. It was my moment of sin. I do not know if Robert Dechesney was killed by a bullet from my gun or Gordon's, but I know that I pulled the trigger out of fear, panic, self-preservation. It was there in the car that I chose premeditated evil. It is for this that I can never be forgiven—by myself or anyone. And it is this that has terrified me about myself all these years.

I failed my one big test. And I am not forgiven. So I continue my purgatory. I leave those I love, alone and ashamed. I am broken and empty, and I do not deserve any better.

All this I have explained in the note I am leaving for Charlie and Amber. It is a suicide note, of sorts; Annie is facing her death. So must Charlie and Amber. I am unsure how to sign this letter. It is the first time I have been completely honest with them and I do not wish to sully that truthfulness in any way. Which of my names is the honest one? Annie has been a lie since the moment I first uttered her name, and I have never been Lucinda to them. Neither is the truth, and so I leave the paper unsigned.

Now, where to leave this awful letter? Amber will likely be home first, but she cannot read it before Charlie. He will need to decipher it, filter the awful truth for her. She will need Charlie's goodness to offset the evil that is me. I place it then, on Charlie's pillow, where he will rest his head alone tonight. I linger over this pillow, then press my face into it and breathe in deeply the smell of Charlie. *Goodbye, my love. I will miss you forever.*

I hide this terrible note under the blue and white quilted bedspread that I bought just a couple of months ago (can it have been so recently that everything was so normal?), and I tuck the spread in neatly so everything will look right and fine and ordinary in the world. I must leave quickly now. I must move, and not think, or it will break me. My suitcase is heavy with remnants of Annie's life, things that do not really belong to me, but I welcome the strain of carrying its weight. This is a physical burden for once, and it is an agreeable change of pace. It is the things I leave behind that weigh most arduously on me. The antique lamp that Charlie surprised me with after I'd admired it in a shop window winks at me seductively, but it clearly belongs here, in the living room corner where Annie so meticulously placed it. I also cannot take the lovely Native American carved table in the hall that Charlie and I fell in love with—I cannot cram it into my suitcase. And it is just as much his as mine, in any case. The framed photo of Amber performing in last year's school play would fit, and I would love to have it. It captures the very essence of her bright spirit and passion. But I have seen the pride in her face when she looks at herself in this picture, and I would not take it from her even if I could justify doing so. All these little pieces of a life I have lived as my own must remain here. Even those items I did take, I do not truly have a right to take. They are Annie's memories. And yet, who, if not I, am entitled to Annie's memories? Tears stream down my face and I wipe furiously at the wetness, but the tears continue to come I am unable to keep up. In any case, I cannot brush away the sorrow.

Outside on the front step, I close the door behind me, listening for the metallic click of the lock catching. I have left my house key inside, on Annie's dresser. I will not be returning.

It is as I am driving down Annie's street, away from Annie's house, that I see the blue FROGS van heading toward me, Jarvis at the wheel. He sees me also and waves at me through the windshield, honks his horn and motions me to stop. I cannot speak to him. He saw Lucinda run out of the office in a panic yesterday and I do not believe I can be Annie to him any longer. He cannot stop me. He has no authority, and someone really ought to tell him that someday. I drive on past him, and although I try not to look in his direction, I see the dismay and the worry on his face, and they follow me all the way to the bank.

My cell phone rings as I am leaving the bank with one fifth of Charlie and Annie's savings. I do not wish to cause Charlie and Amber any hardship, but I will need some money just to survive. I will not be so lucky to find another Charlie this time, and I would not trap another good soul in my lies if I did. The phone continues to ring. I should not even have brought Annie's phone; I am Annie no longer. The display says it is Darlene calling. I have not yet said goodbye to my daughter, so for her I will be Annie one more time.

"Hello Darlene." I hope my voice sounds kind and loving, although I do not delude myself that she will think of me that way once I have gone.

"Mom. Oh god, Mom I need your help."

Her voice is warbly and urgent, much like the night she called from the diner, and my heart leaps to high alert. "What's wrong? Are you hurt?" *Please be okay.*

"No. No I'm not hurt but…oh god, Mom I really screwed up. Really, really bad."

I close my eyes in silent relief. "What happened?"

"I…I…there's this man. In my bathroom. And he's…he's not moving. I can't wake him."

"What man?"

"Just some guy," she whimpers. "But I can't wake him. He's really out bad."

"Just some guy? Do you know him? Did you let him in, or did he break in?"

"I...I don't know. I don't know him but I must have brought him home, I guess. I don't know. But he's not *moving*. I can't wake him up."

Oh dear god. "Is he...Darlene, he's not...?"

"He's breathing. But just barely. I thought...I really thought he was dead. And even now he doesn't look too good and...I don't know what to do."

"Well did you call 911?"

"I can't! I'm still on probation. I can't have him found in my apartment like this. Especially if he does end up, you know."

"So you're going to sit around and wait for him to die? That's your plan? Goddammit Darlene! What the hell is wrong with you? A person may be about to die! Do you get that? Dead! Hang up and call 911 right now."

"I thought maybe we could just take him to the hospital and drop him off anonymously."

Oh my god, can this really be my child? "I'm a good half hour away," I say slowly, distinctly. "He may not have that much time. You are going to have to put someone else first for a change. Call 911 and deal with the consequences."

I hear a sigh, and then a whiny, "Okay."

"Actually, never mind. I'll do it."

"Really?"

"It's not as a favor to you; I just don't trust you to do it, frankly. I'll call and then I'll get there as soon as I can." I disconnect from Darlene and dial 911. I wish I knew how much time Annie has before the police discover her secret and come after her. My daughter could not do more damage to Annie's getaway plan if she were deliberately trying.

CHAPTER 30

Catherine squinted up at the gold letters over the door of the large, white building with ornate columns astride its heavy wooden door. Morrisville Public Library. She maneuvered her silver Buick into the driveway that led to a side parking lot. Who knew Morrisville was so close? It had only taken her a few minutes to get here. She glanced at her watch. Okay, so forty-two minutes. Still.

Turning off the ignition, Catherine sat and stared at the building for a moment. How could it be that she had lived her whole life just a half hour away and had never been to Morrisville before? Well, obviously, because there was no reason to come here. It seemed to be a nice enough little town, much like Dunlee Mill. Nothing here for her that she couldn't find in Dunlee Mill. She reached for the newspaper on the seat next to her, and looked again at the license photo of Pamela. Nothing here, and yet Pamela chose to die here.

Catherine closed her eyes, shook her head vigorously. The thought that kept creeping into her mind was almost too much to bear. She got out, locked the car, and walked briskly into the library. It was quiet and solemn inside, as a library should be, with shelves of books lining the walls and heavy oak tables clustered in the center of the large main room. At an ornately carved desk, a middle-aged woman sat primly, as a librarian should, with upswept hair and dark-rimmed glasses. "Excuse me," Catherine whispered in her proper library voice. "Where would I find a copy of the local newspaper? The current issue."

The woman pulled a pencil from behind her ear and pointed with it. "Down those stairs and to the right. In the Reference section."

"Thank you." Catherine clumped briskly down the stairs, her hand resting lightly on the railing. She located the shelves of newspapers against a wall in the dim, windowless room, and quickly found the current issue of the *Morrisville Gazette*. Opening the first page, she found the Police Log for the week at the top of page 2. Catherine scanned the entries and found what she was looking for about a third of the way down. 7:14am: Body reported at 42 Mockingbird Lane. She fished a little notebook and pen from her purse, opened to a blank page and scribbled the address. She capped the pen, closed the notebook, and replaced both in her bag. Now to find a street map of this town.

Two green plastic recycling bins lay on their sides, their contents spilled out over the floor of the studio. Charlie sat on the linoleum tiles near the closet, open boxes of old photographs scattered around him. Pulling pictures out by handfuls, he riffled through them urgently, fearfully. And then abruptly stopped.

Hands trembling, he withdrew a few ancient photographs, taken forever ago, in those very first moments he'd found Annie huddling alone on a park bench in Chicago. She had asked him to destroy these pictures and he had promised to do so. But they were just too beautiful—she was too beautiful. And what was the harm, really, if he just tucked them away where no one else could see them?

Now, he selected a front view of her lovely face, then hesitantly reached for the newspaper from a few weeks ago he'd found at the bottom of a recycling bin. Exhaling loudly, he craned his head backward, searching for courage in the ceiling tiles before dropping his head forward to look at what he held in his hands. He slid the picture of Annie up next to the old mug shots in the newspaper. Past the three men, up next to one, then the other woman. The hair was different, and in one she was smiling and the other somber. But the eyes, the slender nose, the curve of the chin; this was the same woman. *God, no!*

Full comprehension flooded him in a wave of stinging heat, even as he tried to drive the truth from his mind. He'd expected it, knew it to be true, but how could it be? How could this possibly be true? It couldn't be. It was a mistake. Annie could not possibly be this…he glanced at the name beneath the photo…Lucinda Whittendon. She couldn't be. She wasn't.

But she was. God, what a relief! Despite her denials, he'd worried that there was someone else, that he was losing her, and he had no idea what to do about that. But this, perversely, was a relief. And also devastating. He'd known this woman for two thirds of her life—and her entire adult life—and there was just no way his sweet, wonderful love could have possibly held a gun in her hand and shot a man to death. She hated guns! Charlie looked down at the photographs in his hands. Maybe this is why.

He pressed his palms against his temples, hard, until it hurt. Oh god, could she really have done this? Murdered someone? He shook his head. No. There must be some explanation.

But the world made sense now. Everything, not just the past few weeks, but their entire life together. Why she was on the run in the first place and why she seemed afraid to be photographed. But then, if this was true, then everything—absolutely everything!—else was a lie. Everything from her name and the abusive stepfather, all the way through 37 years of phony I-love-yous to the cancer scare. *Every…god…damn…thing!*

He hurled the box of pictures against the wall where it smacked loudly and fell, photos fluttering through the air. *"Nooooo!"* he roared into the empty studio.

How does your world start to make sense just as it falls apart?

The collapse of everything he'd built his life on triggered his first true understanding, which in turn spawned the collapse. It was both a relief and agony to finally know the truth. Was the entire past 37 years all a lie? How could he believe that? The love they shared was real. Wasn't it? Or was he just the biggest kind of asshole? Duped for 37 years by a cunning and manipulative con artist?

No, no, no! She was his Annie. She loved him. But why hadn't she told him? She must know, after all these years, that she could trust him. Instead, she'd kept it secret and put him—all of them—through hell these past weeks. She'd let him go crazy with worry and jealousy. Damn her for that.

Catherine held the newly purchased street map against the steering wheel as she rolled slowly along the narrow, tree-lined streets of Morrisville. Right onto Whippoorwill, then second left onto Mockingbird Lane. She slowed and scanned the mailboxes along the street for number forty-two. There, across the street. A little white Cape with a quaint wishing well in the yard and flowers on the front stoop. Catherine smiled. It was cute, well cared for. A nice house that was obviously the home of nice people.

She maneuvered the car to the side of the road—might have hit the curb a little there—and turned off the ignition. But what nice people? Could it possibly be, that all this time...no, don't get your hopes up. She squinted at the lettering on the mailbox. Pulkowski. No first names, just initials, and neither of them an L.

Catherine sighed. It was probably nothing. Nothing but the wild goose chase of an old fool. But if poor, suicidal Pamela (Catherine had seen the poor girl was troubled, but how could she have known she was this tormented?), had to take her own life, it makes sense she would do it someplace familiar. One would have thought she would have chosen her old house where she grew up, but if not there, where? Catherine stared at the modest white house. Why this yard, this house? If it turned out this actually was

Lucinda's house—it was almost too much to even put into words, even silently, in her head—then she would never forgive herself for telling the police about Pamela. How could she have been so stupid? Careless? Clumsy? Whatever the word for it, she may well have led the police right to Lucinda. Wouldn't Colin be proud?

Well, she was here now, wild goose chase or not. Might as well get a look at the goose. Catherine got out of the car and locked it. She shuffled tentatively across the street to the little house. There were no cars parked in the driveway, but maybe they were in the garage. Or maybe no one was home. She climbed the three small steps up to the front door, admiring the pretty potted plants on the stoop. Big breath, just for courage, then she raised a hand to the shiny brass knocker in the shape of a pineapple. Oh, dear God, what would she say?

Oh grow up already! She lifted the knocker and smacked it hard three times. If it was Lucinda, she would not have to say anything, of course; a mother and daughter would certainly recognize each other. And if it wasn't Lucinda, it didn't matter what the heck she said. Eagerly, nervously, she waited. But the door did not move, and there were no noises from within. Catherine looked about. To her left, a small, bowed picture window hung just five feet or so off the ground. Could probably see into the living room from there. She shook her head adamantly. No. You didn't go around peeping into other people's houses. It just wasn't done.

She stepped gingerly down the steps and glanced up and down the street. There was no one around in the entire neighborhood. Edging toward the tantalizing window, Catherine examined the flowering shrubs along the front of the house. Nothing wrong with admiring someone's landscaping. It was a compliment, really. She stopped in front of the window to examine a particularly interesting bush, and her eyes flickered over the glass in just the tiniest, barest of glances. Not even a glance, really, more of a glimpse. A fleeting glimpse.

Catherine was pressed up, nose against the glass, peering

intently through her hands when the voice spoke to her from behind.

"Who are you?"

She whirled around, clutching her hands to her chest. In the yard stood a girl, a young teenager perhaps, with blond hair pulled up into a high ponytail, hands firmly planted on hips. A child. "Oh," Catherine wheezed, "you frightened me." She peered closely at the girl's face. There was something…the eyes, maybe…or the mouth. Something familiar. Or perhaps she was just seeing things. "Who are you?"

"I asked you first." The girl thrust her chin out defiantly. "And what are you doing peeking into my house?"

"I'm not—I wasn't peeking. I was just…I thought I saw…I think I might know your mother."

"Uh huh," The girl looked around the yard as though searching for something.

"What are you looking for?"

"Your accomplice."

"My what?"

"Well, you're snooping around here for some reason, so maybe you're a robber. But you don't look like you could do much yourself, no offense, so I'm thinking you must have an accomplice."

"I don't have an accomplice," Catherine sputtered. "I mean, I'm not a robber! I'm eighty-three years old, for Pete's sake. Do I look like a robber?"

The girl shrugged. "Could be a disguise."

"What? My oldness?" Catherine shook her head in exasperation. "It's not a disguise. Oh, for crying out loud." She grabbed a fistful of hair and tugged hard. "See, not a wig."

The girl raised her eyebrows and shrugged again. "I'm going next door to call the police."

"Wait!" Catherine shouted. "No! Look!" She reached into her mouth, detached her dentures and waved them at the girl. "Shee, denshures are real."

"Oh, gross!" the girl cringed, her pretty face screwed up with revulsion. "That's dis*gusting*. Put them back."

Catherine pressed her teeth hastily back onto her gums. "Now do you believe me?"

"I believe you're old. But I can't think of a good reason you'd be sneaking around my house."

"I told you. I think I know your mother."

The girl dismissed this with one quick shake of her head. "If you knew my mother, which I doubt because she doesn't exactly hang out with people like you, then you'd know she doesn't live here."

"Oh. Then who…?"

"I live with my grandparents."

Her *grandparents?* Well, could be. "How old is your grandmother?"

"You know, this is getting like, weird. None of your business."

Catherine pressed her lips firmly together. "Listen, young lady," she snapped, then softened her tone, "I suppose this does seem a little weird. But I promise you this is very important. What harm will it do to tell me how old your grandmother is?"

The girl pursed her lips, flapped her arms against her side. "She's like, fifty-five, I think."

Fifty-five. Lucinda would be fifty-six. "What…what is her name?"

"You know what? No! I'm not answering any more of your questions. I'm not supposed to talk to strangers at all, and they don't come any stranger than you, lady. You're poking around my house, you're asking all kinds of personal questions…that's it, I'm calling the police."

"No! Honey, please. I know this is all weird. And you have obviously been well-trained about the dangers of talking to strangers. But I think…I might not be a stranger. I think maybe it's your grandmother I might know. And I haven't seen her in a really long time, and I just wanted to find her, and I knocked on the door but no one answered. Do you think, and this is going to sound weird too, but I saw inside what looked like family pictures on the wall. Do you think—if there's a picture of your grandmother, do you think I could see it?"

The girl blinked with alarm, shook her head. "No!"

"Oh, *please*. I've come all this way. And it's really important. And…and I'll stay out here. I don't need to come in. You could just bring it to me. Please. I just really need to know if it's she's the person I think she is."

The girl searched Catherine's face curiously. And again, in this girl's expression, Catherine thought she saw a hint of something familiar. Something daughterly.

"An old picture," Catherine said, "from a long time ago would be best."

My daughter sits, cowered and huddled, and so very tiny. She is a mere speck on the couch, in danger of being swallowed up by its scruffy green fabric. One thin breeze, I fear, and she will blow right over.

She does not look at me, but at some distant spot on the wall. Yet she knows I am here. I look about the room, and I see nothing out of place besides the usual clutter my daughter lives in. "Where is he?" I say, and still she does not move.

"Darlene." I sit beside her and she falls against me, a fragile waif in a wispy nightshirt. Her body shakes as though she is sobbing, yet I hear no sound. I wrap my arms around her and hold her, my silent, helpless little baby.

When her voice comes, it is muffled, airy. "I really screwed up." She sniffles softly. "Really, really bad."

"Did the ambulance come?"

She nods. "Yeah."

"Why don't you tell me what happened."

"They came and took him—"

"I mean last night."

She blinks doleful eyes at me. "You want me to say I screwed up. I think I already have."

"I want you to admit you need help. That you aren't capable of beating this problem alone."

She drops her head, stares into her lap. "I sat here, for ten minutes before I even called you. All I could think of, was how do I get out of this mess? I didn't even think about the guy, except that it was good that he wasn't dead because then I would really be in trouble." Shame and a real agony cross my daughter's face. "If I hadn't called you, I would have just let him die. What kind of a horrible person could do that? I'm terrified of myself. I'm afraid to even be trapped here, inside me." She straightens her back, raises her face level to mine. "Do I need help? Every possible kind."

I barely recognize this daughter before me, and yet I have never felt more of a mother to her. She is broken, at her lowest point, her bravado stripped away and her confidence destroyed, and I love her all the more for her courage in facing all that. She is my child. I want to hold her and protect her.

"You know what, Mom?" Darlene says. "Just go. You didn't need to come out here. I'll check into any rehab place you want." She stands, looks down at me. "I'm going to get dressed. Wait for my probation officer to call."

"Darlene, I came here to help you."

"Yeah, and you did. You saved that guy's life, saved me from having a death on my conscience. But the truth is, I'm a screw-up, Mom. And you're perfect. And just being around you makes me feel even worse about myself."

"I'm not perfect."

Her face twists into an uncomfortable smirk. "No. Poor choice of words. Not perfect, but…flawless. Like a Stepford mother. You do everything right, every second of every day. You don't make mistakes, so you have nothing to be sorry about, or feel guilty about, or try to improve on." She smiles weakly. "You're the anti-me."

I cannot allow her to believe this. "Darlene. You're wrong

about me. I don't do everything right. I'm not perfect. I'm no better than you."

"I'm sorry. I didn't mean that to sound like a compliment. It's not. I didn't at all mean to imply that you're the perfect mother. You are far from that. You're a cardboard cutout of a mother. I'm a mess, and I know it. I have trouble staying clean. And this," she waves a hand toward her bathroom, "definitely proves that I need help. But you...you're so clean you're antiseptic. And that means you and me, we got nothing to latch onto between us." She shakes her head sadly. "We just got nothing."

Her words crush me. How have I let my daughter get so far from me? *Come back to me, Darlene. I love you.* And yet, I am about to leave her, and all of them. She is walking away from me and I am losing her, and I cannot bear it. Yet I thought I could leave.

"Darlene."

She turns back toward me.

"I love you."

She nods. "I know. But it's not enough."

"What do you need from me?"

"It's too late, Mom. What I needed, I needed when I was five, and ten, and fifteen. Now, I am what I am. And I need to face my demons on my own."

In this moment, my daughter has passed me. In the pursuit of human decency and valor, she has come from behind, in a faulty, sputtering jalopy, and sped on by me with a simple pop of the clutch. Perhaps she does not even know what it is she is saying, yet she stands here, acknowledging her truth, and willing to endure the future it will bring. She has passed me by without so much as a wave in the rearview mirror and I am left behind on the empty road by myself. I am now in last place.

"Darlene," I say, the idea slowly forming in my head. "Come for a ride with me. There is something I need to tell you. A confession. That I've never told anyone."

God damn woman was laughing at him. Lying there on the floor, amidst all the other scattered papers, her black-and-white face in the newspaper grinned maliciously up at him. Taunting him, mocking him. Charlie glared back at her. *I believed you.* A few feet away, the glossy photo he had taken, also black-and-white, stared up at him with the somber, pained eyes that had so captivated him. That was the face he'd believed. That desperate, fearful vulnerability had just completely sucked him in. It couldn't be faked, could it?

He eased himself slowly out of his chair. No. She certainly would have been afraid then, and with good reason. She was a fugitive, running to escape the police for a violent crime, and her picture—this picture—was everywhere. He leaned over with a muted grunt and picked up the newspaper and the damning photo, and held them side by side. How could he have missed it? Yet even now these did not appear to be pictures of the same person, even beyond the obviously different hair. One was a happy, open person, and the other was very much closed, haunted, and hurting. One girl was lighthearted and carefree, while the other was serious, desperate to escape a horrific past. He searched the clear, intelligent eyes staring out from each photo. Neither had the look of a brutal, gun-toting killer.

Yet if she were a gun-toting killer, so many things over the last few weeks fell neatly into place. She had reacted strangely, he remembered, when the story of this old crime first broke. And now that he thought more about it, that was the beginning of all of the weirdness lately. She'd explained it away by saying she'd dated one of those guys. Maybe that really was true. The fact was, Charlie had no idea what was true and what was not. All of their life together could be a lie. Everything. But he could not believe that. And not just because it would break his heart to do so.

Why could she not have told him? Maybe not right at first, because she didn't know him, but at some point in their life together they had built up enough trust for her to be honest with him. Sometime in the last 37 years, couldn't she have found the time, found an appropriate moment to tell her life partner the truth about herself? Certainly sometime in the past few weeks, when he was tormented with worry and jealously she could have put him out of his misery. It would have been the decent, considerate thing to do. If she truly cared about him. Which she did, of course. But she didn't trust him enough to be honest. He wiped at damp eyes. Why didn't she trust him?

Charlie looked from the photo to the newspaper, the two images of his wife. Obviously, he had to confront her. He pulled a brown leather portfolio from underneath his desk and slid the newspaper and photo into it. He would see what she had to say about it— maybe there really was some sort of good, or reasonable at least, explanation. Maybe…she had an evil twin, or something. Oh god, he was pathetic.

He lifted car keys from a hook on the wall, turned and surveyed the papers and photos strewn about. That mess would have to wait; this other mess was far more urgent. Through a window, Charlie glimpsed the tail end of a car turning into the small parking lot outside his studio. He frowned. He had no appointments right now, and no time for a walk-in, sorry. He opened the door and peered out, squinting in the bright midday sun. Damn. A Morrisville police cruiser with Bob Sifert stepping out from behind the wheel. A knot of dread wrenched Charlie's stomach. Why was he here?

"Charlie!" Bob called out cheerily as he approached the open door where Charlie waited. "How's it going?"

Charlie exhaled heavily. *Maybe it's nothing.* He raised a hand in greeting. "Hi Bob."

Bob sauntered leisurely up to Charlie. "You got a minute?"

"I uh, I was just on my way out."

"Just take a minute," Bob shrugged. "It's important. It's about Annie."

Charlie gaped, speechless, felt the blood drain from his face.

"Oh no," Bob said hastily, "there hasn't been an accident, or anything like that. She's fine, as far as we know."

Charlie nodded slowly. "Then...what?"

"Well, do you know where she is?"

Charlie blinked. "At work."

Bob shook his round head. "She called in sick today."

Charlie squinted, confused. "Sick? Are you sure?"

Bob nodded. "Yeah. I was over there this morning. The girl in the office there tried her home phone and her cell; no answer at either. I just came from your house, and she's not there either."

"Well, I can't imagine," Charlie said, genuinely puzzled. "Maybe she went to a doctor? But I don't know. She would have told me if it was something that serious. I think." He looked quizzically at his friend. "Bob, what's going on? Why are you looking for her?"

Bob met his gaze. "Can I come in?"

Charlie took a deep breath, released it slowly. "It's a mess in there. But yeah, sure." He backed away from the door and back into the studio, leaving Bob to follow.

"Whoa," Bob whistled, looking around, "you weren't kidding about the mess."

"I was looking for something, and I got a little...frustrated, I guess."

Bob shrugged his eyebrows. "I guess." He waded through the papers strewn about the floor, glancing at them as he walked. He stopped and turned, and as he did so, Charlie saw near his right foot one of the old photos he had taken of Annie on the bench. It was partially obscured by a manila envelope, but her eyes peered up through the mess, daring to be discovered.

A cold sheen of sweat erupted on Charlie's forehead. "So. Talk to me."

Bob slid a hand over his thinning hair. "It's a weird one Charlie. We think we may have an ID on the woman who died in your yard. We got a call from a nurse at Mass. General in Boston. She saw the license photo of the dead woman in the paper today and recognized her as a visitor in the hospital Monday night—the night before she was found in your yard. She was looking for that guy who confessed to a robbery/murder in 1969—you probably saw that in the papers? A group of five of them, four of them never caught? Anyway, a person matching this same description apparently visited an elderly woman in Dunlee Mill, who she identified as Pamela Mercurio, another alleged perpetrator in the '69 crime. So we think it's the same person."

Charlie leaned heavily against the wall. *He knows.* "What," he said hoarsely, "does all this have to do with Annie?"

"So this Pamela Mercurio," Bob continued, "grew up in Dunlee Mill, and she and her best friend, a Lucinda Whittendon, were both involved—allegedly—in the crime. And the elderly woman who she visited is Catherine Whittendon, Lucinda's mother. We're still waiting for verification that the woman from the hospital is Pamela Mercurio. There's an officer in Dunlee Mill waiting for Catherine Whittendon to return and positively ID the license photo."

Charlie pressed his lips together. *He's fishing. Looking for a reaction from me.*

"So, what it comes back to Charlie, is Pamela Mercurio decided to commit suicide in your yard. She grew up just a few towns away, but she came here, and chose your yard to die in. And we're just wondering if maybe Annie might know her. You know, and not even realize it. Maybe she knew her a long time ago; Pamela has changed quite a bit over the years. So I just wanted to show her a younger picture and see if it sparked anything."

"Oh, well, you know Annie saw those pictures in the news when they were printed a few weeks ago. And she never said anything to me about recognizing any of them. She would definitely have told me."

"Yeah, um…here's the thing, Charlie," Bob said uneasily. "Remember how I told you that Pamela Mercurio had started using a dead girl's identity in late 1969? Well, we ran a check on Annie, and—"

"You did what?"

"And you too, because she was found in your yard. Pretty standard to check you both out. Of course I didn't expect to find anything. But the thing is, Ann Stabler, who married Charles Pulkowski in 1970, didn't exist before 1969." Bob looked somberly at his friend. "Same time frame as the dead woman, Charlie."

Charlie's knees buckled under him and he sank into a chair. "I know," he said, "about the false identity."

Bob swallowed, cocked his head. "You do?"

Charlie looked at him. "I got it for her. She...had run away from home, which was somewhere in New York state, to escape an abusive stepfather. I went to this guy, this kid on campus who could get stuff like that. She was really...damaged." He steadied his gaze on his friend. "She has a sad secret in her past, Bob, but she wasn't involved with those people. I can't believe you thought she was."

Bob pressed out a deep breath. "Wow. I had no idea. I'm sorry. Well, that certainly changes things. But you know, I'd still like to talk to her. Fact is, it's a weird coincidence that the dead woman in your yard got a new identity same time as Annie. Charlie," he pressed his lips together uncomfortably, "any chance she was lying to you back then?"

"No!" Charlie said. "No way. I know my wife, Bob. You know her too, for God's sake. You know she couldn't do something like that."

"No. No, course not. I um, well, when she turns up, could you have her give me a call? I'd still like to ask her about it."

"Yeah. Sure. No problem."

"Um, just for the record, what was her real name? You know, maybe I can verify her history and get it all cleared up."

Charlie smirked unkindly. "The stepfather's name was Joseph Carter, but hers, I don't remember. She told me once, but it was a long time ago. She didn't talk about her family at all. She really wanted to forget all that. She was just in so much pain." He looked down at his hands, then met the policeman's cool stare. "It's not her, Bob. It couldn't be her."

"Joseph Carter," Bob muttered, scribbling in a small notebook. "And you said New York state. Any town name, or anything? "

"No. I honestly don't think she ever told me."

"Yeah, okay. I'll look into it. I'm sure we'll get it all cleared up. In the meantime, what about your daughter? Could Annie have gone to see her?"

"Well, sure, I guess. Darlene has a way of needing help often." He shrugged. "It's possible."

"All right," Bob said, heading for the door. "It's all going to work out, Charlie. I just got to check all this stuff out. But I'm sure you're right; it'll turn out to be nothing." He stopped with his hand on the doorknob. "I should probably tell you, there's some detective from New York on his way up here, because of the connection to this open case for them. It would be nice if Annie could talk to me before he got here. You know, friend to friend. Probably easier for her."

Charlie eyed his friend coldly. "Yeah. Of course."

He watched Bob through the window as the officer climbed back into his cruiser and drove away.

Damn! Bob knew the truth. And he probably knew Charlie was lying. So when he found Annie, would he arrest her? For being this other person four decades ago?

Where was Annie? Not at work, not at home, not answering her phone. Well, maybe not answering her phone for them, but she would for Charlie. He grabbed the phone off his desk and pressed speed dial one. Holding the receiver to his ear, he listened to the repeated rings, then the automated voice inviting him to leave a voice message. Dammit! He tossed the phone irritably onto the desktop.

Charlie strode across the studio in a few large paces, kicking papers and photographs along the way. He glared at the phone from across the room. Maybe she had gone to Darlene's and was in the middle of some Darlene crisis. He retrieved the phone and dialed Darlene's cell phone. No answer. Which could be significant, or not. Damn, it was so frustrating. He had no idea where to look, no idea who to call. Annie wasn't close to many people; she tended to keep most people at arms length. But...Charlie riffled through a small rolodex, then stopped and pulled a card from the pack. He tapped numbers into his phone and waited.

"Hello," came a husky voice through the line.

Charlie cleared his throat. "Hi Jarvis. It's Charlie Pulkowski."

"Oh," Jarvis said. "Charlie. Hello."

"Jarvis, I um, I'm looking for Annie. I know she called in sick today, but I thought, I don't know why but I thought you might know where she is."

A steady nothingness replied in Charlie's ear. "Jarvis? You there?"

"Yeah," Jarvis' voice was slightly raspy. "Yeah, I'm here. I... where are you?"

"At my studio. Why?"

"I thought you might have been with her."

Charlie looked at the phone, puzzled. "You thought I was with her where? Do you know where she is?"

"No," Jarvis breathed heavily. "But I think she's running."

"Running?"

"I think," Jarvis said slowly, "she did something. Really bad. And now she's got to run."

Charlie swallowed hard, his face burning. *How did Jarvis know? And what would he do about it?*

Amber peered out through the shallow bay window in the living room. The old lady was still there in the yard, waiting. She was definitely kind of weird, but what harm would it do to let her see a picture of Nonny? Maybe she really was an old friend, and Nonny would be happy to see her. That would be fun.

She looked at the framed photo in her hand, rubbed at the dust on the glass and went outside, closing the front door tightly behind her. The old woman looked up hopefully as Amber walked toward her. "I know she used to have one from when she and Grampa got married," Amber said, "but I couldn't find it. This one is pretty old, though."

The old lady's hands shook so badly as she reached for the picture Amber was afraid she would drop it. Wrinkled, knobby fingers gripped the wooden frame tightly as she turned her cloudy gray eyes on the image behind the glass. "Ohhh," she whimpered. "Oh, dear Lord." The woman's legs swayed and crumbled under her, the weight of her body falling against Amber.

"Oh my god!" Amber said, struggling to hold the small, flopping body from hitting the ground. "Oh my god, what's the matter? Don't have a heart attack right here, lady. What am I supposed to do?"

The woman clawed at Amber's arms, holding on desperately, trying to pull herself upright.

"Come on," Amber said. "Get up." she slid an arm under the woman's shoulders and steered her over to the concrete steps leading up to the front door. With difficulty, she eased the woman down onto the second step, so that she was sitting upright. "You okay?" Amber asked, keeping her arm around the woman's back until she was sure the woman could sit on her own.

Amber stood over the woman, panting slightly. "You going to be okay?"

"Yes. Thank you. I'm sorry dear. I was just…"

"That's quite a reaction. I thought you were going to be like, happy if Nonny was your old friend."

"I am happy." She looked up at Amber intently. "I'm so happy it's terrifying."

"Yeah, well, this is all so weird, now you're like, terrifying me. Are you sure Nonny will be happy to see you?"

"I think she will. Yes." The old lady nodded. "Where is she now?"

Amber hesitated, glanced at her watch. "At work."

"Where is that?"

"In Springfield."

"Can we go there? I have a car."

"You can go there. I'll give you directions."

"I don't know my way around Springfield at all. I could really use your help to direct me."

Amber shook her head emphatically. "Oh no. I am definitely not allowed to get in cars with strangers. You know what? I'll just call her. Tell her you're here. She can decide what to do."

"No! No, I'd really like to see her in person. Surprise her, you know?"

"Well, I'm sorry, but those are your choices. I can give you directions, or I can call her. But I'm not getting in a car with someone I don't know."

The old lady smiled suddenly. "What's your name, honey?"

Amber scowled. "Amber."

"I'm Catherine."

"Knowing each other's names isn't like, really knowing each other."

Catherine nodded as she pushed herself up to standing. "I know. But I want to show you something." She reached into her large brown leather handbag and rummaged about. "Here, Amber," she said, "look at this."

Amber took from the woman a photograph. It was old, black-and-white, and slightly faded. It was of a pretty girl with long blond hair, not much older than herself. Why was this old lady showing this to her? Amber raised quizzical eyes at her.

"Look closely," Catherine said. "And compare it to your picture you just gave me. The hair is different, but look at the faces."

Amber squinted from one photo to the other. "This is Nonny? Really? How old was she?"

"She must have been about sixteen, there, I think."

Amber examined the elderly woman skeptically. "Well, you weren't girlfriends. You're like, way older than her. No offense."

Catherine smiled. "You're right. Here," she said, pulling another small photo from her purse. "Here I am with her in this one."

Amber took the picture and examined it. It was a family photo. The same girl as in the other picture, at about the same age. Two brothers, one a tall, gangly teenager, the other short and slightly pudgy. And two parents smiling broadly in the center of it all, arms around their brood. Amber looked up sharply at Catherine. "Oh my god. You're her mother?"

Catherine's face shone, her mouth clamped in a hopeful smile as she nodded a yes.

Amber backed away, dismay overtaking her face. "Oh my god. She's not going to want to see you. You shouldn't have come here."

The old woman's eyes clouded with pain, sadness. "Why do you say that?" New, full tears threatened to spill, and her voice was a barely audible whimper. "Why?"

"Because you didn't help her," Amber said with contempt. "She was your daughter and you just let her suffer alone. Why didn't you help her?"

Catherine looked confused. "How could I help her? I didn't know where she was. She ran away and I had no idea how to find her. I would have done anything—"

"I mean before!" Amber shouted. "When she was still living with you. You didn't protect her; you just let it happen!"

"What are you talking about? Let what happen?"

Amber shoved the family photograph at Catherine's face. "Him! You just let him happen to her! This is him, isn't it? The evil stepfather? And you, the pathetic mother who let him get away with it. Just leave! I'm not even going to tell her you were here. She's tried all her life to forget you all."

"No," Catherine's head shook vigorously. "No, that's not right. She never had a stepfather. I was married to the same man for sixty-four years, until he passed away last year. And he was a wonderful father, and never did anything bad to any of his children. We," she sobbed, "we were a happy family!"

"Well," Amber said, "Maybe you've got the wrong person, then."

"No," Catherine said. "I don't have the wrong person." She

shuffled over to the stairs and eased herself back down to sitting. She let her face fall into her hands for a moment, then looked up at Amber. "I didn't have any right to come here," she said quietly. "Lu —your Nonny, created something here with you, with this new family. And just being here, I'm destroying it."

"So what are you saying? Nonny made up that whole story about an abusive stepfather? No. She wouldn't do that. Why would anyone do that?"

"Because the truth was even worse."

"How could anything be worse than that?"

"I should go. You're right not to tell her I was here."

"No. You can't just go after telling me all this. I want to know the truth."

"It's not my truth to tell."

"You just told part of it already. You told me Nonny's lied to us all these years. And we have a right to know the truth. My mom has a right, and I do." Amber stopped, hesitated before continuing. "She told us that this horrible stepfather of hers was my mom's real father. My real grandfather. But if you're right, then I have like, some other grandfather out there. Maybe someone who's not so terrible." Amber turned with her own tears beginning to form. "I don't have a dad. And I don't see my mom much. All I really have is Nonny and Grampa. And they're great. The best, both of them. But it's such a small family, you know? If there's more out there…"

"There is more out there. And there's more right here."

Amber's eyes widened as she grasped the significance of this woman sitting before her. "Great-grandma. Wow." Amber smiled uncomfortably. "Wow. That's like, huge."

Catherine nodded, unable to suppress her own weepy smile. "It is incredibly huge."

———

Jarvis was waiting for him. As Charlie drove up to his house, he could see the blue FROGS van out front and the hefty bulk of

Jarvis leaning against it. He had refused to tell Charlie anything more over the phone, since he might be wrong, he'd said. He wanted to meet here, so Charlie could see if there were signs of Annie leaving in the house. Charlie pulled into his driveway and climbed out quickly as Jarvis strode up to him.

"Charlie," Jarvis said, thrusting his hand forward in greeting.

Charlie shook the proffered hand, his own hand disappearing into Jarvis' huge beefy one. He had forgotten just how large this man was.

"How you doing?" Jarvis asked with real sincerity.

Charlie examined Jarvis' face closely. *What do you know?* "I'm worried."

"I know. I hope I'm wrong." He exhaled loudly. "But I don't think I am."

Charlie eyed the big man skeptically. If Jarvis intended to turn Annie in to the authorities, there was no way Charlie was going to help him by offering any information. On the other hand, it could prove helpful to find out what Jarvis knew. "Why do you think she's run away?"

Jarvis squinted uneasily. "I could be way off base."

Charlie regarded him silently. "Maybe." He turned and walked up the path to the house, unlocked the front door and turned back to see Jarvis still standing in the driveway. "Well, come in."

Jarvis hesitated, then nodded and followed Charlie into the house. The dark, warm wood furniture in the living room shimmered softly in the dull late afternoon light that floated in dappled currents through the large bay window. Charlie dropped his leather case onto the couch and turned to face Jarvis. "If you know something, tell me."

Jarvis turned to stare out the oversized window into the front yard. "I wrestled all morning with whether or not to call you. I kind of thought you must know, and were helping her get away." He turned toward Charlie. "The dead woman that was found in your yard. It wasn't a coincidence. I saw her picture on the morning news, the day before they ran it in the newspaper, and I recognized her. I couldn't remember from where at first, but then...Annie knows her, Charlie. I'm sure of it." He rested his frame on the windowsill and laced his fingers over his belly. "A few weeks ago, Annie and I were on our way back from Stockbridge and we stopped for some food. That woman was there, and when Annie saw her, she just lost it. The two of them stared at each other like a couple of ghosts. Ghosts that hated each other." Jarvis stopped, hesitated. When he spoke, his voice was quiet, strained. "She must have done it."

Charlie looked up sharply. "Done what?"

"She was scared of that woman, Charlie. It was obvious. I mean, I know, it's Annie. She must have had what seemed like a good reason. But still."

"You think Annie *killed* that woman? No! No way. You're crazy!" Charlie glared at the bigger man. "It was a suicide, Jarvis. The police are sure about that."

Jarvis shook his head sadly. "I wasn't sure. And I knew if I asked her about it, she'd just deny it, and if I was wrong, it would ruin our friendship forever. So I sent her a note. Anonymously. It said, I know what you did." He met Charlie's glare. "I made sure to be there to see her open it so I could watch her reaction. If she wasn't guilty, she would have just laughed the note off as weird, or tossed it away as trash. But Charlie, she panicked. She went white as a sheet; I thought she was going to faint. And then she went flying out of there like she was being chased.

"It's hard to believe," Jarvis continued, "it's Annie, for god's sake. But she's feeling guilty about something. And now she's disappeared. She's definitely running."

Charlie slumped against the back of the couch, dizziness swirling in his head. Could Jarvis be right? It was one thing for Annie to have done something all those years ago. You could assume she deeply regretted it, based on how she'd lived the rest of her life. But now? Could she have done such a terrible thing just a few days ago? Maybe this woman had threatened to blow her cover, to go to the authorities. Maybe Annie had to stop her. No.

This could not be true. Less than an hour ago, he'd thought he'd learned the worst. But this, if it was true, was more devastating than he could bear.

"Maybe," Jarvis interrupted his thoughts, "you should check to see if her suitcase is gone, any of her belongings. Because, you know, maybe I'm wrong."

Charlie felt his head to be heavily weighted, turning in slow motion. "Yeah. Right." He heaved himself upright and shuffled down the hallway to the bedroom he shared with Annie. He stood in the doorway and peered in, afraid to step inside to see what might be seen. The bed was neatly made, closet doors and dresser drawers all closed as they always were, and everything looked just fine and dandy. Perfectly normal, nothing wrong. Could he not just stay here in the doorway and believe that nothing was wrong?

He pressed forward into the room and stopped in front of Annie's knotty pine dresser, the top covered with a neat array of small jewelry boxes, bottles of lotions and perfumes, a box of tissues. He sighed. He would not know if anything was missing or not. He pulled open a large drawer halfway down. Same thing. The drawer was about half-full of sweaters, but he did not know if that was normal. He closed the drawer and approached the closet he shared with his wife. He pulled open the double doors and felt his heart deflate in a sad gasp. The left side of the closet—Annie's side —was drastically more empty than normal. A few dresses and silk blouses hung alone on wire hangers, abandoned. And the gray tweed suitcase that lived in the back corner on the floor; gone. She was gone.

Charlie sank heavily onto the edge of the bed. She was really gone. He looked skeptically into the closet. She did still keep the suitcase in that corner, didn't she? Yes. Annie was a creature of habit; that suitcase had been there for years and would not move except for a good reason. Like it was in use.

"Charlie." Jarvis' voice called from the living room. "You find anything?"

Charlie exhaled deeply. Jarvis. What the hell was he supposed to do about Jarvis? Jarvis actually thought Annie killed that woman. Was he right? Would he now go to the police with his theory? If so, then why come to Charlie first? He didn't; Charlie had called him. Jarvis didn't seem to know the real identity of either Annie or the dead woman. Charlie covered his face with his hands. Knowing who they were, didn't that make it even more likely that Annie would have had motive to kill her? But it was Annie! It was *Annie*! How could Jarvis even think like that? It was his sweet, wonderful Annie. Charlie pressed fingertips into his eye sockets until tiny white lights of static clouded his vision. That was just it, though, wasn't it? She wasn't Annie.

CHAPTER 31

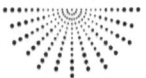

I have told her everything. Everything except how it all relates to her. Darlene sits beside me in the Prius as I drive west on the Mass. Pike, toward a blinding sun low in the sky. My daughter is utterly silent as she considers me. I do not think she believes this fantastic story I have told. She has not said a word since I stopped speaking several moments ago. I do not blame her. She cannot possibly recognize the overblown character from this farcical tale. It is no one she knows.

"I don't shock easy," Darlene says finally. "But I think, Mom, we're both going to be locked away in hospitals. Me in rehab, and you in the psycho ward."

"I know it seems unbelievable."

"No seems about it. There is no way you could have done all that. You don't have it in you to do anything like that."

"I don't. But she does."

"She who? You just said you did it."

"I did. She is me. Or was me."

"Yeah. Mental hospital. I think we should call Charlie."

"You don't think people can change over time? You're much different now than when you were nineteen."

"Not so much, really."

"Sure you are. You were much more hopeful then. You had bigger dreams than just staying sober."

"I have bigger dreams now!"

"I'm sorry. This is not at all about you." Even now, in the midst of my grand confession, we fall into our old habits of antagonism. I own the blame for that. "This is about my character flaws, which are much bigger and worse than yours."

Darlene flinched, her eyes growing wide. "I don't even know how to respond to that. You've never said anything like that. You don't even seem like you."

"That's what I'm trying to say. The person I've been all these years is not who I am."

"In reality," Darlene's words drip with sarcasm, "you're a renegade, anti-war activist, bank-robbing killer."

I do not answer this. I do not need to. "Darlene," I say, "there is more I have to say, to tell you. And I do not in any way intend it to be a defense of my actions. But it is the truth, and I must finally tell it.

"In those early days, I was so frightened. Scared of getting caught, of course, but also terrified and horrified at what I had done. I was scared of myself. Afraid to be me, if that's what me was capable of. So I tried not to be me. I pulled back from, and out of the world. I had to watch every word I uttered. If I didn't think before I spoke, I could let slip some tiny bit of information that could condemn me. I created the story of Annie, and then I was stuck in it." I stop for a breath, for strength. "But I was learning it myself, and I needed to dispassionately assess every situation, every word I spoke, so it would not contradict some other previously revealed detail about Annie. I had to train myself to lose any spontaneity; impulsiveness was much too dangerous. And the truth is, I felt safer being Annie, because Lucinda was such a monster. I was afraid Charlie would find out I was her, but mostly I was terrified that I actually was her."

I maneuver the Prius into the slow lane to the right so I may focus less on driving and more on my confession. Darlene watches me, her eyes steady, lips pressed tightly together. "All of my energy I poured into becoming Annie. I remember the stress, the constant pressure to not say the wrong thing. I had to become Annie. To evade the authorities, to get Charlie to love me, to allow me not to hate myself. I am not sure I succeeded in that last part. In any case, I think I just did not have anything left over." I steal a glance at my daughter. "Perhaps I was incapable of being a good mother; certainly Lucinda is no role model for a child. But Annie had nothing left to mother with. It was too much effort just to be her. And eventually, I did become her. Unemotional, cautious, guarded. Annie was safe."

A squeak of skin against vinyl interrupts as Darlene shifts abruptly in her seat. She no longer watches me but stares straight ahead through the windshield. "I loved you. With all my heart I loved you. And love you still. You were a sweet, adorable child. And it broke my heart that you could never know your real family. Or your real mother, even. Every holiday or birthday, which we often spent with Charlie's parents, I felt a gaping hole where my family should have been. I missed them so horribly! My parents would have adored you, just as Charlie's did. And I felt shame and guilt at denying you each the pleasure of knowing one another."

I am crying now, so badly that I am forced to pull the car to the side of the road. I put the car into park, and I look at my once-lovely daughter. "I have made a mess of things, Darlene. I have ruined so many lives. They all torment me; those that are dead, and those that survive. But perhaps the one that tortures me most is you. My own child. The most unforgivable of the indefensible."

She watches me cry for a long while. When she speaks, her voice is hushed, airy, and I can barely hear it. "Who," she says, "is my father?"

I am not done yet, I realize. I still have much to tell her.

"This story," Darlene says impatiently, "about the stepfather, was just a story. So who is my father? Really?

I wipe the tears from my face with the heels of my hands and try to smile as I face her. "His name was Michael Strickland. He was handsome and idealistic and charismatic. He was a good man."

She blinks, and I see tears brimming in her own eyes. "So…you didn't hate him?" she says. "Or me."

"What? Of course not! How could you think that?"

"I thought, especially since you told me about the stepfather, I thought you didn't want me. Because I came from a rape."

This lands with an excruciating thump in my chest. *What have I done?* "Darlene. Oh sweetheart, I am so sorry—"

"Where is Michael Strickland now?"

"I'm afraid he just died recently. You may have heard about it in the news; he was one of our group that committed the robbery."

"So I'm the product of two criminals." It is matter-of-fact, without self-pity.

"Michael was a good man," I say again. "He drove the car. He didn't carry a gun and he believed ours weren't loaded. He had no idea this could happen."

"But you knew the guns were loaded?"

I exhale heavily, forcing myself to meet her gaze again. "I did."

She watches me for a long moment, as though waiting for me to offer something else in my own defense. But there is nothing to say.

"So where are we going?" Darlene says finally, nodding toward the highway beyond the windshield.

I shift the car into gear and ease it back onto the road. "Kelsey, New York. You're facing your demons, and now I need to face mine. And I need you."

"Me? *You* need *me*?"

My daughter does not yet know what I am about to do or how much it frightens me. "Yes," I say quietly. "I need you, Darlene."

———

Catherine drove, as was proper, with both hands on the steering wheel and eyes straight ahead on the road, except when she darted them to the side to steal quick little glances at this newfound great-granddaughter. Absolutely thrilling, spine-tingling, goosebump-inducingly delightful, she thought, turning toward Amber once more—and was caught by the girl staring back at her.

"You look nothing like Nonny," Amber said bluntly.

"Neither do you," Catherine shot back. But the words were defensive, she knew, and not entirely accurate. "Actually," she said, "there is something, maybe around the mouth, something in you that very much reminds me of your grandmother."

Amber pressed her lips together self-consciously. "So, my mom knew Grampa's parents," she said. "They had holidays together and stuff. But they both died before I was born. And I know Grampa had a brother who died like, really young. But that's it for relatives. Nonny would never talk about her family. And Grampa said not to ask her, that it just made her sad. Take a right at that light," she pointed through the windshield. "So you don't know who my real —biologically speaking—grandfather is?"

Catherine switched on the blinker signal and a loud clicking filled the car. "I don't. I'm sorry."

"You wouldn't tell me anyway."

"I would prefer that your grandmother tell you," she admitted, slowing to a stop at the red light.

"Is her name really Annie?"

Catherine hesitated. "No."

"And you're not going to tell me what it is."

Catherine turned sideways in her seat to face Amber. "Is my daughter happy? Has she been, all these years? Is her husband, Charlie, you said, is he good to her?"

"He's great—to everybody. He's the absolute best. And yeah, I think she's been happy. They laugh a lot, they seem really close, like they understand each other. Except these last few weeks. Nonny's been like, really weird, and Grampa's definitely bothered by it." Amber's eyes narrowed, scrutinizing Catherine. "And then this dead person pops up in our yard, and then you show up. All this is related, somehow, right? Something happened to make her act so weird and all this other stuff happen."

Catherine turned back toward the windshield. "Will we be there soon?"

"We're there," Amber huffed. "Couple more blocks."

Across the street from the FROGS office, Catherine bumped and lurched her way through a parallel parking job until Amber said she thought they were close enough.

Catherine stopped and looked out the side window past Amber. "Are you sure? How close are we?"

Amber opened the door and looked out. "Just a few…yards. It's fine. Really."

"I don't know," Catherine said, but Amber had already gotten out so she did the same. "Oh, for crying out loud," she exclaimed as she considered the nose of her silver Buick jutting out into the road. "It's sticking way out. And look how crooked."

Amber shrugged, nodding in agreement. "Come on. Let's go see Nonny."

Catherine allowed Amber to take her arm and gently steer her across the street. "I don't get much practice parallel parking, you know."

"It's okay. You did fine."

"What is this place?" Catherine asked, reading the words on the FROGS door. "Some sort of food bank, or something?"

"Yup." Amber pulled open the heavy glass door and held it, allowing Catherine to go in ahead of her.

A pretty blonde woman looked up from behind a desk. "Can I help you?"

"Yes," Catherine said. "We're looking for, um," she turned to Amber for help.

"My grandmother," Amber said. "Annie Pulkowski."

"Oh. Hi. Amber, right? I didn't recognize you. I'm Lindsey, remember? Your grandma's not here. She called in sick today."

"Sick?"

"Yeah, kind of weird. And then…there was a cop here looking for her. Even weirder."

"Oh, dear Lord," Catherine said.

Amber's eyes grew big as they looked from one woman to the other, settling finally on Catherine. "What is going on?"

"Did…did they find her?" Catherine asked Lindsey, her voice hoarse.

"I don't know," Lindsey said. "I called her cell phone while they were here, but there was no answer. And then, I tried a few more times since they left, but still, nothing. It's like she's turned it off."

Amber continued to stare at Catherine. "Why are the police looking for Nonny?"

Catherine looked intently at her great-granddaughter. "Where else might she have gone? To see your grandfather, maybe? Where is he?"

Amber folded her arms across her chest. "*Why*," she demanded, "are the police looking for Nonny?"

Catherine glanced over at Lindsey. A nice girl, she seemed, but not family. "Come," she said quietly to Amber. "I'll explain while we're driving."

"Is Nonny in trouble?"

Catherine met Amber's worried look with anxious eyes of her own. "Maybe," she breathed. "I think so."

Jarvis watched Charlie shuffle despondently down the hall toward him. This man was crushed, devastated. He clearly had not expected her to run. But how much did he know about everything else? About the dead woman in his yard, about why Annie had to kill her, if she did in fact kill her? "Her stuff gone?"

Charlie looked at up him, a heaviness in his face. "Are you going to turn her in?"

Jarvis spread his arms wide. "Why would I do that?"

"You think Annie killed that woman in our yard. Annie always says you're all about justice and doing the right thing. What's the right thing to do?"

"I don't know what's the right thing to do. But I know that the right thing is not always easy to recognize. And justice is very often not what the law says it is." Jarvis shifted his bulk from one foot to the other. "Annie is my friend. I've known her for a long time. She's a good person. *If* she really did kill that woman, well, I don't know, there must have been a reason. Maybe that was justice in some way."

Misery crossed Charlie's face as he looked warily at the bigger man. He opened his mouth to speak, hesitated, and began again. "What," he asked hoarsely, "if it was just to avoid getting caught for another crime?"

"Oh, Jesus," Jarvis breathed. "What did you find?"

Charlie walked over to the leather portfolio he had dropped on the couch earlier. He pulled out the newspaper and his old print of Annie and handed both to Jarvis. "I took this picture of Annie years ago, the day I met her." Jarvis took the photo and newspaper and looked at them silently for a moment, then eased himself down onto a chair.

"Holy. Shit."

Bobby grunted as he forced the faux wood-paneled accordion door off its broken track. "Don't see why this can't wait until after the game." The door came off with a jolt and Bobby lurched backward, thudding hard against the corner of the kitchen table. "Godammit!"

The heavy wood table skidded on the floor and the yellow ceramic bowl of apples atop it wobbled noisily. Dim late afternoon sunlight flickered weakly through gauzy white curtains over the dark wood cabinets of the kitchen. Angela frowned at the long metal piece in her hand. "Do you think this new track will fit? It looks like it was made for smaller wheels."

Bobby glared at her, wide-eyed. "What, are you kidding? I can't do this no more. My back!"

Angela reached out a hand and massaged her son's back absently. "It'll be fine. Just a bruise. Take more than that to put a man like you down."

A brief smile played across his face, then quickly disappeared. "That flattery bullshit ain't going to work on me."

Angela smiled. "It's true, isn't it? Nothing wrong with flattery if it's true." She held the new track out to him. "You're almost done. That was the hard part."

"Ma. That was the easy part. The hard part's putting it back together." He took the track from her and set in on the table. "I'll finish the rest of it later. Dean's coming over any minute to watch the game."

"Good, he can help you." She picked the track up and handed it back to him. "It'll go faster with both of you working. And then, you know what? I'll make up some of my buffalo wings for you boys to have during the game."

"Really?"

"Sure. They'll be ready by halftime."

Bobby smirked down at his mother. "There's no halftime in baseball, Ma."

"Oh. Really?" She shrugged. "Well, whenever the halfway mark is. An hour or so."

He nodded, licked his lips. "How about some chili too? And mac and cheese."

"I'll see what I can do." Angela waved a hand at the broken door. "See how much you can inspire me."

Bobby pursed his lips. "That's bribery."

"Yup."

Three loud knocks sounded on the front door. "That's Dean," Bobby said, turning toward the door.

"I'll get it," Angela laid a hand on her son's chest, steering him back toward the broken kitchen door. "Next week," she said, walking through the living room, "you're replacing this broken window." She leaned over the window next to the door, pulled aside the curtain and peered out through the cracked glass at the two strangers standing outside on the front stoop. *Who on earth?*

The rural greenery of upstate New York has given way to dusty roads and tiny, tired dwellings here in the town of Kelsey. There is a dreary sadness in these streets, as though the entire town has lost hope, given up on dreams. Darlene stares out the window silently, as though she, too, pities this place.

We are almost at our destination and I feel one more confession bursting through the seams of my conscience. I find a strange comfort and strength in admitting all my flaws and errors, in tearing down my perfect wall. Perhaps it is just the relief of no longer pretending, but it seems that the truth possesses a power of its own.

"There were many times," I say, then hesitate, "I thought about taking the same way out as Pam."

Darlene turns to me and shakes her head adamantly. "No way. You didn't think about that. You would never do anything like that. It would never even cross your mind."

"I *think*," I say with an emphasis I can not aptly express, "about everything."

Darlene challenges me with a look of skepticism.

"But you're right," I admit. "I would never do that. And it has nothing to do with right or wrong, or sending a message to my family. It's that I do not deserve to be granted such an easy way out. Life under my great guilt is my penance for those deaths."

She says nothing to this but drops her head back onto the seat heavily.

"I think," I say as the thought forms in my head, "maybe that's why I've been so hard on your mistakes. It was my own guilt I couldn't tolerate, and I took it out on you."

"You did tolerate your guilt. You lived with it for almost 40 years."

"Badly, though. Look what it's done to me. To you."

Again, she says nothing, and I feel the sting of her silence harsher than any words.

I slow the Prius to peer at a twisted street sign. "Is this the street we want?"

Darlene consults the directions scribbled on the back of an envelope that we got from the little shack they called the Kelsey Post Office. "Yeah," she says. "And then Elworth Road is the second left."

I turn the car onto Elworth Road and we bump along the rutted dirt path, past faded houses set back into the woods. The few homes on this street are all tiny, each comprising no more than two or three small rooms. Number seventeen does not stand apart from the rest in any significant way. Dingy yellow paint peels off its clapboard siding and the glass in one of the two front windows flaunts a jagged diagonal crack. Any semblance of a lawn that may once have existed is reduced to a scattering of sickly weeds sprouting from the ashy dirt. Off to the side, a rough assortment of small animal pelts hang drying on a tattered clothesline.

Now that I am here, finally, I find I cannot move. My body is suddenly heavy, anchored to the seat by a cold, leaden terror. Nausea churns in my gut; a tinny echo swells in my ears. Even the smallest breath seems a great effort.

Darlene stares at me, waiting. "Are we just here to look?"

"I'm scared," I whisper, and this first naked honesty toward my daughter startles and confuses me. I do not know who just said that, Annie or Lucinda. I do not know who I must be now, for this task, and the indecision paralyzes me. Inside that house is a lonely old woman who I have harmed, yet I am terrified of her.

"We drove all this way," Darlene says, "so you could make your big confession to her."

I feel my daughter's eyes on me, yet I am too cowardly to meet them. This was perhaps not such a good idea. This woman will not want to see me. There is nothing I can say to her to undo the damage I have caused.

"Fine," Darlene says. "If you're not going in there, I'd like to go home now. You've had this on your conscience for thirty-seven years. What's another thirty-seven, right? Let's go."

It is the poppiest of pop-psychology, yet I am unable to ignore the truth in her words. "Come with me."

"I have nothing to say to her," Darlene says, alarmed. "This has nothing to do with me."

"*Please*, Darlene." I do not know why I need her, only that I am unable to find in me a self with which I am familiar. "Please."

She examines me curiously, also unable to find me. "All right," she exhales heavily. "But you're doing all the talking. I'm just there…just to be there."

Outside the safety of the car, I feel exposed and out of place. I do not belong here, in this dusty, sorry neighborhood. The deepening gloom of a fast-approaching evening diffuses the place with an eerie solitude. I am glad Darlene is with me.

We approach the little house together, Darlene's hand resting on my arm, for comfort or as a restraint to keep me from running, I do not know. At the door, Darlene waits a moment for me to knock, but my arm will not move. As she raps on the scarred wooden door, it occurs to me my daughter may be enjoying being the one in control, rendering assistance to me. Perhaps it is good for her.

Within seconds, the blue-striped curtains in the cracked window flutter aside abruptly and a face peers out at us. *I cannot do this!* The old woman's eyes roam over us with suspicion, assessing our threat potential. She has no idea.

Her eyes lock onto mine and hold them, and I feel awkward and intrusive. "Mrs. Dechesney?" I call to her. "Are you Angela Dechesney?"

There is acknowledgment in her face in the instant before it disappears from the window. The door in front of us opens with a quiet click, and Angela Dechesney stands before us. "What do you want?"

The air in my lungs catches and will not release. I feel dizzy and befuddled, and yet I know I must speak. "My name," I say, my voice quivering badly. I stop, inhale deeply, and let the words drop one by one, like a series of punches. "I. Am. Lucinda. Whittendon."

"Tell me what's going on," Amber shouted as she followed Catherine across the street toward the inelegantly parked Buick. "Why is Nonny in trouble? Why are the police looking for her?" She caught Catherine by the arm and spun her around. "Please," she begged. "Please tell me what's going on."

Catherine's eyes softened. "Okay. I will tell you. But let's find her first. Before the police."

Amber sighed. "Okay," she said. "Grampa could be either at his studio or out at a shoot. Give me your cell phone. I'll call him."

"I don't have a cell phone."

"What? How can you not have a cell phone?"

"I never purchased one."

"Everyone has a cell phone."

"You don't, apparently."

"I'm like, thirteen! And anyway, I'm getting one. Nonny says next birthday."

Catherine turned back toward the FROGS office. "Is there a private phone in there we could use?"

Amber raised her eyebrows. "Yeah. In Mr. Chandler's little broom closet office."

Back inside the building, Amber politely asked a bemused Lindsey's permission to use the phone in Jarvis' office. Catherine closed the door behind them and stood, by necessity, within inches of Amber as the girl dialed the telephone.

Amber held the receiver to her ear, listening impatiently to the dull ringing. Finally, Charlie's voice burst through the line. "Hello?" Amber could hear the anxiety in his voice.

"Grampa? Hi."

"Amber? Wha—where are you calling from? Are you all right?"

"Yeah. I'm…is Nonny with you?"

A slight pause. "No. I'm not sure where she is. I'm trying to find her. Where are you?"

"I'm at her office. I think…Grampa, they said the police were here looking for her. I think maybe she's in trouble."

"Yeah, I…what are you doing at her office? How did you get there?"

Amber glanced up at Catherine. "I um, I'm with someone. They have a car."

"Someone? Who are you with?"

Amber exhaled loudly, looked Catherine in the eye. "I'm with…Nonny's mother."

The quiet shush of an empty phone line whispered in her ear. "Grampa? Did you hear me?"

"I…did you say, her mother?"

"Yeah."

"How—?"

"She was at our house when I came home from school. She's looking for Nonny too."

"How do you know she's who she says she is? You got in a car with a stranger?"

"She has pictures. And she knows things, and she's really worried about her. It's really her, Grampa."

A breathy exhale. "Wow. Okay, listen. I'm home right now. Come home. Both of you. Can…can you do that? Will she drive you? Or should I come there?"

"No. We'll come there. Grampa. Do you know what's going on?"

"Just come home, Amber. We'll talk when you get here."

Amber felt her cheeks redden as a silent scream filled her head. *Somebody tell me!* To Charlie, she said, "All right. When I get home, you'll tell me." She hung up the phone and turned to Catherine. "He doesn't know where she is. But he said to come home. Both of us."

Catherine looked grim. "We have to find her. What about your mother? Or friends?"

"Grampa said he's been looking for her too. He must have tried calling everyone."

Catherine's eyes fell shut briefly. "He can't find her? Oh…" the word trailed off somberly. She steadied herself with a hand on Jarvis' oversized chair, then sunk weakly onto its cushion.

"What?" Amber pleaded. "Please tell me what's going on. You promised you would tell me. Please."

Catherine looked wearily up at her. "Your grandmother," she said slowly, "was a bright, shining, beautiful, confident, wonderful girl. Young woman. But she made a mistake. A bad one. And a man died. Your grandmother ran away. And I've never seen her since."

Amber swallowed, her face ashen. "She like, killed someone?"

"She was with some people when they shot a man. So that makes her automatically guilty. Even if she didn't pull the trigger herself. Which…I don't believe…she could have."

"No," Amber's head shook involuntarily. "She couldn't."

"And now," Catherine said, her voice subdued, "if no one can find her, I'm afraid maybe she's running again. I've lost her again."

"Running? Away, you mean? No. She wouldn't run away from us. Not from Grampa and me. We—we're a family. She wouldn't leave us."

Catherine's eyes held both grief and pity. "That's what I thought too."

Charlie paced his living room, fists clenching and unclenching, stopping every now and then to peer out the front window. "I should never have told you."

Jarvis shrugged his bushy eyebrows. "But you did. And Charlie, I know you can't be objective, but you can't ignore the facts either."

"She has lived such a good and decent life since then," Charlie said. "It was a horrible mistake, but she's atoned for it. She's helped so many people over the years. You can't believe she deserves to be locked in a cell."

"If that was the end of it, maybe, although the family of the victim deserves to see justice done. But if she killed that woman just last week…"

"She didn't! The police said it was suicide. They were positive."

"Police make mistakes. And maybe, you know, maybe it was suicide. But if it wasn't," Jarvis hesitated, "if it wasn't, and she's out there on the loose, and she's desperate, and maybe not thinking straight. And if your daughter is with her, she might be in danger."

Charlie gaped in disbelief. "You. Are. Insane. Annie would never hurt Darlene."

"No, I know," Jarvis sighed heavily. "But the fact is, neither of us knows her like we thought we did."

"No. You're wrong. I know her. Inside and out. This old thing," he gestured toward the damning newspaper, "is ancient history. A different person. Lucinda somebody. Annie, I know. Annie did not kill that woman. And she won't hurt Darlene. Or anyone."

"I hope you're right. But do we have the right to just hope?"

"It's not just hope, Jarvis. I know I'm right. Tell me, is Annie stupid, too?"

"No. Of course not."

"So what kind of idiot kills someone and then leaves the body in their own front yard?"

A flicker of doubt crossed Jarvis' face. "Someone who doesn't have the physical strength to move it. She was a big woman, the deceased, and Annie—"

"No, no, no! She didn't do it, Jarvis. She didn't. There was—I saw Annie take something off the body. Before the police got here. Amber said she saw something in the victim's hands, but then it wasn't there when the police got there. It must have been a note, or something. A suicide note."

Jarvis rubbed pudgy fingers over his cheeks. "Maybe. Possibly. But it could also have been—" he stopped, met Charlie's gaze. "It was probably a suicide note."

Charlie shook his head, barely appeased. He peered out the window yet again. "Here they are." A silver Buick pulled cautiously into the driveway. Amber emerged from the passenger side, and an elderly woman stepped out of the driver's side with surprising energy.

Charlie strode across the room and pulled open the front door. Amber walked, then ran, to him and wrapped her arms around his midsection, squeezing tightly.

"Are you all right, honey?"

Amber pulled away and looked up into his face. "She says," jerking her head back toward Catherine, "Nonny used to be a bank robber."

Charlie nodded, eyeing the old woman making her way toward the house. "Come inside."

"You knew?" Amber spun around.

"I just figured it out today." To Catherine he said, "Welcome. Please come in." He closed the door behind her and said, "I'm Charlie Pulkowski. This is Jarvis Chandler, Annie's," he caught Jarvis' eye, "friend."

"I am Catherine Whittendon. You are married to my daughter?"

"I am married to a woman who has always called herself Annie. But…"

"But her real name is Lucinda Whittendon. My daughter."

Charlie shook his head in amazement. "Incredible. So you still live around here."

"In Dunlee Mill, yes."

"And you and Annie have been seeing each other secretly all these years," Charlie said, more a statement than a question.

"Oh," Catherine said, surprised. "No. I haven't seen my daughter since 1969. I can't believe she was so close all this time."

"That can't be coincidence," Jarvis interjected.

Catherine squinted, confused. "But why be here if she wasn't going to come see me?"

"Maybe she did," Jarvis said. "Dunlee Mill is up ninety-one a bit, isn't it? Near Chesterford?"

"Yes," Catherine nodded.

Jarvis blew air at the ceiling in a low whistle. "She was always asking for that assignment, making the trip to Chesterford. Always disappointed when she couldn't go. Extremely disappointed."

"She was?" Catherine's eyes glistened. "My poor girl. I wish she'd knocked on the door."

Charlie ran a hand through his thinning hair. "How did you find us?"

"I saw Pamela's picture in the newspaper, poor girl. I had no idea she was so distraught."

"You knew her?"

"I've known Pamela since she was a child. She and Lucinda were best friends." Catherine smiled forlornly. "She disappeared the same time as Lucinda. But then she came to visit me last week. A couple of days before she died." She dropped her head, stared at her hands for a moment. "She was so depressed. Deeply, like a lost soul. But I didn't realize...I should have realized. I feel just terrible. Poor Pamela."

"So she was depressed?" Charlie shot a glance at Jarvis. "Enough to take her own life?"

"Well, yes. Evidently. She took it, didn't she?" Catherine pressed her hands to her face. "And now Lucinda is out there somewhere. I've gotten this close. And now she's gone again. She's run away. Again."

"I don't know about that," Charlie said. "She may not be alone. My daughter may be with her."

Amber startled. "Mom's missing too?"

"It seems so," Charlie said. "And if Annie were running away to hide, I'd think she'd go on her own. Not take Darlene with her."

"You're right about that," Jarvis said. "So the question is, where would they go together?"

Charlie shrugged, shook his head. "God, I wish I knew."

She stands at the door, this widow I made, glaring daggers of hatred. She has let me speak, heard my halting, weepy apology, but she says nothing in return. I do not know what I expected. I have told her how I have agonized over the aborted life of her husband every day since. And that I am tired of running and will turn myself into authorities. And that I am aware that nothing I say will relieve her pain or my guilt, but that I want her to know how terribly sorry I am. And yet, these words that I believed would somehow create closure seem only to have dredged up the pain and the hatred in her and pulled into sharper focus the chasm between widow and widow-maker.

I have not told her how hard I worked to live a good, noble, charitable life in the attempt to make amends in some minor way. It will only anger her more, I fear. Feeding the hungry in Springfield has in no way brought her peace or returned what I have taken from her.

I do not know how long we should stand here. Is it rude to leave while someone is hating you? Darlene fidgets nervously at my side. Angela Dechesney seems not to notice my daughter, so intent is her gaze upon me. I meet her eyes, because it is the least I can do, to allow her to hate freely and directly.

Behind her, there is a shadow in motion, a break in the stillness, and a face slowly emerges from the deep gloom of the house. It is pale and slightly flabby around the jowls, framed by shaggy dark hair. Angela Dechesney does not move as the face settles in above her shoulder.

"It's okay, Bobby," she says without turning around, but her voice wavers and cracks and does not sound okay.

"I been listening," Bobby says. "It's really one of them?"

This is her son, obviously. The little boy, a baby at the time, who never even knew his father. "I am," I confess, misery lashing my heart.

His head bobs slightly as he scrutinizes me with contempt. "It don't make it okay, you know," he says, "just coming and apologizing. That ain't enough."

I know.

"You think," he says, "you can just come here, say you're sorry, and clear your conscience and everything's fine. You feel better."

That is what I had expected. Hoped for. "I don't feel better," I say truthfully, and while it is an enormous disappointment, I feel guilty even for having hoped.

"You don't deserve to feel better."

"No."

"You weren't expecting forgiveness?"

"No." *I guess not. Was I?*

"All the other kids," he says, "most of them, had dads. Not me."

"I know." I force myself to meet his glare. "And I know my apology is not enough. But I wanted you to have it anyway."

"It ain't even close to enough. You got to pay for what you done."

"I am going to turn myself in." I say. "I will be going to jail." Speaking this aloud makes it more real and I am suddenly frightened. I will not be happy in jail. And that is the point.

"Who's that?" Bobby nods his head toward Darlene.

"This is my daughter, Darlene."

"Is it?" His eyes widen.

"Yes," I say. "She never knew her father either." It is a stupid thing to say, and I regret it immediately. I am simply desperate to find some common ground, something sympathetic between us, but it is a mistake to equate this man's loss with Darlene's, to demean his in some way. It was rash and imprudent, and Annie would never have given in to such a reckless impulse.

He stares at us with obvious disgust, and then melts, slowly, back into the murky shade of the house. I do not blame him. I could not stand to look upon me either. I have made this horrible situation worse, and I must go.

"I am sorry," I say to Angela Dechesney, who still stands in the doorway, "for everything." I take hold of Darlene's arm to steady my wobbly psyche as we turn and walk down the broken concrete steps.

"Are you the one?"

The wobble is gone from her voice, and it is stronger, firmer than I would have guessed. I turn back to face her. "Excuse me?"

"Are you the one?" she repeats. "The one who sends...the money."

"Oh." I had not thought to tell her this. Why not? "Yes," I say. "It's not...it could never make things right, I know."

"No," she agrees. "But it shows you have a conscience."

Yes. Yes it does. And I feel its grip loosening, this oppressive heaviness under which I have existed, until it lifts off of me and floats away, and I feel lighter, freer than I can ever remember. That is all I ever wanted, I realize. Just for her to know I have a conscience. That I am human after all. "Thank you," I say, and now it is my voice that is cracking. I am overwhelmed with such gratitude that I wish to hug her, even as I know how inappropriate and unappreciated such a gesture would be.

From the darkness behind her, Bobby's pudgy face appears once more. He pushes past his mother to stand outside on the top step, his movements a bit awkward, and I do not realize why until the rifle in his hands swings forward and is leveled at us. My breath catches in my throat and I feel Darlene stiffen against me. I am utterly unable to move, at a time when I realize it is most crucial that I do so. Darlene also seems immobilized by fear.

"What the hell you think you're doing?" Angela Dechesney says to her son.

"She's got to pay."

"She's going to jail."

Bobby grimaces, ugly and cruel. "So she says."

"You shoot a person," Angela says, "and *you're* going to jail."

"No." He shakes his head emphatically. "No, she's trespassing on my property. Threatening me. It's just self defense."

"Bobby." Angela's voice is steady, slow, as though calming a young child. "You can't do this."

"Why? Why can't I Ma? She deserves it."

Angela takes a deep breath. "You remember how unsatisfying it was when the other man died in the hospital? You were so upset he never had to do any jail time. He got off easy, you said. Well, don't let her off easy Bobby. Make her do her jail time."

Bobby's eyes waver, the barrel of the gun dips slightly. "Maybe you're right."

"Course I am."

"But jail time ain't enough. She needs to be punished like I was punished. Like you were punished."

"What," she says, "are you saying?"

"She took a husband and a father." He raises the weapon and a loud click resonates ominously through the dingy yard. "She should lose a daughter." I hear myself gasp as he swings the rifle slightly to his left and I can see that it is pointing at Darlene.

Time is still, or at least tremendously slowed, and I swear I am able to see his finger squeeze the trigger and the bullet emerge from its slender barrel and bear down on my daughter that I have brought to this place of danger and I do not know if I am still unable to move but only that I can not allow my Darlene to be harmed. I have seen the bullet emerge from the gun but I have not been able to follow its path and something must have happened because now I am on the dirt, or more precisely, on top of Darlene who is on the dirt. I do not know how I got here because it seems I am still incapable of moving, yet here we are in the dirt together. I hear Darlene screaming and I know she is terrified because I am also. I want to comfort her, send away the danger, but how to get the gun away from Bobby Dechesney when I am lying here immobile in the dirt?

"Mom!" Darlene screams. "Are you all right? Mom!"

Yes, I am all right, except that I cannot move. It is you he is aiming for.

"Mom!" Darlene squirms out from under me and now I am completely in the dirt. "Mom are you okay? Talk to me. Please." She is crying and I see that it is she who is afraid for me. She turns away from me abruptly and screeches toward the house, "Get away from us you crazy bastard!"

I see the Dechesneys over Darlene's shoulder; Angela's hands clapped over her mouth, Bobby's dark eyes grim and confused.

"What happened?" A shout that seems to be floating, unattached, until I see a bald man with a red-striped shirt stretched tightly over his belly rush from a neighboring yard toward the Dechesneys, followed more slowly by a woman in equally tight-fitting pants.

"He shot my mother," Darlene cries. "Call an ambulance! He shot my mother."

This must be true, I realize. This makes sense. I do not feel pain. Or anything at all. But it explains why I lie here in the dirt. I must make Darlene stop crying. I am okay, I say, but perhaps I did not speak aloud because she is still frantic. "I am okay." My voice is raspy, but it is there, and Darlene hears it.

"Oh god, Mom. Hang in there. We're going to get you an ambulance."

"I can't feel anything," I say.

"Well, good. You're probably in shock and can't feel the pain. That's good."

That is not what I mean, however. I cannot feel *anything*. "Okay," I say in my raspy voice. "But Darlene. Don't call an ambulance. Take me to the hospital yourself."

"What? No. No, I don't think I should move you. We have to get an ambulance."

Behind Darlene, on the broken concrete steps to the house, Angela and Bobby huddle together with their neighbors. She is crying, the earlier hatred in her eyes completely gone; replaced by horror, torment. The rifle hangs low in his hands. *Trespassing*, I hear him say loudly, but there is a naked, fearful urgency in his voice.

"Darlene," I wish to place a hand on her arm, but neither hand will obey commands. "I don't want him to get in trouble for this. Take me to the hospital yourself."

"Mom! He shot you!"

"He deserved to."

"No! No he didn't. And anyway those people know now so he's going to get in trouble anyway."

"They're his neighbors. Friends. They'll protect him." I swallow because my mouth is becoming dry. "I don't want that woman to lose her son because of me."

"Mom."

"Please, Darlene. Please do this for me. This….this is what I need. My body can take what it has to. My conscience can't take anymore."

"But moving you might kill you. Please," her voice catches in her throat, "just hang in there."

I lie here, an accusatory bullet aimed at the already damaged Bobby Dechesney and his mother. "If you leave me here to send that man to jail, it will kill what's left of my soul."

"No," she wails, her face wet with tears. "Mom, please. I can't risk hurting you. I can't," she mumbles, just barely coherent through her deep sobs, and holds my hand up to her face. "Please Mom. Please."

I see my hand pressed against my daughter's cheek, yet I cannot feel any physical sensation of warmth or pressure. It stirs something much deeper within me, something far more awe-inspiring. What an extraordinary way to discover my daughter loves me.

Her face grows murky and a cold fatigue settles over me. I would like so much to sleep. "Darlene," I say, and it is a much greater effort to speak now. "This is what I want. This is what will save me. Please. Save me."

CHAPTER 32

It was hushed and still in the hospital waiting room, but not in the polite, respectful manner of a library. This was an eerie quiet that pervaded the bland space, and somber, as behind the pale green-painted walls roiled the struggle to stave off death, mitigate the damage to life.

Alone in this bleak, perilous room, hugging her knees to her chest, Darlene huddled on a gray vinyl couch. Her face was down, forehead resting on her knees, eyes closed. She was hiding. Taking cover from all the possibilities this room represented, from all the futures she could not help but contemplate. The tears were not unfamiliar. She often cried, alone, late at night, though few who knew her would believe that, she knew. But those were tears of self-pity, loneliness. Despair. These were so very different. Except for the despair, maybe.

Commotion bubbled down the hall and Darlene lifted her head reluctantly, yet hopefully. Her relief at seeing Charlie's balding head approaching overwhelmed her and the tears surged again. She stood and went to him silently, falling heavily against him.

"Charlie," she sobbed into his chest.

"Is there any update?" Charlie's voice was clipped, urgent, though he folded his arms about her tenderly.

Amber slid up and into the embrace, wrapping her arms around her mother. Darlene hugged her, kissed the top of her head. To Charlie, she said, "No. I would have called you. She's still in surgery." Darlene glanced distractedly at the other two people with Charlie and Amber, a man and a woman, neither of whom she recognized. "Nobody's told me anything."

"That's not right," said the very large man Darlene did not know. "You deserve some kind of information. I'll go find out what's going on." He looked up and down the hallway, chose a direction, and strode off with purpose.

"Who?" Darlene asked.

"That," Charlie said, "is Jarvis Chandler, your mother's boss. And friend. Haven't you ever met him?"

Darlene shook her head. "No. I don't think so."

"Jarvis was with us when you called and was worried about her," Charlie explained. "And this," he said, turning to the elderly woman beside him, "is, well…"

"I am your grandmother, dear," the old woman smiled.

Darlene blinked. "What?"

"She's Nonny's mother," Amber burst out. "Isn't that, like, amazing?"

Darlene gaped, unable to speak.

"And she says you have an aunt and uncle," Amber continued, "and some cousins, and I have some second cousins. And Mom," she hesitated, "they're not the bad family Nonny said. That was just a story."

Darlene looked with affection at her daughter. "I know. She told me the truth today." She turned toward Catherine. "Well. Hello."

Catherine smiled. "This is all very sudden and strange for you, I'm sure. But I've known about you for a long time. Your mother wrote me a letter years ago, when you must have been about Amber's age. She told me all about you. She said you were beautiful and spunky and wonderful. That you were just perfection."

Darlene felt the rush of water in her eyes again. "She said… that? Perfection?"

Catherine nodded. "Her exact words. She adored you, that was obvious."

"Did you find out anything?" Charlie's voice interrupted, and the rest of them turned to see Jarvis standing quietly in the doorway.

"I did," he nodded. "Although it's like pulling teeth around here." He crossed his big arms over his chest and spoke slowly, evenly. "The bullet is near her spine, apparently. They don't know," his voice dropped, "if they can get it out."

"Oh god," Charlie breathed heavily, collapsing into a vinyl chair.

Catherine, too, sought out a chair, with Amber's arm under hers, helping to guide her. A grave, dismal silence filled the room, oppressive and domineering, forbidding all else.

Darlene covered her face with her hands and, after a time, spoke into them. "It was supposed to be me."

Charlie and the others looked at her quizzically.

"The guy was aiming for me," Darlene said. "Mom jumped in front of me." Her sobbing was deep and loud, nearly engulfing her words. "She saved me. And now she might die. Because of me."

I can see myself. How odd it is. I see my body far below, tubes springing from my face and chest. A gaping, bloody hole in my belly. People in pale blue clothing hover over my body, their hands in the blood. The lights are so bright, but there is no sound. I see me, but I know that is not me. I am up here, looking down at me. How can this be?

They work to save me, I realize. Or, save my body. I do not need saving, I want to say, but they will not listen. They think that is me, there on the table.

I must leave now. I feel this urgently, although I do not know to where it is I must go. Yet I am not permitted to leave. I am unsure if this pleases me. Perhaps if I knew my destination I could decide if I wished to go there. It is not a fair question. I should not have to decide without all the information.

And the truth is I am not really sure that I do not need saving. I do not know. If I knew I was saved I could go peacefully, willingly. Wherever it is I am to go.

It seems I do not have a choice. My own fate rests in others' hands. This does not seem fair either, yet I have long since lost the expectation of fairness. And I am befuddled and uncertain as to which to choose anyway, so what does it matter that I have no control? The uncertainty is disconcerting, however. I am a little afraid. I am frightened of going into the unknown. I am frightened of staying in my purgatory if I am not saved. I see no choice which is comfortable. I see no choice at all.

The bright lights go dim. The silence grows more quiet. I lose my grasp on myself. I am going. Somewhere. Am I going or am I staying? Which me is real?

Voices now. I can no longer see anything, but I hear voices and a steady, insistent beeping. It is unsettling, this transformation from deafness to blindness.

The choice has been made. I know this with certainty without really knowing why. It was not my choice. It was made for me, and here I am.

The voices become louder, bolder, demanding to be heard. I listen, because it is all I can do, and the hearing is much clearer because there is no seeing. I know these voices. They are the voices I love.

"Can she hear us if we talk to her?" It is Amber's voice, except that it is timid and thin.

"I don't know, sweetheart." Charlie's soft, throaty rumble.

I am smiling, am I not? Can they not see my smile? I am so

happy they are here. I want to talk to them. But they cannot even see my smile.

"Maybe, though. It's worth a try. If she can hear you, it'll make her so happy." Darlene. She is here too. My whole family. My everything.

"Hi Nonny. I love you."

Hello, my bright, shining light.

"I wish I'd said it before."

"She knows," says Charlie's voice.

I know.

"She's still so lovely." A familiar voice, yet not quite known.

"Mom." The word is no more than a sob.

Yes, Darlene?

"Thank you. For saving me."

You are very welcome, my sweetheart. It is all I ever wanted to do.

A steady, faint beeping fills my ears. My eyes still see only dark. I have been sleeping, I think, although I do not know for how long. I feel myself breathing, the air passing into my lungs and out again. My heart beats, I know, and not just because of the beeping machine. My mouth feels dry and I would like something to drink. I am not dead. This comes as both a surprise and a relief. I am not dead!

The joy I feel at this also surprises me. I was so tired of keeping up the deceit, I believed I could go, or not, and it would all be the same. I believed I did not care. How very wrong I was. How very wrong I have been about so many things.

There is another sound in here with me. A murmuring in the darkness. Hushed voices. I am not alone. Who is with me? I wish to see. Will my eyes open? Please. I need to see.

It seems a great effort. They are just tiny things, eyelids. How can they be so heavy? A murky light filters through, a grayness, then soft, muted forms. The plain walls of a plain room emerge from the colorless gloom, a plain chair in the corner. And there, beyond the foot of this bed in which my body lies, two people. One is Charlie! My love. He whispers to a person in pale, loose clothing. *Charlie!* I wish to call to him but my mouth does not seem to work. *Come to me, Charlie. I want to see you. I am alive now, and I want to see you. Please come to me.*

Charlie glances toward me, perhaps randomly, but I would like to believe he hears me. Our entire adult lifetime has been spent listening to one another; it is not so unreasonable to believe he can hear my thoughts. Anyway, I believe it to be true.

"Oh. My god," he breathes, and rushes to me, leaning over me, his hand on my face. His mouth opens to speak. No words come, nothing but airy, raspy breath, a contorted smile, molded by the raw emotions on his face: joy, relief, sorrow, gratitude. Love. His lovely, warm, gentle eyes fill with water which he allows to spill down his face unselfconsciously and unrestrained. It is as though he empties his entire self, everything he is and everything we are together through his tears and they fill the empty place inside me. He cries for me and about me. And about us. All that he feels lies naked on his face. This precious face. My love. We, the two of us, are everything at this moment. We are this moment.

CHAPTER 33

Six months later

My chair holds me, embraces me, supports me, traps me. I despise my chair and I adore it. Mostly, I need it. It is my savior. It is my jailer.

My limbs do not function, and never will again, the doctors tell me. This ugly metal chair with its oversized wheels and mechanical hum is all that affords me mobility, other than my mouth to speak and eat. This fabricated, motorized, non-living contraption grants me the human need to roam, to alter my surroundings from time to time.

I did not see this one coming. Of all the outcomes I may have imagined to have ensued from Annie's predicament, this is not one I ever dreamed. And yet now that it has happened, it seems it must always have been so. Almost as though it were preordained, not that I believe in such things. If I did, I would not have felt guilt for so long over an act that was not my choice, only my destiny to commit. Yes, it does fit. I have lived trapped by my invented identity and now I exist trapped in my physical, immobile body. Really, how could it be any other way?

It was not immediately so clear. When I still lay in my hospital bed, my mind not yet accepting of what had happened to my body, the frustration and anger bubbled through me fiercely. How could this have happened to me? Yes, I deserved to be punished, but did I deserve *this*? This helpless, hopeless fate worse than death? I lay there, my truth exposed, powerless to escape the many pitying, disdainful eyes that ran up the length of my body apprehensively before resting on my head. Forced to submit as Charlie and Amber and the others all came with their sad, sympathetic looks to see my shame exposed. I could no longer hide myself. My façade stripped away, I could not turn my back for a moment to put some distance between us, or even hide my face in my hands. I could close my eyes; that was all. Not nearly barrier enough.

Police officers came, probing me with questions that I was expected to focus on and answer. And I did answer, absently, while my brain concentrated on willing my body to work, or making sense of odd, phantom limb sensations. The district attorney, a prim young woman in a dark gray skirt suit, babbled legalese at my head, indicting me for murder. Did I understand the charges against me? My ears heard her droning voice, my eyes beheld her crisp efficiency, and my mouth dutifully answered the yeses she wished to hear. How like a separate entity my head was from my body; it could move and react and express itself while the rest of me lay dead.

The deputy posted at my hospital room door seemed both amusing and an insult. Standard procedure, I was told. I wondered if the uniformed man appointed to guard me felt silly and embarrassed to be assigned the challenging task of making sure a quadriplegic did not run away.

Those days in the hospital, a blurred tableau of monotonous and excruciating repetition, stretching out with agonizing sluggishness, seemed endless in their torment. Surely this was all a hallucination, a masochistic delusion designed by my guilty brain to punish me.

Yet every morning I awoke from my nightmare with relief that it was finally over, only to find that it continued. And it continues still. But I have grown accustomed to the nightmare, and have even come to appreciate its benefits. The world, the people around me, are different here in this hideous reverie. Everything has changed.

My daughter seems overwhelmed by what she perceives to be my act of heroism in saving her, taking the bullet meant for her. That was not heroism, I have told her. I did not think about it. I did not weigh the risks and dangers, steel myself to the hazards, and then choose to take action. I did not consider my safety versus Darlene's. I did not even think, "I must save Darlene." I simply could not bear my precious girl being damaged. I never could. All these years of fights and tears and tantrums about her lifestyle; that is what they have been about. I hope she truly understands that now.

Happily, it is not just Darlene's physical life that was saved. My daughter has re-found her ego. Not the ego of self-centered, arrogant, dismissive disregard for society and personal safety. That had not been lost, and in any case is only a false ego. No, she has regained her sense of self. Her confidence in her ability to function, not just satisfactorily, but exceptionally. I sit here, in my own home and not some medical facility for felons, because of Darlene. Squeezed between her classes, outpatient visits to a rehab counselor, and her regular visits here to her family, Darlene has had a number of conversations with the Dechesneys and their lawyers, in which she has convinced all of them that her memory, as witness to the shooting, would depend a great deal on the Dechesneys' willingness to make a statement in court on my behalf when my case is brought.

The issues, as Darlene has researched and explained them to me, in deciding a criminal's fate, are fourfold: deterrence, rehabilitation, punishment, and justice for the victims. Clearly, it is unnecessary to incarcerate me to deter me from committing future crimes, as I am not even able to feed myself without assistance, much less launch an attack. My rehabilitation occurred the instant I committed my crime and continued every moment since as I attempted to do enough good deeds to offset the one bad one, impossible a task as that is. And I am punished. In all the many possible ways, physically, mentally, emotionally, I am so very punished. I am rendered useless and helpless. Long ago I was rendered identityless.

All these things, the Dechesneys will say, cause them to no longer seek reprisals against me. I have suffered enough. Justice has been done. The New York authorities will have little appetite for prosecuting a quadriplegic for an almost 40-year-old crime if the victim's family does not wish to press the issue, according to the lawyer Charlie and Darlene have hired.

For her part, Darlene will recall that she and I trespassed on Angela and Bobby Dechesney's property, were warned to leave and did not. No serious charges will be filed. Everyone will be happy. Or no one will be happy. Perhaps happy is not the precisely accurate word choice.

"Don't worry Mom," Darlene tells me. "They'll go along with it. That old lady doesn't want her kid sitting in jail."

"And my kid doesn't want this old lady sitting in jail." I smile as I say this.

"I didn't mean—," she says hastily, then breaks into a grin. "Yes. That's it exactly."

It is the jokes, in many ways, that delight me the most. Her willingness to be playful with me, and the trust that it will be okay. "Thank you," I tell her yet again, "for honoring my wishes. My conscience simply could not have handled inflicting any more suffering on that woman or her children. And I will say it again, if it will ease their suffering to pursue this and see me go to jail, that's okay. Really."

Darlene turns steely eyes toward me. "No."

And that, in a final, powerful word, is that. My concern for the Dechesney's peace of mind is no match for my concern for my daughter's. And if I believed Darlene was doing this as some sort of repayment for my perceived heroics, I would perhaps stop her from putting pressure on the Dechesneys. But I have seen the change in my daughter this new role has brought. She is the fixer, the competent one. She is getting me out of a jam, taking care of me. It is good for her to help someone else. Especially someone she believed she hated for so long. This is a mother-daughter relationship that may work, finally, now that our roles have been reversed.

Jarvis says he will hold my job for me, but we both know there is nothing I can do for FROGS or for anyone. I am useless and a burden. But he says no, that I have knowledge and I have dedication and I have the respect of all who have known and worked with me. And I may take as long as I require to adjust to my new self and decide to come back at any time. And they will make any and all accommodations necessary for a handicapped person such as myself because I am worth it, Jarvis says.

"You don't have to say all that," I tell him. "I'm not buying it anyway."

"I don't have to say anything, Annie. And you don't have to buy it." He shakes his big head. "I'm trying to help."

"I know," I say. "It's what you do. But I'm your friend."

"Always," he says, surprised.

"So you need to be honest with me."

"There are things you could do," he says, "like supervision, scheduling."

I smile at my friend. "Maybe Charlie or Darlene could bring me in for a visit once in a while. Just to say hi."

Jarvis nods slightly, accedes with a weak grin. "Yeah. Come say hi."

Jarvis has never once mentioned my former life as Lucinda-the-killer. It does not seem to affect his friendship with Annie in the least. I am fortunate to have such a loyal, considerate, charitable friend. There are few gems like Jarvis in this world. Would Jarvis have befriended Lucinda? Would she have been receptive to such a friendship? I can only guess.

My nurse comes in to exercise my limbs. She is a kind young woman who is quick and efficient and she is here almost all the time with us. Charlie said he wished to take care of me himself, but I do not believe him. I am burden enough on this dear man who does not deserve any of this hardship I heap upon him.

It is costly, retaining this nurse, but I simply cannot be such a terrible encumbrance on my family, and my mother has some money she is willingly, even happily, contributing. It is the money I should and would receive as my inheritance, she says, and there is no reason I should not have it early if I have need of it. Still, the money will not last forever.

Astonishingly, Charlie still loves me and the fiction no longer stands in the way of a true and honest bond between us. And yet, his love for me is different now. Where he once loved Annie for her strengths, his love for this feeble cripple is steeped in pity. I cannot be the same wife to him in almost every important way. He must take care of me. We are caretaker and invalid. Parent and helpless infant. Gardener and houseplant. All his words of love and devotion, sincere as they may be, cannot mask that hideous truth. All his smiles and playful jokes cannot hide the sorrow and sympathy in his face. As difficult as it is for me each time I see that pity in his eyes, I watch them closely. For the pity will surely turn with time, first to fatigue and then boredom, and eventually resentment. And if it does not, then Charlie is an even better human being than I have ever given him credit for. Line him up for sainthood. Beatify that man.

But that is the crucial reality. Charlie is a man. Not a saint. He will tire of this. He will grow resentful that his life has become an endless monotony of nursemaid duties. And when the money for the nurse runs out, which it surely must, Charlie will feel compelled to take on the many dreadful tasks of maintaining this houseplant. His final memories of me will be those of repulsive chores and my helpless indignity. How could he possibly endure that? How could I? I have not spoken with Charlie about what should be the course of action when that day arrives, for I know he will not want to hear it. There will be time for that later.

My mother comes to see me nearly every day. She has so many

questions, and I have so many, about the years that we each missed, it seems we will certainly run out of time before we run out of questions. Still, after all these months, she bursts into tears upon seeing me and throws her arms around me in a hug. She is making up for all those years of lost hugs, apparently. I only wish I could embrace her in return.

"Lucinda," she will say, her face bright with recollection, "do you remember when we used to hunt for wild blueberries in the woods? Remember how we used to let you play hooky from school and spend the day at the beach? Remember that crazy pet lemur the neighbors used to have?"

Almost always these remembrances are from when I was a very young girl, not the teen years just before Lucinda disappeared. It is as though my mother is reclaiming Lucinda's childhood, which somehow was destroyed by Lucinda's crime and disappeared in Annie's adulthood. Or, perhaps, she is simply reassuring herself this person before her truly is her lost little girl.

Equally fascinating to my mother are all the many stealthy visits I made to watch her and the rest of my family. "Were you there Fourth of July of…ninety-three when your father almost blew up the garage with firecrackers?"

"I was almost never there on holidays or big events," I tell her. "Usually, the only time I could get away was a weekday, when I was up that way for work. I saw the quiet times, for the most part. You and Dad sitting at the old picnic table. Reading the paper. Sometimes talking. It was very comforting really. Like nothing had changed."

"I wish I'd known you were there. Your father, oh he would have loved to have seen you. Just to have known you were alive would have been a thrill, but to think you were right *there*." She raises teary eyes to me. "You could have trusted us, you know."

"It wasn't trust, Mom. It was…I was paranoid, I guess, that they might possibly still be watching the house. And I was so ashamed. And I knew you must be too. And Dad was so…Republican. And disapproved of my involvement in the antiwar movement. I just thought he would be so disgusted with me. I was disgusted."

"It was an accident. Wasn't it?"

"What? The shooting?" I shake my head sadly at her. "We didn't plan to shoot anyone. But no, it wasn't an accident."

"But if you didn't plan it…"

"We were robbing a bank, Mom. With loaded guns."

She nods. "But it wasn't…Lucinda, you weren't the one. It wasn't *your* gun that killed that man." She has stated this as though it were established fact, rather than a desperate hope from her own heart.

She needs to cling to this hope I know, and yet I must tell her the truth. "I honestly don't know."

"You don't." This seems to deflate her beyond despair. "Well," she says hopefully, "we should find out. I'm sure forensics now can figure out if it was your gun or the other man's."

"It doesn't matter."

"Of course it matters. If you find out you weren't the actual shooter, it will give you some peace of mind. Imagine the load off your conscience."

"Mom," I say, "I shot my gun. More than once, I think. In the direction of one of the guards. Whether or not one of my bullets hit him is just chance, happenstance. Irrelevant."

She stares at me, a despondent face of misery.

"My conscience can't be eased," I tell her. "But it has learned to live with itself."

So. I have told my mother the truth of me. And still she comes to see me.

My brother has also come to visit me. Once. He does not know quite what to say or how to treat me. Of all the people I expected to be angry with me when my awful truth was discovered, I would never have guessed Colin would be the most furious. Perhaps it is more resentment than anger, but I can see it there in his eyes, as he does not make any attempt to hide it, especially as he watches my mother fawn all over me. I truly believe he is unhappy my mother has rediscovered me, although I hope that is only my own paranoia.

"I've missed you so much Colley."

He raises his eyebrows self-consciously, and I realize how silly it sounds to call a grown man by that childhood name. "Am I the only one," he says, "who has a problem with what you did?"

"Everyone has a problem with what I did."

"Maybe," he nods. "I guess so. And I don't mean to be such a hard ass about it, but I can't seem to get past it so easily."

"Easily?" I cannot suppress a smirk. "I will never be past it."

I do not know when I will see my brother again.

Colin's daughter, Vanessa, has written to me from California. Her letter was a cordial expression of welcome to her long lost aunt, and included photos of her new baby. She has promised to visit when she next comes east, she says. We shall see.

Oftentimes, because my mother is here so frequently, and because Darlene comes to visit more often, they are both here when Amber arrives home from school. My mother will invariably make some comment about the four generations being together at last, and for a while we will talk and laugh just as though we had all grown up and grown old together. It has become something of a formal title for our gatherings: The Four Generations, as though we were some sort of official committee or social club.

My mother knows nothing of Darlene's past and can only judge her by the competent, take-charge woman she has observed these past months. It is unusual for Darlene to be treated with such outward respect and admiration, I am sorry and ashamed to say, and she is genuinely enjoying becoming acquainted with her grandmother, just one of the many things that has been missing from my daughter's life.

Amber, I believe, is simply beside herself with happiness these days. Not only is her mother clean and sober and pleasant to be around, she is actually *around*. Much of the time. Amber has always loved her mother, has always hoped fervently that her mother loved her in return. Now, I believe, she knows for certain.

And now she can be proud of her mother. And she thoroughly delights at being included in our grown-up conversations among The Four Generations.

The truth is we all do. They are wonderful times for me. I never believed we would all be together in the same room. Not happily. I thrill to see the joy on each of the three faces I love so much. The joy of connecting and of reconnecting, the laughter that makes us forget, for a time at least, that this closeness has come at an enormous cost. And then, when they think it might be time for a walk outside, maybe, or a cup of tea in the kitchen, and someone has to wheel me to the new destination, the reality of my plight dampens both moods and faces. Make way for the big chair! Quadriplegic coming through! For a quick instant before they rush to conceal it, I see the pity in their faces. The sorrow. A touch of shame. Do not pity me, I want to say. Don't you see? This had to happen to me in order to bring us all together. Were I still able-bodied, I would be in a prison cell, and we would not be having these lovely warm regular gatherings of The Four Generations.

I see the pity in Charlie's eyes also, and that is the place where it causes me the most agony. He tries to hide it, disguise it, but I know his face well enough to know what I see. I believed Charlie would be so angry when he learned the truth of me, that he would despise what I had done and despise all my deceit since. But he loves me still. He tells me so regularly, and I believe him. I have to.

"Good night, my love," he says in that quiet moment after he has turned off the light before we sleep. "Sleep well."

I feel his damp kiss on the tip of my nose and I want so much to wrap my arms around him and hold his body against mine. "I am so sorry," I whisper, unable to hold in the tears.

"Enough. You've apologized every single day."

"It's not enough. I lied to you every day for thirty-seven years."

"So I've got thirty-seven years of daily apologies to look forward to?"

It is meant as a joke of sorts, but falls flat as a reminder that, with my body as damaged as it is, I have considerably less time than that remaining. "I am so sorry, Charlie, for having deceived you. You have been just everything to me. And you were always so honest with me, and I reciprocated with a never-ending string of lies." I hesitate, for I do not know how he will receive this next confession. "But you know what? If I could have another thirty-seven years with you, like I was, not like this, I would lie all over again."

Charlie exhales loudly in the dark, and we lay in silence for a long moment. "I wouldn't have imagined I'd say this. But if we could get it back, and that's what it took, I'd want you to lie."

"It was good, wasn't it?"

"It was great. Best life I ever had," he says, attempting humor once more.

"If I could smack you for that, I would."

"Seriously. I couldn't have asked for anyone or anything better. My life was perfect. Until this, of course."

"I'm sorry for this too."

Charlie rolls onto his side, facing me, head propped up on his hand. "Maybe this makes me a terrible person," he says. "I'm very sorry a man died. But if he hadn't, we would never have met. You wouldn't have been on the run, and you wouldn't have run to Chicago for me to find you." Though I can barely see him, I know he wears his sweet dimpled grin. "It's selfish of me, I know. But how am I supposed to regret that?"

My eyes water and blur and I can no longer see his beautiful face at all. "God, I so don't deserve you. I never have."

"Annie." He holds my face between both his hands. "It was a terrible mistake. You don't need me to tell you that. I've never seen anything but good in you. And it's not just because I'm a sucker for your pretty face," he grins. "You're a good person. I can't speak for that Lucinda person, because I didn't know her. As far as I'm concerned it was Lucinda's mistake." He presses his lips gently onto mine. "You're not her."

Is this true? All these years I have been hiding from Lucinda, knowing she lurked inside, waiting to take over again. And yet, now I wonder. Could Charlie be right about this? I am not Lucinda? At some point between the moment I introduced myself to Charlie as Ann and this moment, I have morphed from Lucinda pretending to be Annie, into Annie believing, incorrectly, she was really Lucinda. How could I have missed it?

I chose, all those years ago, the name that seemed the most bland, nondescript, unlikely to draw attention I could think of in those few seconds I had to think. One syllable, only two distinct letters, flat-sounding, commonplace. Yet over the years this plain-Jane name, this static sound, has taken on a complete personality, has grown into a human being with attachments and responsibilities and connections with other humans. This simple, false name now has people who love her.

I am Annie. What a stupendous and simple revelation! Lucinda may have haunted me all this time, but she did not pursue me as I had imagined. She was not trying to wrest control, to take her life back. Lucinda was truly dead and gone like the man she killed, and both ghosts haunted Annie equally.

Even my mother realizes this, I think. Though she still calls me Lucinda, she does so because she has never called me anything else. And when Charlie calls me Annie, I can see in her face that she knows it is right. She knows this is who her daughter has become, and she is content, even pleased by this. Annie is good. Annie is the best Lucinda could have hoped for.

Annie has been Charlie's wife. Annie has been Darlene's flawed mother. Annie has been Amber's doting grandmother. Annie has done a lot of good in her life for a lot of people through both her work and her volunteer activities. Would Lucinda have been so charitable had she lived? I believe, in her heart, she would have wanted to be, tried to be. I know she would have liked the chance.

With Lucinda gone, however, I am free. Free! How silly that may sound when I am bound by a metal chair and others' willingness to roll me from here to there. Unable to open a book or turn on a light or scratch an itch. I have simply traded one form of bondage for another.

I have also traded one freedom for another. I am liberated in ways I have not been since Lucinda was nineteen. I am free to be honest with all those I love, and everyone else as well. I am free to allow thoughts to flow from heart or head through vocal chords unimpeded. I am free to be the me I truly am without pause or second-guessing or calculation of any kind. Everyone knows all of me, including the very worst.

Bobby Dechesney has exacted his revenge on his father's killer. I have finally been dealt the punishment I had evaded all these years. Justice has been meted out. I am free!

Though trapped inside this useless body, these final days afford me everything I have so yearned for these past decades when I took my physical wellbeing for granted. These days are happier than I could ever have imagined. The laughter and voices of my family trill a blissful music in my ears. My soul, fettered and constrained for years by guilt and deception now dances freely with exhilaration and joy. It is the only dancing I will ever do, and yet, if given the choice, I would make this trade again.

These cannot last, these wonderful days, for they must surely dissipate with failing health and dwindling funds. In the meantime, for as long as it does continue, I will enjoy this time with my family that I never believed I would have. It is more fantastic than I could have imagined. Blissful and deeply gratifying. An undeserved miracle. It is glorious.

THE END

AUTHOR'S NOTE

The story of Annie/Lucinda is loosely inspired by that of peace-protester-turned-bank-robber, Katherine Ann Power. Power, along with her small gang of renegades, stole weapons and ammunition from the National Guard Armory in Newburyport, MA, in 1970, and a few days later robbed a bank in Brighton, MA, during which a Boston police officer was shot and killed. Power drove one of two getaway cars. Like Lucinda, Power went into hiding, changed her name, and built a new life based on this false identity. Unlike Annie, Power turned herself in to authorities after 23 years of hiding and served six years of an eight- to twelve-year prison sentence.

In reading Power's story, I became fascinated by what a lifetime of hiding and lying—of pretending to be someone else—would do to a person's emotional and psychological wellbeing. Annie's story was intended to be an exploration of that, although it ended up being more. Her story grew into an examination of the corrosive effect of guilt, as well as the often-complicated but powerful bond between mothers and daughters.

A profound thank you to my husband, David, who believed in me and in this book, even when I had doubts. Your love and support are everything.

www.ingramcontent.com/pod-product-compliance
Lightning Source LLC
Chambersburg PA
CBHW021230250626
47155CB00008B/2947